Praise for ⎯⎯⎯⎯ and *Eternal Hunger*

"Dark, ⎯⎯⎯⎯ a stun ⎯⎯⎯⎯ new se ⎯⎯⎯⎯ I can't wai ⎯⎯⎯⎯ from Laura Wright."
—⎯⎯⎯⎯ *New York Times* bestse ⎯⎯⎯⎯
author of *Bonds of Justice*

"Dark, sexy vampires with an urban bite make *Eternal Hunger* a must read!"
—Jessica Andersen, author of *Demonkeepers*

"Action, passion, and dark suspense launch a riveting new series. Laura Wright knows how to lure you in and hold you captive until the last page!"
—Larissa Ione, *New York Times* bestselling author of *Ecstasy Unveiled*

"Paranormal fans with a penchant for vamps will find *Eternal Hunger* a must read, but be warned: You will quickly become hooked!"
—The Romance Readers Connection (4½ stars)

"*Eternal Hunger* is deliciously dark while making you believe in the concept of soul mates." —Fresh Fiction

"An exhilarating vampire romance . . . dark, passionate, and utterly intoxicating!"—Reader to Reader Reviews

"In a field brimming with rehashes of the same theme, Wright has managed to create a sound, believable vampire culture with plenty of tension and interesting plot points. The pacing is smooth with well-developed characters, and the satisfying conclusion leaves ample room for more from this strong new series."
—Monsters and Critics

"A bold new voice in vampire romance."
—*Romantic Times* (4 stars)

continued . . .

"Just when it seems every possible vampire twist has been turned, Wright launches a powerful series with a rich mythology, page-turning tension, and blistering sensuality."   —*Publishers Weekly* (starred review)

ETERNAL KISS

MARK OF THE VAMPIRE

LAURA WRIGHT

A SIGNET ECLIPSE BOOK

SIGNET ECLIPSE
Published by New American Library, a division of
Penguin Group (USA) Inc., 375 Hudson Street,
New York, New York 10014, USA
Penguin Group (Canada), 90 Eglinton Avenue East, Suite 700, Toronto,
Ontario M4P 2Y3, Canada (a division of Pearson Penguin Canada Inc.)
Penguin Books Ltd., 80 Strand, London WC2R 0RL, England
Penguin Ireland, 25 St. Stephen's Green, Dublin 2,
Ireland (a division of Penguin Books Ltd.)
Penguin Group (Australia), 250 Camberwell Road, Camberwell, Victoria 3124,
Australia (a division of Pearson Australia Group Pty. Ltd.)
Penguin Books India Pvt. Ltd., 11 Community Centre, Panchsheel Park,
New Delhi - 110 017, India
Penguin Group (NZ), 67 Apollo Drive, Rosedale, North Shore 0632,
New Zealand (a division of Pearson New Zealand Ltd.)
Penguin Books (South Africa) (Pty.) Ltd., 24 Sturdee Avenue,
Rosebank, Johannesburg 2196, South Africa

Penguin Books Ltd., Registered Offices:
80 Strand, London WC2R 0RL, England

First published by Signet Eclipse, an imprint of New American Library,
a division of Penguin Group (USA) Inc.

First Printing, April 2011
10 9 8 7 6 5 4 3 2 1

To my husband, Daniel Ionazzi, who, at times, was both mother and father to our children while I wrote this book. I love and appreciate you so much.

ACKNOWLEDGMENTS

The world in which Nicholas Roman lives is a dark and complicated one, but with Danielle Perez by my side, it was an extreme pleasure and honor to tell his story. Thank you, Danielle. You are not only a brilliant editor, but a patient and kind one.

Thank you, Maria Carvainis and the entire staff at MCA. Your endless support is invaluable.

Thank you, Julie Ganis, Barbara Ankrum and Jennifer Lyon for your critical eyes and impeccable ideas.

Thank you to my friends: old, new and ETERNAL, on my Facebook author page—your support and humor amaze me daily.

GLOSSARY

Balas—Vampire child.

Breeding Male—A *paven* of purest blood whose genetic code and structure were altered by the Eternal Order. He has the ability to impregnate at will and decide the sex of the *balas*. He is brought in by Pureblood families and/or to repopulate one sex or the other in times of dire necessity. He is uncontrollable, near to an animal and must be caged.

Credenti—A vampire community ruled and protected by the Eternal Order. Both Purebloods and Impures live here. There are many all over the world, masked by the Order so that humans barely notice their existence.

Duro—Tender word for "brother."

Eternal Order—The ten Pureblood vampires who have passed on to the middle world. They make the laws, punish the lawbreakers and govern every vampire *credenti* on earth.

Eyes—The New York City street rats who run the sales of drugs, blood, and body to both human and vampire.

Gravo—Poisoned vampire blood.

Imiti—An imitation vampire, one who can take on the characteristics of vampires if they drink blood regularly.

Impureblood—Any combination of human and vampire. No powers, heartbeat, can live in the sun, only has fangs when blood is consumed. Males are blood castrated, their sex drive removed through the blood by the Order. Females are blood sterilized and the insides of their thighs are branded with "I"s.

Meta—A Pureblood female of fifty years, can still remain in sunlight, but needs the blood and body of her true mate.

Mondrar—Vampire prison.

Morpho—A Pureblood *paven* of three hundred years; as powerful as a *paven* can get, is sunlight intolerant, and the need to find his true mate becomes impossible to deny.

Paven—A vampire male of pure blood.

Pureblood—Pure vampire. Powerful, no heartbeat, will go through *morpho* and *meta* and find their Pureblood true mate.

Puritita—One who is chaste.

Sacro—Dirty.

Similis—The Impure guards of Mondrar.

Swell—Vampire pregnancy.

Tegga—Nursemaid/nanny/governess.

True Mate—The one each *veana* and *paven* is destined for. Each shares the same mark somewhere on their skin.

Veana—A vampire female of pure blood.

Veracou—The mating ceremony between two Pureblood vampires.

Virgini—Virgin.

Witte—Animal.

MARK OF THE VAMPIRE

Nicholas Odysseus Claudius Roman did not fight. In fact, as he lay on his back, strapped down to the stone table, bare as the day he slipped from his mother's weary body, he projected an almost eerie calm.

The leather restraints placed on his upper arms, belly, neck, and ankles by the Order sliced into his skin like dull razor blades, but he ignored the pain. It was as it must be. Inside the Tomb of Nascita, the massive hole cut deep within hundreds of layers of rock, the Order performed the morphing ritual several times per year. When a *paven* hit his three hundredth year on earth, he was brought to the tomb, laid out on the slab of stone, and more often than not, held his position without restraints. He was, after all, being gifted with the strength and power of morpho. But the ancient ten were a bit unsure of how the Son of a Breeding Male would react to the final strikes of the maturation ritual. After all, their body and brain chemistry were so very different than the average *paven*. Would Nicholas Roman's pain override his good sense and spur on the instinct to attack, to drain, to kill? No one was sure. So imprison him they must.

"Get on with it," Nicholas said with grave irritation, lifting his chin. "My brothers search for a way here even now."

One of the female members of the Order sniffed her disbelief. "Surely they wouldn't come without an invitation."

"There is no one who wishes to incur the wrath of the ancient ten," said the *paven* beside her.

Nicholas laughed bitterly. "If you think that, you're all even bigger fools than I thought you were."

Several low, bloodthirsty snarls sounded behind him, but one very cool head prevailed and the *paven* said, "We waste time with things that matter not. Prepare yourself, Son of the Breeding Male."

There was a sudden crack, and above Nicholas, the perfectly painted night sky split apart. The sounds of day echoed all around him—birds waking one another, insects searching for a meal, and in moments the cold, happy darkness ceased to reign. The brilliant white light of a fabricated sun spilled into the stone room, its greedy fingers reaching for every dim corner and crevice.

And for the skin of a newly morphed *paven*.

No stranger to pain, Nicholas remained still as death, even as the hot branding iron of the false sun went to work on his forearms, carving the daggers and his true mate's marks into his skin. It took only minutes, but when it was done and his arms smoked in the light, he cursed his ancestry as he had many times in his one hundred and fifty years. For most *pavens*, this would be it, the end of the physical torture, but not for Nicholas. He was a Son of the Breeding Male and his pain had just begun.

Up the heat traveled, over his chest and shoulders, up his neck, trailing his jawline in savage pursuit of its target until the blazing sunlight reached his cheekbones. A hiss escaped his lips as the needle of fire carved the second set of brands into his cheeks—the Breeding Male circles, and his true mate's symbols within it.

As quick as the light had come, its return to the makeshift heavens was even quicker. The sounds of day died off and the ceiling fused, and once again he was bathed in darkness. Breathing heavily, his head feeling as though it had been rammed against a brick wall forty times in succession, Nicholas heard the gentle footfall and swish of the Order's burgundy robes as they approached him. The ancient rulers, the treacherous ten, gathered around the stone table and trained their eyes on him.

Cruen, as he so often did, spoke first. "Dare has been in hiding these past months, licking his wounds, eerily silent—like a rat. But he has emerged, calling Impures to his fold—filling their heads with lies, filling their hearts with a need for freedom. Find and kill him," he said, but through Nicholas's mind he uttered, *Or your brother will have stone at his back, leather around his extremities, and no doubt two empty circle brands on his cheeks.*

Nicholas hissed and pulled at his binds, strained to get up and extinguish the pale blue light in Cruen's malevolent eyes forever. But he was held, caught.

The image of Lucian, circle brands on his cheeks with nothing inside, no mark of his true mate because he would never have one. No love, no life—only the cries of a near-animallike *paven* bent on feeding and breeding.

The possibility that any one of the Roman brothers could have the Breeding Male gene was a good one, but Nicholas and Alexander had long suspected that Lucian, with his pale features and insatiable sexual appetite, was the carrier.

It appeared as though Cruen believed so as well, and if Nicholas wanted to keep his oath, his private promise to protect his younger brother, as Lucian had once protected him—resurrected him—on the dirty, dangerous French streets all those years before, Nicholas would heed the monster before him.

"Release me," Nicholas demanded. "Now."

Cruen grinned, his red fangs—a symbol of the Order's end of blood consumption—were pin-prick sharp. "I appreciate your eagerness. Will you be a good little *paven*, then?"

It took every ounce of mental restraint for Nicholas to spit out the words "I will."

The thick leather straps around his arms, belly, neck, and ankles evaporated like boiling water, and before another word was spoken, before he could even sit upright, he was flashed from the Tomb of Nascita and dropped naked, his brands still smoking, onto the mountaintop next to the cave.

Night covered the sky, a spring mist coated the air, and his brothers stood at the mouth of the cave, matching expressions of rage on their faces.

1

Vermont credenti

As the blue light of day succumbed to the pale lavender of evening, a bitter cold moved over the land, shook the snow from the trees, and curled around the *veana* and the *balas* who sat on the front steps of the small *credenti* elementary school. The snow on the ground that had been melting just a few hours earlier now glistened under the rising moon as water quickly turned back to ice. It was nearing six p.m., and in accordance with the laws of the Order, it was time to end the labor of the day and begin the calm of night. Most residents of the *credenti* had left their work or schooling and had entered their homes for family meal and reflection. Kate Everborne, however, had no family to go home to. What she did have was a belief that reflection was for unthinking drones and the unwelcome responsibility of a seven-year-old *balas* who once again had to be watched until his mother showed up.

"She's not coming."

Kate glanced down at the boy. With his large black eyes and shock of white hair he didn't blend in well. She knew how that was. "She's coming. She's just late."

"She's always late," he grumbled.

"Give her a break, okay, kid? She's doing the best she can."

"She should work inside the *credenti*. Like you. Do what *veanas* are supposed to do."

The smile on Kate's face was tight and forced, just like the white purity bindings on her wrists and throat. The last thing in the world she wanted to be doing was living inside the *credenti*, or any vampire community, for that matter. And her work at the elementary school, passing out lentils and fruit during midmeal—well, it was utter bullshit, a way to keep her in plain sight, see if she could live among society again.

But she didn't have a choice in where she resided. Not yet.

"She dishonors my father's memory by leaving the *credenti*," the boy continued.

"You're a good kid, Ladd Letts, but right now you're acting like a brat."

He crossed his arms over his chest. "I don't care."

"Yeah, I can tell."

"I don't care about me and I don't care about her." He puffed out his lips. "Maybe I wish she'd never come."

Kate sniffed. "Maybe she wishes that, too."

Ladd's eyes grew wide and *balas*-wet as he stared up at her, took in what she'd just said and molded it into the worst possible abandonment scenario.

Ah, shit. Kate released a weary breath. She could be a real asshole sometimes. "Listen, kid, I didn't mean it like that. I was . . ."

"I'm here. I'm here." Mirabelle Letts came running across the tree-littered play yard toward them, her feet sinking calf-deep in the heavy snow. She was a pretty *veana*—small, curvy, with soft brown doe eyes that did their best to exude happiness. Slightly breathless, she called out, "Sorry, Kate."

"No problem," Kate returned, coming to her feet. She was just relieved the *veana* had shown up. She really sucked with kids, wasn't sure what to say to them, how to comfort them. Sticking her in a school wasn't the Order's smartest move, but hell, she wasn't about to complain. She had two months left on her work release, two months until she could finally consider her time spent in the vampire prison, Mondrar, over and done, the debt for another's crime paid.

Until then, she was keeping her nose clean and her fangs retracted.

Ladd jumped to his feet and waved his arms like he was landing planes, all anger gone now. "Mommy! I see you!"

Kate chuckled at the quick recovery. At Ladd's age, it seemed that no matter what a parent did, said, or forgot, they were always a welcome sight.

Give it a few years, kid.

No more than ten feet away, Mirabelle waved back at her child as she waded through the snow. "Training went over and there was a gardening demonstration—"

It happened in an instant. Something shot out of the shadows of the trees, cutting off Mirabelle's words. A *paven*, tall and dark. In under a second, he was on Mirabelle, ripping the scarf from her neck, searching her flesh. Kate opened her mouth to scream when she saw a silver flash. A knife! Oh, shit. No! Terror locked the scream in her chest, and she fought the dual urges of running to help the *veana* and protecting the young *balas* at her side.

Before she could make her choice, the *paven* plunged the knife deep into Mirabelle's chest, then yanked it back out again and took to her thighs, slashing at her skin until he severed the two main arteries. Blood exploded from her legs in violent sprays.

Her attacker released her, let her limp body drop to the ground, and a piercing scream whipped through the night and jerked Kate from her horror.

Ladd.

His face contorted with panic, he ran at his mother, but Kate caught him in her arms and held him back.

The dark-haired male suddenly glanced up, locked eyes with Kate, and grinned. *Fuck.* It was there in his eyes, in his smile—hunger to spill blood. He was going to take her out and the kid too if she didn't run or fight him off.

The butcher *paven* started toward her and Ladd, his movements graceful, catlike. Knowing she couldn't outrun him, not with the boy, Kate shoved Ladd behind her back, opened her arms to the evil coming at her, and flashed her fangs. *Come and get it, then, ass-*

hole. His smile widened, the moonlight catching the tips of his fangs. Then suddenly he stopped, lifted his chin, and sniffed the air. With a growl of annoyance, he turned around and ran back across the field, into the trees.

What the hell?

Kate sucked in the bitterly cold air scented with blood and screamed, "Help!" Silently praying that Mirabelle was still alive, she raced to the female's side, Ladd at her heels. The *veana's* eyes were open, but her quick, shallow breaths signaled how close to death she was. Kate dropped down in the snow and pressed her hands to the gaping wound in the female's chest. Forcing up the healing energy all Pureblood *veanas* possessed, she blew on the wounds in Mirabelle's thighs—back and forth, back and forth, each breath a show in pure determination and desperation. But the cuts were so deep, the femoral artery calculatedly severed. Red death seeped between her fingers, over the *veana's* chest, spilling out onto the pure white-powdered floor.

"Goddammit!" Kate screamed. "We need help here!" Darkness had come. Where were all the selfless, community-first, pious bastards when one of their own needed them?

Ladd laid his head on his mother's belly and howled in misery.

Mirabelle's eyes were glassy as she hovered somewhere between this world and the next. Her gaze flickered toward her son, then back up to Kate. "Take him," she uttered through short gasps of breath.

"Don't talk," Kate said.

"Take him. Please. He can't be tested."

Lifting her head again, Kate yelled into the frigid air, "We need help!"

"No!" Mirabelle rasped. "Please. Before they come . . . take the *balas.*"

She was delusional, had to be. Kate shook her head. "He'll be okay. Don't worry."

Mirabelle whispered something.

"I can't hear you . . ."

"Come. Please."

Kate lowered her head, her ear to the female's mouth.

"He will be . . . caged if they find out."

"Find out what?" Kate uttered, keeping her ear close to the female's lips.

In the last seconds before her death, Mirabelle revealed not only her secrets, but her desperate plea to save her son's life, all to the one vampire on earth who, if she wanted to gain her freedom, could do nothing for her.

The steady beats of the Impures' hearts beckoned.

They always did.

Ethan Dare was one of them and yet the males that hovered so near within the Vermont *credenti* woodlands would be hard-pressed to see his merciless destruction of a Pureblood *veana* as a sacrifice to the cause. No. They'd been raised to serve, protect, and defend their Pureblood masters, not rebel against them. And when

Ethan had finally left the vicinity, they would run back to their quarters and squeal to the very ones who had once upon a time turned them over to the Order for blood castration. Yes, taking away an Impure's ability to breed or even enjoy sex could not spur the inferior class into running away.

Ethan closed his eyes and flashed out of the woods.

According to the Order, his Impure brothers and sisters of the *credenti* were sterilized for the good of the Breed. Keep things nice and pure. Well, the Order could keep their precious purity. After a slow recovery from the bullet wounds he'd suffered at the hands of Alexander Roman, Ethan and his recruits had begun anew, and soon he would be coming back to the Vermont *credenti* just as he'd done in the Maine and Pennsylvania communities to offer each Impure a new life.

From frosty air and heavy snow to arid, oppressive heat, Ethan touched down on the iridescent sand of the Supreme One's existence. His partner in the Uprising could command time, place, mood, and, much to Ethan's irritation, temperature. The *paven* got off on heat—intense, land-of-Satan kind of heat—and for a male who had a hard time regulating his body temperature as of late, it was a real pain in the ass for Ethan to take a meeting there.

But he never complained. After all, he would always go where the power meal was.

Sweating like a whore in church, Ethan trudged down to the water's edge. His arms hung at his sides, empty. They should've held the *balas*, but his attempt to get Ladd Letts hadn't been successful. Not that he really gave a shit, but the one who fed him, the one who gave him power did, and Ethan knew he was in for a fang-lashing.

No sympathetic breeze caressed his face as he drew nearer the water, just incessant blasts of wet heat. The Supreme One's reality was a massive one-room beach setting, open to the elements, dressed with plant life and flowers, and three white walls adorned with Hockney miniatures. As Ethan passed by a stand of palm trees, he took in the sight of his human female, lying on a beach chair sunning herself. Pearl McClean's eyes were closed and her hands were on her round belly. She was a "guest" of the Supreme One's. Instead of staying with Ethan at his new compound, which had been given to him by a Hollywood actress with a penchant for males with fangs, the master had insisted she remain with him. The sweet, stupid little thing had happily agreed before he'd even had a chance to persuade the *paven* otherwise.

Poor Pearl. She had no idea she was collateral.

Ethan kept walking until sand gave way to sea. Over the water, lying in a hammock supported by nothing at all, the Supreme One reclined, his gnarled hand passing back and forth over the blue water, manipulating the speed of the waves as they rushed to the shore. Slowly at first, then a bullet train of salt water crashing against Ethan's thighs, followed by the ever-popular freeze in midair trick.

Ethan sighed. Oh, the drama.

When he reached the Supreme One, he inclined his head. "It is done, my lord."

The Supreme One dragged his gaze from the water and narrowed it on Ethan. "You're certain?"

"Her blood ran like sweet wine into the snow."

"And you saw the mark? The eternal kiss?"

"It was on the back of her neck, as the genealogist claimed."

The Supreme One grinned. "Nicholas Roman's true mate extinguished."

"Yes, sir." It was a bizarre partnership, Ethan thought, wiping the sweat from his face and neck. The supposed ancient Pureblood teaming up with an Impure who was hell-bent on the destruction of the Pureblood race—but they both had much to gain, it seemed.

"And the boy?" the Supreme One said. "Where do you have him hidden?"

There it was. The dreaded question. Ethan forced out his chin. Fucking up was one thing, but he must never appear the weaker to this *paven*—even if they both knew he was. "I couldn't get to the boy."

The Supreme One sat up. "Fool!"

"There was a *veana* with him, and Impures close by, watching. I didn't want the whole of the *credenti* on my ass."

"Of course you didn't," the Supreme One muttered with undisguised sarcasm. "Impure coward."

Ethan sniffed. Impure coward indeed. Though the Supreme One had great and awe-inspiring power, he had revealed to Ethan the truth about his own blood—

the drops of Impurity that lay dormant in his cells, his secret lineage—a male on his father's side who had been born of a human woman. The Supreme One hated his Impurity, even as he had given his support to the Uprising.

"I will get to the boy," Ethan assured him. "I just need to rest, gain more strength. Perhaps if you had fed me more regularly during my recovery I could have remained and fought—"

Ethan shot into the air, flew forward and slammed headfirst into the water. A light thread of panic jumped in his blood and he tried like hell to lift his head out of the rushing current, but his neck refused to give. He couldn't move. Not even a fingertip. He knew better than to criticize the Supreme One.

Holding his breath as long as he could, he whimpered his exhaustion, his eyes scanning the empty seafloor. Then his lungs gave out and he inhaled, swallowing the salty water in gulps. Pain surged through him, an empty ache. Recognizing he was in the moments before death, Ethan conjured an image of the child he'd created yet would never see. He barely felt the force yanking him up out of the water and tossing him onto the sand.

Choking on the water in his lungs, weak as a *balas*, Ethan tried to sit up. He clutched his skull and whimpered as stars played on his eyelids.

"Open your eyes, Impure."

Ethan forced his lids back.

The Supreme One still lounged in his hammock, a

soporific smile on his lined face. "You want your feed, do you?"

Ethan could only nod. What he would give to make the Supreme One choke, just once.

"You may have it."

Once on his knees, Ethan tried to capture a clear breath, then attempted to stand.

"Remain," said the Supreme One.

Ethan lifted his eyes. "My lord . . . ?"

"Remain on your hands and knees and crawl to me."

Because he had to, *for now* he had to, Ethan did as he was told, inching toward the master—a dog looking for a scrap—as his human female watched from the sanctuary of her lounge chair, her eyes losing a thread of their admiration.

Someday he would be the one who controlled all. Someday he would make the Purebloods—and the *paven* before him—crawl.

2

The collar of his coat flipped up to mask the brands that were now seared into the skin of his cheeks, Nicholas pushed his sunglasses to the bridge of his nose with his index finger and moved through the crowd. On the stage to his left, an all-female heavy-metal band rocked out, their hands working their instruments, their bodies gyrating against their mike stands. The guitar player, a tall redhead with ripped fishnets and dragon tats up both arms grinned at him and tried to catch his eye, but he was on the hunt for one hidden somewhere in the strobe-lit shadows.

The Eyes, the New York City street rats who ran the sales of drugs, blood, and body to both human and vampire had texted Nicholas twenty minutes ago—just as he was getting bawled out by his brothers for going it alone before the Order. It had been a real shame to have to bail on Alexander's lecture, end Lucian's rant regarding his bullshit actions and inconsiderate stupidity. But hey, the Eyes were claiming to own some information Nicholas wanted pretty badly, and rescheduling his brothers' tantrum for sometime next century seemed the wisest course of action.

Pissed at the lack of control they had over the situation with the Order, Alexander and Lucian had made it clear they'd wanted to be at this little meet and greet. But the Eyes tended to clam up around blood they didn't know, and Nicholas wasn't going to risk that.

He walked around the bar, his gaze sliding from one face to another. His brothers would ease off, calm down, and get on board once he came home with the location of Dare and his recruits. Because Dare's whereabouts was the reason for this meet.

Had to be.

Better be.

His gaze shifted to the hallway leading to the emergency exit. *There. Bingo.* A tall, lean figure stood under the pale red sign, deep in the shadows, the agreed-upon Mets cap tilted low. Nicholas headed in that direction, but even before he reached the hazy spotlight of red, he knew something was off. Way off. The one waiting in the shadows wasn't a member of the Eyes, wasn't an Impure—and definitely was not a *paven*.

Another step forward and her blood scent hit him like a battering ram—up the nostrils, into the lungs, and straight down to his cock.

Holy shit. His hands dropped to his sides, hovered near his weapons. What the hell was this? As one who'd spent years selling his flesh, only the scent of currency made his body react like that. He inhaled again, filling his lungs with that luscious, highly addictive scent she was throwing off, as his brain searched for clues into what was waiting for him under that Mets cap besides a few strands of escaped blond hair.

She was a Pureblood *veana*, and if the abilities of his newly morphed status could be trusted, untouched by a *paven*.

What the fuck was going on here? Had Dare orchestrated this meet? Or was this something else altogether? Some*one* sent through the wrong channels—the Nicholas Roman for-hire channels—the one he kept private for . . . private clients.

The *veana* lifted her head then and he saw her face for the first time. *Jesus*. She was gorgeous. Drop-dead. Her skin was smooth and tantalizing, like cream with a touch of honey mixed in, and her nose was small and perfect. But it was her lips that really made his cock stir . . . full and pale pink. Christ, he wanted to run his fangs, his mouth up one cheek and down the other, catch her lips as he went, suckle the dark pink top, then the extra-plump bottom.

Then there were her eyes. Large, deeply brown, tough as a brick wall, and screamed disaster. They were the most beautifully haunting things he'd ever seen. And he'd seen many pairs of fine eyes.

She was his perfection, and well, that just couldn't be an accident, now, could it?

As he headed for her, his hands stole inside his coat, closed around the guns at his waist. She was tall for a *veana*, perfect height in fact, and even in the *credenti* rags she wore, he could tell she was built for a *paven*'s hands—his hands.

He released the safeties on his twin Glocks as he met her under the red glow. He didn't want to shoot up the place, but he wasn't about to walk into a trap unprepared either. "Who are you?" he asked her.

Her eyes met his with an abrasive wariness. "A messenger."

Her voice coated the air around him, like satin for the ears. Whoever had sent her knew him well. "Have a message for me?"

She nodded. "If you're Nicholas Roman."

But who knew him that well, save his brothers?

"Are you?" she asked. "Nicholas Roman?"

He wanted to see how this played out. He nodded. "Yes."

She turned then, called out to someone behind her. "Ladd. Come here."

Nicholas reached out and grabbed her, had her back to his front and his gun trained on her temple in under a second. "Don't move, *veana*."

She didn't. But she did growl at him. "Put the gun down, asshole."

"Not a chance."

"You're going to scare him."

"Scare who?"

"Don't do this."

"Scare *who*?" he said again, his tone lethal, his hand crushing against her ribs.

"The *balas*," she uttered between gritted teeth.

A boy stepped out of the shadows and into the pale red spotlight where the *veana* had been just seconds ago. His hair was snow white and his dark eyes were wide and filled with fear as he took in the sight before him.

Nicholas dropped his gun at once, but didn't release the *veana*. His tone went dry and deeply suspicious. "What is this?"

The *veana* didn't struggle against him, but she turned her head and looked up into his face, her large, haunting eyes threatening to bore a hole right into his skull. "This, Nicholas Roman, is your son."

3

.

Kate stared up into the hard-angled, menacingly dark face of the devil himself and loved what she saw.

But that was her way, attracted to pain and torment in any form.

Within the greasy, blood-spattered walls of Mondrar prison, the stories of the Breeding Male were whispered from cell to cell late into the night. As Kate had huddled close to the bars, trying to gather warmth from the coal fire that sat in the very center of the cell block, she had listened, heard all about his offspring who roamed the earth. She'd heard of their escape when the Breeding Male program had ended abruptly a few hundred years ago. She'd heard they were predators, animallike Purebloods who lived in the shadows, waiting for the day they were morphed, waiting for their genetic codes to awaken and set them free to rut any female they encountered.

She wondered about this one who held her against his painfully hard chest, his thick black hair licking at his neck, his cruel mouth ready to do battle. Was he on the hunt? Had he awakened? Was that a trace of lust in his black gaze?

"Are you going to let go of me anytime soon?" she said, remaining still, calm, despite her instinct to jab her elbow deep into his groin. She knew when to fight and when it was wisest to play the soft *veana*.

"No," he uttered, pulling her closer, forcing her elbows to lock straight, allowing her to feel the true force of his size.

"Any closer, *paven*," she said, "and my relations will force you to mate me."

"Who sent you?"

"The mother of the *balas*."

He didn't believe her; it was clear as hell in those severe black eyes. "How did you text me? How did you get my number?"

"The Eyes passed it along."

"Those Impure pieces of shit," he muttered. "They'd sell their mother's beating heart straight from her chest if they could get enough for it."

Sounded about right, Kate thought.

"What it is you want, *veana*?" he asked, his voice a hotbed of irritation. "You need money?"

Kate didn't blame him for not trusting her, but she didn't have time for this. "I need to get this done, get the boy with his father, and move on."

His eyes scanned every inch of her face as his lower half pressed closer to her hips. "Are you working for Dare or one of his recruits?"

Heat rushed through her, proving once again that fear and hard handling were the keys to getting her hot. Jesus, she was pathetic. "Don't know anyone named Dare."

He chuckled. "Nice."

"Listen, I'm here for the *balas*. That's it. We came on the train from the Vermont *credenti*." Her gaze slid from his to the boy. Ladd, who remained in the pool of hazy red light, wore an expression of confused anguish. Kate felt her chest constrict. She hated it, hated what had happened to him—hated that she was going to have to leave him here with this *paven* who appeared closer to predator than parent. But shit, she had no choice.

She turned back to the Roman brother and laid it all out. "Mirabelle Letts asked me to bring her son to you. Your son."

His grip on her suddenly eased. "Mirabelle."

"That's right." She watched the aggressive ire slip from his expression and knew a nerve had been hit—knew that if she was going to get away she'd need to amp it up right now. She whispered so the boy wouldn't hear, "Remember her, do you? Pretty, dark hair, soft eyes. Maybe eight years ago? Your bed? Or was it against the wall in a club like this?"

He released her then, thrust her toward Ladd. "Enough of that."

The pain in his face was evident. Kate wasn't a fan of playing with people's emotions, but she did what she had to do to get free, stay free.

"Why didn't Mirabelle come herself?" he asked.

"She couldn't."

He sniffed bitterly. "How convenient."

"She couldn't," Kate repeated darkly, moving closer to Ladd, "because she's dead."

At that moment, the redhead with the dragon tats sent her electric guitar into a perfect high-pitched scream. It resonated throughout the club, and vibrated through Nicholas's body. Hell, in that moment, it was his emotional fucking sound track. It wasn't as if he'd loved Mirabelle Letts. God, he didn't love anyone, least of all the bodies he screwed for money. But he remembered her, her gentle face, her tears when he'd made her climax. And he remembered how lonely she was. Her mate hadn't been into females, but had mated with her out of duty, and had never touched her after the first night they were together.

Nicholas stared at the *balas* before him. He remembered Mirabelle Letts because, like him, she had been dying on the inside for a long time.

"When did it happen?" he nearly shouted over the guitar solo.

"About ten hours ago," the *veana* said.

"How?"

When she didn't answer, he looked up. She had her arm around the *balas*, and her eyes trained on him. She shook her head, as in *Not in front of the boy, dumbass.*

His gaze returned to the *balas*. Eight years ago. Yes, that sounded about right. "What's your name, boy?"

The *balas* looked tired, scared shitless, but he said in a strong, clear voice, "Ladd."

"And yours?" Nicholas said, shifting his gaze upward.

The *veana* shook her head. "Doesn't matter."

"Like hell it doesn't."

"Let's stick with Messenger. How's that?"

"Hiding something, *veana*?"

"Aren't we all?"

The question hidden inside a statement thing made his blood heat and he closed the distance between them. Her scent pushed into his nostrils again, clawed its way into his lungs, and if the boy hadn't been there, he was pretty damn sure he'd have yanked her back into his arms and taken her mouth, tasted her tongue. But the *balas* was there, huddled against her hip, and Nicholas needed to get to the whole truth of what was before him.

Then, like a magic trick revealed, he spotted something, something on the *veana*'s alabaster neck. What the hell was it? The mark of her true mate? The bruise of a sweet, hard suck—a blood drain from a hopeful lover?

He cocked his head to one side, narrowed his eyes.

No.

Fuck him. No.

A growl vibrated in Nicholas's throat, and grew in both volume and ferocity until the *balas* ducked behind the *veana* and clung to her waist.

He knew it. Goddammit! The scent of her, the overwhelming desire he felt—it was all a deception, a trick by an Impureblood who knew that the Romans were after him, and that his time was almost up.

And this *veana* had the cheek to stand there looking confused, pissed off even as strands of her long blond hair attempted to hide the whip marks branded on her neck.

Nicholas leaned in and took a count. One, two, three . . . Ten in all. Ten years in Mondrar, the vampire prison. His nostrils flared. A fucking criminal, punished by the Order. And to use a *balas* . . . No wonder she knew the Eyes. No doubt one of them had been a cell mate or a fellow yard scum.

The *veana* suddenly saw where his eyes were trained and blanched in the red light, pushed her hair forward in an attempt to hide the marks.

Nicholas shook his head and grinned at her. "You nearly had my sympathy, *veana*. Nearly." He felt her stiffen as he leaned in and whispered in her ear, "Listen well, *sacro* bitch. Tell Dare he can send a hundred *balas* my way, but the only trap to fall into is the one I'll be setting for him."

Without another look at the pair, Nicholas turned and walked away. *Veana* who used their *balas* deserved nothing less than misery.

Nice, France
1892

"Wake her up!"

The male who had come blustering into their flat

stank of liquor and refused to leave, even though Nicholas had told him that his mama could not service tonight. She was sick. More than usual. More every day. The vampire drug *gravo*, the dried, poisoned blood she loved so dearly, was taking her mind away, her body too, perhaps even taking away her love for her son.

"I will have my suck, *boy*," the male slurred, gripping the wall for support. "Wake her up or I will shove *mon grand bitte* up her ass."

Frightened now, Nicholas hurried to his mother, who lay prostrate on the sofa and shook her. "Mama, Mama, please. *Un homme* is here for you."

"I will pay well," the male put in, grinning. "If she uses *des crocs*, that is."

Fangs for francs. It was what the humans always wanted from her. Nicholas didn't understand why they would want to feel such pain.

"Nichola," his mother rasped, her eyes flickering open.

Nicholas dropped to his knees beside the sofa. "Mama."

"What is it he wants?"

"I want *turlutte*!" the male said with a drunken chuckle. "The wee *garçon* can watch if you'd like—see how his mama's open mouth and willing throat earns her her francs."

"Nichola," his mother whispered. "Will you help me?"

"What is it, Mama? What can I do?"

Her eyes, so red from the *gravo*, her lips so pale.

She needed blood, but Nicholas couldn't give her his anymore—he had grown too weak. And she could not feed him, as her own blood was near to poison now.

She turned her head, tried to focus on the male. "My *balas* will care for you, monsieur."

From his position near the wall, the male looked down at Nicholas. There was no shock in his eyes at the suggestion, only mild irritation. "He has barely *huit ans*."

Nicholas nearly told the male that he was indeed eight years. Last Sunday was his birthday. But he didn't have a chance. Stumbling toward him, the male grabbed Nicholas off the ground, stood him up, and forced open his mouth. As his rotten breath beat down on Nicholas's face, the male ran his thumb roughly over Nicholas's tongue and fangs. When he felt the ridges, he smiled. "Yes. This is good, nice. I will accept him."

"Go with him to my room, *mon petit*." Nicholas's mother started coughing, a bitter, harsh sound that he was more than used to. "Get his ten francs first."

Nicholas understood what his mother was asking him to do and his entire body shook with fear and revulsion. "No, Mama. Please. No."

"Just this once, *mon petit*." Her eyes implored him. "For Mama. I am so tired. And we need to feed."

The fear inside the boy was nothing next to his love for his mama. He would eat crushed glass for her if she asked it of him. He supposed that to eat another male would be nothing.

And yet, when the monsieur led him into his mother's room and closed the door, he nearly froze in terror.

"On your knees, boy," the male commanded, taking down his pants and releasing his thick manhood. "And drop your fangs."

Kate watched Nicholas Roman disappear into the sea of writhing, sweat-drenched bodies and tried not to panic. What the hell did she do now? Time was running out. She needed to get back to the *credenti* before the Order knew she was gone, before they connected Mirabelle's body and Ladd's disappearance with her—before they took away the one thing that mattered in her unlivable life—her freedom.

She reached for Ladd's hand and led him toward the back door of the club. "Come on, kid."

"I'm tired."

"I know." *Me too.*

"Can we go back home?"

"No."

"Where are we going, then?" he whined, though it wasn't the sound of the petulant seven-year-old on the *credenti* steps anymore. This was a child who was truly and understandably scared.

"I'll let you know when I figure it out." She looked down, gave him a weary smile. "Okay?"

He bit his lip, but nodded.

Taking the boy's hand, Kate headed out of the club into the dimly lit alley. Screw Nicholas Roman. Seriously, what was she supposed to do? Run after him and beg him to take the boy? It was clear he thought she was a con and that the boy was part of that con. And there was something in him that wanted it that way, expected it, was relieved by it.

She'd figure something out, always did. Maybe the Eyes knew where she could take Ladd, where he'd be safe for a while. She just needed two months and then she could come back—

A sudden jerk of fear moved through her, made her tighten her grip on the boy. She glanced around, her eyes hitting every dark corner, her ears listening for any sound that wasn't expected. Nothing. Nothing she could connect to and yet she felt something.

Some*one*.

Again, her gaze jumped from dark corner to dark corner, to windows with bars slashed across them, her skin prickling at the feeling of whatever it was that was watching from the shadows.

She shoved the boy behind her back and slowly turned around in a circle. A come out, come out, wherever you are that she hoped wouldn't be fruitful, and yet the need to know what was out there nearly had her shouting into the black.

Finally, when nothing appeared or advanced, she gave up. Time to hit the road. And fast. Pulling at Ladd's hand, she hurried him forward, down the remainder of the empty alleyway. The energy of whatever it was followed them, but Kate just kept going. At first she wondered if it was the *Similis*, the Impure guards of Mondrar, come to take her back, but she knew their scent—had felt their eyes on her every moment of every day for ten years.

This was something else.

"Let's go, Ladd," she urged the boy. "A little faster."

If they could just get into the light, into traffic, maybe whatever it was would back off.

Half a block. That was it.

She caught her heel on the edge of a pothole and stumbled a little. Loose gravel went flying, but she remained upright and moving, sensing the nearness of the hidden presence, the shadow of whatever followed them gaining ground. For the first time, she wondered if maybe this thing was after the boy, not her. What if it wanted to hurt him? Shit! Maybe she should just take him back, go back to the *credenti* right now, give up . . .

Suddenly, like a miniature bolt of lightning, the alley exploded with white. Panicked, Kate glanced behind her and saw Nicholas Roman practically flying toward them, sunglasses, black hair, long coat—a devil with angel's wings. In under a second, he scooped both her and Ladd into his arms, and they were gone—flashed out of the alleyway and hovering somewhere between light and darkness.

4

His brain burned, his throat too.

Alcohol moved through Gray Donohue's veins at a hectic pace, gripping every inch of muscle and skin.

It wasn't a cure-all, but, combined with the deafening sounds of the house band, Cage, it tamped down the voices in his mind.

Instead of barks he heard whispers.

For the past month he'd searched the city, even Long Island, for a club he could get lost in at night, a club that drowned out the voices of others. Equinox was it. Auditory perfection—or as close as he was going to get. And night after night he went there to drink, to fuck, and to sleep—to forget that he'd ever wished for the memories of the fire that had taken his father's life to be gone from his mind.

Shit, he'd give anything to be catatonic again.

"Wakey, wakey, little brother."

Gray's eyes snapped open and he snarled at the voice, a strident growl in his ear. It didn't belong to any brother of his—it belonged to his sister's mate,

Alexander Roman, and it had been there before, two months before, searching for the debilitating pain of past trauma, retrieving and eliminating each thread of it through his blood until it was as if it had never been.

Alexander had the gift of speaking into another's mind, while Gray had the hidden curse of not being able to turn off the voices of anyone and everyone around him.

Pretty much yin and yang from hell.

Pushing out of the booth near the back of the club, Gray faced both the dark-haired vampire and his acidic, nearly albino brother. He'd hoped the pair wouldn't be able to track him down, but he knew it was a lost cause. Especially for Alexander. His sister Sara's mate would do anything to make her happy.

Even trail a newly discovered Impure who had made it crystal clear he wanted no part of their clan.

Gray hovered around six foot, not exactly sky-scraper tall like the Roman brothers, but what he lacked in height he made up for in muscle. Another way to shut out the noise. Big fat weights and an iPod cranked up to eardrum-busting loud.

"Not in the mood, boys," he yelled over the heavy-metal din of Cage.

"This is getting old," Lucian shouted at Alexander. "Why do we have to babysit this kid?"

Alexander tossed his brother a fierce glare.

"Oh, right." The near-albino with the fierce almond eyes snorted. "Relatives."

Ignoring Lucian, Alexander focused his gaze on

Gray. "We were supposed to be training thirty minutes ago."

We. There was no *we.* Why couldn't this bastard get that? Thankfully, Lucian and Nicholas didn't give a shit about pulling him into their family, into their training schedule. It was Alexander alone who kept trying to make him into a warrior, trying to get him to fight for their cause. In the beginning, after Alexander had taken the memory of the fire from his mind, Gray had given the *paven* his time, his brawn, even his allegiance. Hell, what else could he do? Alexander had given him an existence, allowed him to feel again, know desire and lust.

That is, until the telepathic bullshit had set in.

Gray grinned. And Alexander wanted him to fight his war?

Didn't the Roman brother know he had a war going on of his own? A secret war—inside his motherfucking head?

Again.

"You're wasting your time here," Gray yelled, as the crowd of a hundred or more in front of them started slam dancing.

Alexander didn't even hesitate. "No."

Gray cocked his head. "You're not going to pull that 'If you're going to live under my roof' bit, are you?"

He shrugged. "If you act like a *balas*, you'll get treated as one."

"Shit," Lucian yelled, loud enough for the pair of females in front of them to turn around and give them the once-over. "How about I pull the 'drag him by the hair like a little girl thing.'"

"Lucian," Alexander said through gritted teeth, skimming a hand over his skull-shaved head. "Shut it already!"

"Why should I? He's been acting like a little bitch for two months. Why you unlocked his mind for this bullshit is beyond me."

Gray laughed. "Damn right! Maybe you should've left things as they were, Alex."

Leaning in near Gray's ear, Lucian snarled, "Hey, I could send you back to oblivion if you'd like."

"Stop, both of you," Alexander commanded, his tone war room heavy now. He eyeballed Gray. "Come with us now."

"And if I don't?" Gray countered.

"You will," was all Alexander said before he turned around and headed toward the door of the club.

Cage's final song ended abruptly with a shattering clang on the drums.

Voices came at Gray like a hundred predatory mosquitoes. But inside the hum he heard two distinct voices.

"Because I don't want to have to drain my mate's little brother. Again."

Alexander. Real pissed, real worried.

"Worthless Impure."

Lucian. Clear and disgusted and . . . true.

Nicholas landed on the exterior observation deck of the Empire State Building, his arms wrapped excessively tight around his companions.

Especially her.

Her.

The wind whipped over the glass enclosures, sending her blood scent straight into his nostrils, teasing him, enticing him. His fangs elongated in his mouth. What was it with this *veana*? Why did he want to tear the clothes from her body and play doctor? His hands curled into fists, bunching the rough fabric of her coat between his fingers, wishing it was her hot, smooth skin. How did she have this power over him? How had Dare managed to gift it to her?

"Make no mistake," he uttered, his mouth dangerously close to her neck. "I did that for the boy."

"Yeah," she said, pushing away from him. "I got it."

When she reached the railing a few feet away, she turned, no doubt expecting the boy to have followed her. But Ladd remained, clinging to Nicholas's leg like it was a lifeline, and Nicholas let him, even put his hand on the *balas*'s head. Hell, it wasn't the boy's fault he'd been brought into this bullshit.

The Mets cap had come off somewhere back in the alley, and under the bright light of the moon Nicholas saw the *veana* fully—her perfect face, those large tragic eyes, and her long hair, pale as beach sand flying about her shoulders in the wind. He itched to touch it, even imagined it wrapped around his fist as he pulled her in for a taste. Goddammit! Goddamn *HER*! His lower half stirred and he growled at the effect she had over him.

"So, what was that?" he said. "Did you piss off Dare,

or was that thing hiding in the alleyway another guest of Mondrar?"

The *veana* said nothing, her gaze dropping to the boy every few seconds as though she wasn't sure if Nicholas was going to keep his hand on the *balas*'s head or drop it to the child's neck for a quick snap.

"Or was it the Order?" Nicholas continued. "They looking for you?"

"Ladd," she said, ignoring Nicholas altogether, "you want to come over here?"

The boy stared at her, but didn't move.

"Did you break out?" Nicholas pressed. "How many years of hard labor do you have left?"

She flashed him her fangs. "You really like hearing yourself talk, don't you?" Again, she called to the boy, "Ladd? Are you okay?"

Nicholas kept at it, hoping she would crack or get so pissed off she'd let the whole story rip. "Are you on the run, *veana*?"

"Goddammit!"

"Are you?"

"Yes!"

Finally. If she was connected to Dare, maybe he could get a location out of her or a meeting place. His tone smoothed out. "And the Eyes? Did they introduce you to Dare?"

"The only answers I'm bound to give you, *paven*," she said through clenched teeth, "are about the boy and his mother. I've done that. I'm done here."

His eyes narrowed. "What does that mean?"

"I did what Mirabelle asked me to do. Bring the boy to his father. I'm done."

"You're not done until I say you're done."

Her gaze dropped again. "Ladd, it'll be all right, I swear."

The instinct to rip into her flesh with his fangs was as strong as the desire to pleasure her with them. "Where. Is. Dare?"

"I don't know who you're talking about."

He looked at her with true disgust. "There are not many females on this earth who would agree to use a *balas* as bait."

Her face went white as a snowfall, and her cheeks pulled inward. But it was her eyes that gripped his soul and twisted, those large brown mirrors that showed a raw misery he completely understood. He knew what had made him look at the world like that, but what had she seen—or done?

She looked down and faced the *balas*, her tone gentle but resolute. "Listen, you'll be okay. Safer than with me, I promise you."

Ladd clung to Nicholas's leg.

She backed up along the railing. Slowly, the city lights spread out in back of her. She pointed a finger at Nicholas. "Take care of him or I swear I'll come after you."

Nicholas laughed. "Where do you think you're going to go, *veana*? And how are you going to get there? You can't flash—you haven't gone through Meta. I can tell."

"No." She shook her head. "I'm not going to flash." She stepped back another three feet, this time into a weak, but undeniable ray of day's first light. "But you are."

Whipping around, Nicholas saw the very raw edges of daybreak. He shot back to face her, stared into eyes that may have carried deep pain, but also rendered an undeniable strength.

"I will see you soon, *veana*." Then he flashed, the boy firmly affixed to his side.

5

"You're an embarrassment. You know that, right?"
Working a light sweat and dressed head to toe
in black fighting gear, Lucian sidled up to the counter
and dropped his new toy, his new weapon of choice—a
Fusion tomahawk—on the granite.

"Watch it," Alexander said, knife in hand, head
down, brutalizing some sad piece of fruit. "Evans just
put this in yesterday."

Lucian's gaze slid over the gleaming slab of ebony
stone. It was a damn shame. "Pureblood *pavens* do not
have kitchens."

"Times have changed, little brother."

"So it would seem. Especially when you're tracking
an ingrate Impure male who wants nothing to do with
our cause, instead of the one who will get the Order off
our asses."

"Ease up, Luca," Alexander said tightly. "You'll never
understand what—"

"You'll do for a female? Hell no. Don't want to.
And forget Gray—look at you. One second out of

sparring practice and you're working on your slice and dice."

That made Alexander grin, shrug. "My true mate desires. I provide."

Yes, the female. They screwed up everything. "Hey, your knife looks a little dull there, brother." Lucian yanked up the tomahawk and thrust it toward Alexander. "Wanna use mine?"

"Pass." Alexander waved the weapon away, his movements causing the lit votive candles on the countertop to twitch.

The house had just gone dark as the sun was up, and Alexander was working this romantic bullshit first thing in the morning for his *veana*.

"We should be continuing to train," Lucian said with obvious irritation. "And you're standing in what used to be our game room, looking like a fucking contestant on *Top Chef*."

Alexander pointed his knife at Lucian. "I knew you watched that bullshit."

"Seriously, *Duro*," Lucian said, using the affectionate word for brother with all the sarcasm he could muster. "If you're going this route then you need to swap out those battle blacks you're wearing for a nice white chef dress—oh, shit, I mean *coat*."

"Hey—can you shut your hole for a moment and help me figure out the best way to serve this?"

"You're talking about the fruit, right? Because you've clearly already served up your balls to that *veana* of yours."

A growl vibrated in Alexander's throat and his eyes flashed red. "Watch yourself, little brother," he said, fangs punching past his lower lip, "or I might be serving up yours."

Lucian grinned at the hunger running all up and down his brother's body language. Fight, maim, kill. It was right, good—how a Pureblood *paven* should be.

"Isn't it a little early to be discussing balls, *gentlepaven*?"

And there it goes . . . Lucian mused darkly.

Still wearing her doctor's coat from a night shift at the hospital, Sara Donohue, Alexander's true mate, walked into the room, went directly over to Chef Pureblood and kissed him, all sweet and possessive. Then she turned to Lucian, her blue eyes sparkling with humor. "I like a little fruit with my blood, Luca—is that a crime?"

"No, but forcing my brother to do the labor is."

She laughed. "Yeah, as if I could force him to do anything. Have you met your brother?"

"It is a labor of love, my dear," Alexander said, his arms going around Sara's trim waist, his hunger to kill replaced by another kind of hunger. "And I can think of no other kind I would favor doing." With a quick tug, he spun Sara to face him once again. Grinning like an asshole in heat, he reached for a slice of fruit, then brought it up to her mouth. "Mango," he said, teasing her lips apart. "It is a wonder. She opens her mouth. I slide the slippery fruit between her lips, down her throat."

"Aww, fuck me," Lucian muttered.

"Yes," Alexander said, his eyes remaining on his mate. "I would say you need someone to fuck you, Luca."

"And to feed as well," Sara added with a grin. "Nothing is as sweet as the blood of the one you love."

"That is far less likely than the fuck, my love," Alexander said with a grin. "Lucian has never fed a female."

Sara looked surprised. "What? Why not?"

"He's a selfish prick." Alexander's grin widened; then he chuckled.

"You're really a funny guy, you know that?" Lucian said dryly.

"I do. Yes."

But Lucian didn't contradict the statement. It was a well-known fact among his brothers that he was only too happy to drink from any female who offered herself up, and maybe one or two who didn't, but he had never given a drop of his red stuff to anyone, ever. Something within him had put the brakes on the equal-opportunity feed a long time ago, even before he'd run from his *credenti*. His mind, and every available vein, just refused to be a giver.

"Well, it's a pity you let Bronwyn go so easily," Sara added, glancing over her shoulder. "She may have changed your mind about both of those things."

Lucian shot her a blank stare. "Who?"

Sara laughed. "Please. Even I can't forget that *veana*. No scientist should be allowed to have a top half like that . . ."

Pulling his mate even closer, Alexander's brows lifted. "My love, whatever you need you know I will agree to . . ."

"Down, boy," she muttered, patting his shoulder.

"Yes, *Duros*," came a male voice from the doorway, "ease up on the threesome talk, if you please."

"Jesus." Lucian turned to face his brother, the anger at last night's secret branding session with the Order still alive within him. "It's about time you showed up."

Nicholas stood in the doorway, looking as though he'd like to rip the heads off everyone in the room.

"What news from the Eyes?" Alexander asked, keeping his *veana* close even as his tone changed to all professional. "Did you get a location?"

"No," Nicholas gritted out. "Wasn't a meet with the Eyes after all."

"No shit!" Alexander said. "Was it Dare?"

"Not in person."

Lucian gripped the wood handle of his tomahawk. "I knew we should've gone. I'm done respecting your judgment. We made a pact. We do this together."

"What does that mean?" Alexander asked, completely ignoring Lucian's rant. "'Not in person?' Did he send recruits?"

Nicholas didn't move, but his black eyes flashed. "He sent bait."

The soft movements coming from behind him had both Lucian and Alexander moving forward, weapons drawn, all kinds of deadly threats streaming from their mouths.

"No!" Nicholas shouted, arms shooting forward to block them both from advancing farther. "It's not what you think."

Lucian growled. "What I think is that you have a pretty little something back there. Bait, my ass!" He stabbed his tomahawk into the countertop. "Bring her out."

"Be cool, the both of you," Nicholas warned before motioning for whatever was behind his back to reveal itself. "And by the way, it's not a *her*."

"One more time," Lucian said, dropping into a chair in the dimly lit library.

"Your son?" Alexander said brusquely, refusing to wait for Nicholas to reply.

Pacing the rug in front of the fireplace, Nicholas shook his head. They were alone now, the three of them, the exhausted *balas* in the care of Alexander's mate, Sara. "It's a lie," he uttered. "A manipulation."

"Who were you with?" Lucian asked.

"That matters not." Nicholas was a closed book when it came to relationships with females, and his brothers rarely inquired—no doubt out of respect for his past. Lucian and Alexander both knew of his whoring only in the past tense, and Nicholas would make sure it always remained so. The continued selling of his skin was his shame alone, his addiction that needed to be fed, and for the past several decades he had been wise about how he took on clients. One per month, the funds in cash and hidden. "The boy isn't mine."

Alexander shot him a dark glare. "How do you know?"

"I don't." *Fuck*. "Not for certain. But I will."

Lucian stared at an invisible spot on the carpet. "He looks a bit like . . ."

"You," Nicholas said. "Yes, I know. The hair." Goddammit he needed . . . something—warm blood or *gravo*, the delectable poisoned blood he didn't allow himself to sample anymore—the drug that had destroyed both his mother and himself. It was really unbelievable how far Dare was willing to go to take out the Romans, get them off his trail. To destroy the life of a *balas* to stay alive . . .

"How did you find the boy?" Alexander asked.

Nicholas tread carefully. "A *veana* brought him to me. She claims his mother died."

"Was the mother a *veana*?"

"Yes. Vermont *credenti*."

"Was she mated?"

Nicholas hesitated, then clipped a nod.

Alexander tossed him a sharp look. "Then the *balas* could be his."

"No."

"Why the hell not? Was he an Impure?"

"Short and sweet—he desired the company of *pavens*."

Lucian snorted. "Well, maybe he had a change of heart one night eight years ago."

"The *paven* is dead," Nicholas said, feeling ready to bolt—go after the *veana* who'd jumped out of his arms and into the sunlight. "Happened a month before the mother and I were together."

Alexander's eyes narrowed. "Perhaps she found a new mate. It has been known to happen after death."

"Possible," Nicholas acknowledged. "But she said nothing to me at the time."

"Where is this *veana*?" Lucian asked tightly. "The one who delivered the boy?"

"Gone."

"Gone where?"

"Back to her *credenti*."

Lucian pushed forward in his chair. "And you didn't try to stop her?"

"I tried."

"Not hard enough. You let her get away."

Nicholas's mouth twitched with annoyance. "I know where she is, where she ran to." He pulled out his BlackBerry. "And as soon as the light dims I will go to her. Squeeze until she tells us where Dare is hidden."

"You're certain she's working for Dare," Alexander said.

"Not a hundred percent." There were the whip marks from Mondrar to consider. "But I don't trust her. In the meantime, you and Lucian can make contacts within the *credentis*, find out if there are Impures missing, any threats, rumors of action going down. We'll hit this from every angle."

"What about the boy?" Lucian asked. "Are we keeping him?"

"What fault of his is any of this?" Nicholas said, snapping the phone shut. "The *balas* will have our protection until we can locate his true sire."

6

Every time the train stopped, Kate made a point of changing cars. It was a bitch and a half, and she got the crazy-chick looks from some of the passengers, but as long as she kept moving the chances of the Order pinpointing her location with any true accuracy declined.

So was the life of a felon. Bugged until the day you were set free.

As the train slowed to a stop somewhere near Albany, Kate ducked out of business class and headed for coach. If she could just get back into her *credenti* without anyone knowing she'd been gone or had been in the presence of Mirabelle and the boy, life could resume and so could her two months of work release. But after a full day and night missing in action at the school and her room, she was willing to bet there'd been some guesses as to her whereabouts, some questions about her involvement in Mirabelle's death and Ladd's disappearance.

Shit. She spied an unoccupied sleeper berth and

stole inside. She closed the door and sat down on one of the chairs attached to the wall. Was she an asshole? A fool for thinking she could walk back into the *credenti*, explain away where she'd been and with whom? Her gaze darted outside the window. Night had descended over the lush New York landscape and snow was falling against the glass in elegant little dots.

Come on, train. Move your metal ass.

But what choice did she have? Run, keep running— always running, the bug in her leg a promise that its master would be forever on her trail? Or return to the *credenti* of her own free will, lie her ass off about Ladd, and beg for forgiveness and the completion of her prison sentence?

Oh, Ladd. Poor kid. She knew he was probably feeling abandoned, pissed off, and was still in shock over the loss of his mother. She'd been there too—the loss of both parents, in fact, in one miserable fucking day. But Ladd was safer than he would ever be with her or in the hands of the Order, and if she had to do it all over again, she'd make the same choice: hand him over to Nicholas Roman and split.

The train lurched forward and started off real slow. Looking at her from the outside, she seemed like one cold bitch, but she hadn't gotten there picking flowers and having picnics by the lake in summertime. Hell no. When you watched one parent slowly kill the other every day of your life, then see that parent turn around and kill her abuser, well it forces you to see the reality of life, especially the ugly, painful, suckass reality.

After her two months were up, she'd go back, make sure Ladd was all right. It was the best she could do.

A sharp knock on the door had her up, her back against the wall beside the door, knife to her side. She'd learned much in the dregs of Mondrar society. "Yes?"

"Tickets, please."

Just do what you normally do. Flash your ticket, act surprised when you're in the wrong place.

Keeping the weapon hidden, Kate opened the door a crack and came face-to-face with Nicholas Roman. *Fuck me!* On a grunt, she slammed the thing shut, but not before his scent got inside. Kate tried not to breathe it in, but it was like ice water to a dehydrated desert dweller. Her lungs demanded it, demanded him. Goddammit, what was with this *paven*?

"Sniff me out, Roman?" she called through the door.

"No need to. You made no secret of your plan. Only one train going to Vermont tonight."

Kate's teeth ground together. "I don't take returns."

"I came alone."

"You left the boy?" she cried, wanting to punch him through the metal door. "What the hell?"

"He's with my brother's mate. He's safe."

Bullshit, she thought. The Order could track morphed *pavens*, and if they had any hint about Mirabelle's relationship with Nicholas or who Ladd's father really was, they could be at his door in an instant. But perhaps sons of the Breeding Male were different? Untraceable. She sure as hell hoped so.

"What do you want?" she called.

"You say you don't know Dare."

"Yeah, about half a dozen times."

"I want to believe you."

"Really? Why's that?"

"I don't enjoy killing *veanas*."

"I almost want to tell you I'm lying to see if you'll actually put some lead behind your threats."

She heard him exhale, loudly, showing off his annoyance to anyone who might be passing by her sleeper car. "We can do this quick and easy," he said, "or I can stay on this carnival ride, follow you all the way back to your *credenti*, and find out what really happened to Mirabelle up close and personal."

The *paven* was quick on the threats, but Kate truly didn't like the sound of that one. She wanted him nowhere near her *credenti* or the Order. With an aggravated curse, she turned and opened the door a crack. Again, his scent rushed in like a damn river, nearly drowning her in its heady, delectable intensity. She had a feeling that if this *paven* ever touched her, she'd melt into the ground and never recover.

He still wore the coat, but the collar was down and she could see his full face now. Damn, it sucked to be her. The devil had come up from hell looking hot, all sharp angles, heavy lips, and blazing black eyes. His Breeding Male brands were round and small on his cheeks and sported some faded-looking symbols inside their circles. As a descendant of the Breeding

Male, he could either be mated to an Impure or a Pureblood, just as his brands could sport a whole symbol or a half looking for its match.

When he saw her, his eyes softened just a hair. "Listen, I'd like to hear the story. From beginning to end. If the *balas* is mine, if you really are an emissary from Mirabelle, I think I deserve it, don't you?"

Interesting way to go, pulling at the heartstrings . . . and well, it was possibly a valid point. "Perhaps."

"Good." He kicked his chin forward, aiming for the inside of the berth. "Can we do this in there?"

Kate hesitated. Having Nicholas Roman in close proximity seemed dangerous in more ways than one, but then again pulling in an audience of passengers and staff while they discussed the murder of a vampire wasn't a good idea either.

Jaw tight, she let him in. His scent moved into the room with him, past her cheek, her shoulder, a life of its own.

Way past six feet tall, he nearly grazed the ceiling as he walked into the room. At once, the space seemed too small to contain him, and Kate moved back in a hurry. He went over to the window, stood with his back against the glass. The car rocked like a piece of driftwood on a stormy sea, but the *paven* remained solid and unmoving.

His black eyes narrowed under long black lashes. "How did she die?"

The memory of Mirabelle's murder flashed through her mind like nauseating bolts of lightning, still shots of a horror movie. "We were outside Ladd's school; Mirabelle was late picking him up." She shook her head. "It was only seconds after she got there—she didn't even get to touch the kid one last time, you know?"

"What happened?"

"A male came out from the trees real fast, jumped on her"—she shrugged, hating herself in that moment—"sliced her through before I could do anything."

Nicholas frowned, his eyes momentarily haunted as he was no doubt coming up with his own version of what she'd witnessed. "Pureblood or Impure?"

"Not sure."

"Did you see his face?"

She nodded.

"Did you know him?"

"Never saw him before."

"Did he say anything? Why he was there? What he wanted?"

"Nothing."

"Did he go after you or Ladd?" There was palpable ferocity in his query, and it surprised her. Maybe he'd loved Mirabelle, maybe still did.

The very thought made Kate both dislike him more and want to jump on him and lick the scent of him off his solid neck.

"He started to come at us," Kate began, trying to force that grotesque revelation out of her mind. "But then he stopped and took off."

"What stopped him?"

"No idea."

He growled with irritation. "You're extraordinarily helpful, you know that?"

"Hey," she returned just as fierce. "I'm giving you the only answers I have. Besides, why should I be all that helpful? You don't believe me anyway."

"There are ten reasons engraved into your neck why I shouldn't," he said.

"And you have two carved into your face that should make me loathe your very existence," she shot back. "Did Mirabelle even want to screw you? Or did you take her by force?"

"Fuck you."

"No, thanks."

"Saving yourself for a *paven* who gets turned on by ex-cons?" he said with a flash of venom. Or was it barely disguised passion? It was hard to tell rage and fervor apart at times, and for a second Kate wondered if he felt an attraction to her too. And if he did, did he despise the feeling as much as she?

His eyes probed hers. "How long have you been working for Dare?"

"Seriously?" she said on a dark laugh. "Are we really going back there?"

He crossed his arms over his chest. "Did he get you out of prison? Did you make a deal? Your freedom for my life?"

"Fuck you."

"No, thanks." He grinned.

She nearly returned that grin. "You have your answers. Now, why don't you get the hell off this train and back to the boy?"

"Oh, I am getting off this train, but you're coming with me."

"Not a chance." She said it all tough and as-if, but her insides started churning with nerves.

"You seem to think you have a choice."

"I'll always have a choice. I'll kill to have the choice."

"I just bet you would," he began, pushing away from the window. But as he started toward her, a hard knock at the door stopped him cold.

And a low, male voice called out, "Tickets, please."

Nicholas had been halfway to her, and if that asshole on the other side of the door hadn't interrupted their little chat he'd have been nose to nose with the *veana* right now.

And wasn't that what he wanted? What his fool body was screaming for? Nose to nose, her breath on his face, her hands brushing his hands—her delicious scent enveloping him as he warned her that she was never getting away from him?

There was another knock. "Come on, now. I know you're in there."

Nicholas hissed. He ought to break the human's neck or at the very least remove his voice box.

"I'll go," Kate said, starting for the door. "I have the ticket."

"Fine. Hurry up and get rid of him."

"Yeah. Sure thing." She went to the door and opened it wide. Too wide, in fact. What the hell was she trying to do? Get him noticed? Instigate a fight? Because that's what was going to happen if the ticket taker saw his vampire ass.

"Evening, miss," Nicholas heard the guy say. "May I see your ticket, please?"

"Of course," Kate answered, all nice and soft and obliging.

There were a few seconds of looking and reading, then a *tsk-tsk*, and the human said, "You don't have a sleeper ticket, miss."

"Oh," Kate said innocently. "Are you sure?"

The guy chuckled softly. "You need to leave now—head back to coach. In fact, I'll escort you there."

"Okay, thanks. No problem. Sorry about that." And that was it.

Nicholas waited.

Where the hell . . . What was she . . .

She slipped out the door without even a look back at him. And then there was the ticket taker, his meaty hand pulling the door closed.

Staring at the windowless slab of metal, Nicholas nearly had an aneurysm. His body was wound so goddamn tight all he wanted to do was rip the door off its hinges, flash down the corridor, and tear that human to bits—drain him dry and take the *veana* back.

"Are you always helping silly girls like me get back to where they belong?" Nicholas heard Kate ask as she and the ticket troll walked down the hall together.

The guy laughed. Yeah, he was into it, into her, the whole flirty female routine. Sucker. Mondrar had been most instructive . . .

"It's not a good trip unless someone's trying to sneak into the wrong room," the guy responded.

Nicholas was panting, sweating, his hands balled into fists.

Christ. Something was off with him.

Way too much predatory anger for the situation.

Had to be morpho—had to be. Or some kind of magic Dare was using to rev up his engines and lure him into a trap. Nicholas didn't even want to contemplate the other option. A blond, brown-eyed *True Mate*, who was as sneaky as a python and just as trustworthy.

Sara enjoyed a quiet house. But she knew that the peacefulness of the moment was nothing more than the calm before the storm.

Another storm. One that wouldn't let up without two very important Impures getting what they deserved— death and life.

Sara glanced down at the seven-year-old *balas* with hair the color of clouds who was asleep on her lap. His breathing was easy now, though a moment ago, he'd been dreaming. His painful, soft cries were difficult on the ears, yet devastating on the heart. As a psychiatrist, Sara understood the stages of grief that a child went through when they lost a parent, but as one who had lost her father at an early age, she felt for Ladd on a whole different level.

"What's all this?"

Sara looked up, smiled. Dillon stood in the doorway, her hazel cat eyes narrowed playfully.

"Are we babysitting tonight?" she asked.

Sara laughed softly. "Not we. Me. You know no one would ever trust you with a kid, D."

"True." The ripped, badass bodyguard to a human senator pushed away from the doorframe and strode in. Her auburn hair had grown in the two months since Alexander had hired the *veana* to guard Sara when her patient had flipped out and done the scary stalking thing. Now D was back working for the senator from Maine, but stopped by once a month or so to bust balls and check in on certain people.

As Dillon dropped into the chair opposite, Sara felt the old rush of teasing antagonism that suited their friendship so well sizzle between them.

"Slumming again, vampire?" Sara asked with a grin.

Dillon shrugged. "Your mate wanted to talk about a few *credenti* males who left the Maine compound last week. My cell is top-of-the-line, even have Skype—don't know why I feel the need to do this in person."

"'Course you do." Sara's grin widened. "You get to see me."

Dillon pointed a finger at her. "You can't flirt with me anymore, human." It was what Dillon had called her back when they'd both thought she was a human. They knew differently now, but a nickname that annoyingly cute just couldn't help but stick. "You're mated now."

"I have had no Veracou," Sara said, referring to the vampire wedding ceremony that was given only to Pureblood mates.

"Technicality," Dillon tossed out.

"Come on, D. You know you'll always be my guilty little secret."

Dillon gestured to the sleeping *balas* in Sara's arms. "Not in front of the kid, Fang Tease. And whose kid is this anyway?"

"Could very well be a little Roman brother."

Dillon's cat eyes grew wide. "Alexander's?"

"Nicholas's."

"No shit."

After helping out Sara with her stalker and the Roman brothers when they were trying to off Ethan Dare the first time, Dillon had become more than just a body for hire. She didn't have much of anyone to call family, and even if she acted like a pain in the ass sometimes, they had all made her understand she was not only needed, but welcome in their house and in their lives.

"Speaking of brothers," Dillon said, kicking her feet up on the coffee table. "How's Gray doing?"

All playfulness ceased, and Sara shrugged. "He's functioning, I suppose."

"Interesting answer."

Sara laughed softly. "It's kind of the only one I've

got. He's barely here and when he is it's like he doesn't hear me or see me . . ." She shrugged again. "He still lives inside his head."

"Is he helping the Romans?" Dillon asked.

"He trains with them sometimes. Alexander thinks it's good for him to be physical, to feel needed and part of a pack."

"What do you think?"

"I think he wants to be anywhere but here. I think he's miserable and has no idea who he is or what he wants." Sara's gaze dropped to the boy in her lap once again. She hadn't been all that much older than Ladd when she'd accidentally started the fire that had killed her father and disfigured her brother. For years, she'd watched Gray turn inside himself, stop talking and give up on life. She'd become a psychiatrist for him, spent every day inventing ways to bring him back to life, spent every night dreaming of ways to remove the traumatic memories from his brain. She'd failed every time. Later, she'd found out it was because he was half vampire, and instead of using therapeutic methods, he'd needed his memories bled.

Dillon shrugged. "The guy was trapped inside himself for years. Blowing off steam, staying out, lack of communication, screwing females—you're the shrink—it's kind of expected, isn't it?"

Releasing a heavy breath, Sara nodded. "I guess."

"But . . . you're worried."

"I don't begrudge him a few wild nights. I just don't want him getting hurt. Again."

Dillon sat forward, swiped a magazine off the table. "He's not a *balas*, Sara. Extend the leash or he'll break it."

Yes, that was entirely possible. But it did nothing to quell her anxiety. "Maybe if you're in the city again soon, or while you're here now, you could check on him?"

"You want me to spy?" Dillon asked dryly.

Sara smiled. "You're so good at it."

Dillon chuckled, flipped through the magazine. "I think you need to let him be. For now. If things get really out of control, I'll check it out. Deal?"

"Yeah. Okay." Sara stood up, the heavy *balas* in her arms. "Want to help me put him to bed?"

Dillon didn't even look up from her *Entertainment Weekly*. Clint Eastwood was on the cover selling his latest film, and the *veana* was a wreck for a good Western. "I'm meeting up with your mate in a minute, and besides, Eastwood will always come before diapers and drool."

Sara laughed softly and headed for the door. "You're so sensitive, D."

After sitting in coach next to a teenager who smelled like warm Fritos, waiting for the ticket guy to get distracted and take off, Kate escaped the car once again and without garnering notice headed for the end of the line—the caboose. She needed off this train, and when it slowed into the next stop she was jumping. Between the watchful eyes of the train service crew and an overly amped Pureblood *paven* who thought he was going to control where she went and when, she was done.

Hell, she could hitchhike if she had to. No one was going to mess with a female with fangs.

She moved down the hall, didn't slow as the train rocked from one side to another like a carnival ride. Son of a Breeding Male—son of a bitch. Nicholas Roman had no idea who he was dealing with. Granted, she had a few soft places left inside her, but when it came to her freedom, she was one hundred percent hard-ass.

She slammed her palm into the black push sign and the doors leading from one car to the next opened. When she saw it was empty, she ran, fast as she could down the corridor, night spilling in through the wall of windows to her left. She knew that if Roman could find her once, he could do it again, and he seemed pretty hell-bent on taking her home despite all the information about Mirabelle she'd given him. Seriously, what more did the *paven* want? Why couldn't he just keep what he had, deal with it, and let her move the fuck on.

And she was moving on. Hell, if she had to she'd jump off this two-hundred-ton bullet at full speed.

Spying the final car up ahead, she hustled forward. Through one set of doors, then to the padlocked door to a large baggage and storage area. Pulling out her knife, she settled the tip of the blade into the keyhole and twisted a few times. When the thing sprang free, she pulled it out and tossed it aside.

Across the storage room, the door to the caboose

was open, the metal slide retracted. Crisp winter air hit her face and neck as she hustled toward it. It was a perfect night for a crazy jump—over the railing, off the side, into the snow and grass—then head south to the highway.

She was nearly through the door to the caboose when a sound behind her made her whirl around.

"Where's the boy, bitch?"

For one brief second, Kate thought it was Nicholas standing there, but the male before her had a heartbeat and was a mouse with a bad attitude compared to the Roman brother. This pale, dark-haired male was a coward, an Impure—and the bastard who'd killed Mirabelle Letts in cold blood before her child's eyes.

"Where is the boy?" he said again.

Kate gripped the railing, but stayed calm. "I don't know."

"Bullshit," he spat.

"Maybe I dropped his little vampire ass somewhere in the city."

"I'm not playing, *veana*," he sneered, walking toward her.

She shrugged, acted casual. "Fine. I gave him to the Eyes, okay?"

"What?"

"Sold him."

"I don't believe you."

"Do you see the kid on me? He's long gone." She shrugged. "I needed the money. Hard life living outside the *credenti*."

His eyes registered just a hint of panic. "What member of the Eyes?"

"Haddad."

"Try again," he said menacingly. Clearly, he knew the Eyes and that she was bullshitting him.

"Fine. It was Cambridge."

"Better."

Kate felt like a shit, but there was nothing for it. Cambridge was the only member of the Eyes she knew. The tricky bastard had occupied the cell next to hers in Mondrar for a year and a half. He was the one she'd gone to for information on Nicholas. Oh, he was going to be thrilled she'd sent this jerkoff his way, but then again, Cambridge was pretty fearless. He knew how to handle any sticky situation he found himself in.

"Now, if you want to live," the male uttered, flashing his fangs, "tell me exactly where you dropped him."

"Maybe I don't want to live," Kate tossed back, even as she slowly eased the knife from the back waistband of her jeans.

There were many days in Mondrar when she'd have asked this piece of shit to send her off the planet permanently with one bullet to the brain. But that day wasn't today. She had a chance, a possible future for herself, and this Impure asshole wasn't going to take it away from her like he had Mirabelle.

"You want to die, do you, *veana*?" he said, closing the distance between them. "Well, I'd be happy to help ."

Forced to move back onto the platform of the caboose, Kate flashed her knife and crouched down. "Didn't say I wanted you to be the one to do it."

Beneath the staccato of snowfall, she jabbed out with her blade, hoping to catch him off guard, hoping to buy herself a moment or two. But the Impure moved shockingly fast, a sudden blur. Adrenaline rushed through Kate's blood. She hated this, hated that this was her life—fighting and escaping, running and praying.

She jabbed at him low, but got nothing but air. When she pulled back, it was the Impure's blade that made contact, slashing her hand. She hissed at the sting of pain.

This wasn't right. He was a freaking Impure. He shouldn't have speed or strength.

She felt the railing at her back, felt the cold—the sting of her flesh wound. And she felt him, the Impure, he was going to kill her. Breathing heavy, wielding her knife at any part of him that came near, she weighed her options. Truth was, when you couldn't win a fight, you knew it in your gut and you needed to turn and run.

Or in her case—jump.

Like a bloodhound, Nicholas followed Kate's scent, stalking through the train cars, his height, facial brands, and fierce attitude scaring the shit out of passengers who were stumbling out of their bunks, half asleep to hit the bathroom. It wasn't his intention, just an unfortunate part of being himself.

He came around the corner and moved through coach, hoping he wouldn't run into any of the crew. His brother Alexander was one lucky Pureblood. The ability to mask oneself from view would've really come in handy right about now. Apart from the regular enhancements of morpho, the only additional talent Nicholas possessed were the ribbed fangs in his mouth—not exactly something he could use to disguise himself.

He pushed through the door leading from one car to the other, headed down a hallway, then came to the end of the line—a storage car and the caboose. He was halfway through storage when he heard her. Her and someone else . . .

Holy shit. He sprinted across the car and sprang through the door to the exterior, winter air, pelting snow and the faintest scent of sewer slamming him full on. But he barely noticed any of it. There was Kate, knife in hand, her face a mask of fear and rage as she slashed in sharp X patterns at a dark-haired male.

"I should have gutted you back at the *credenti*," the male screamed over the train and wind, his back to Nicholas as he easily avoided her stabbing motions, "let your blood run into the snow right alongside that sad little *veana*. But that would've been a waste, wouldn't it?" He grinned. "Now you can be all mine to consume."

Nicholas's fangs shot from his mouth, and he flew forward, had the Impure bastard in a headlock in under a second, gun to his temple. "The lady's spoken for, asshole," he growled into the male's ear.

With one quick glance over his shoulder, the male Nicholas had yet to see grinned up at him, then flashed out of his arms.

Nicholas bared his fangs and howled into the night air. "Motherfucking Ethan Dare!"

7

To stave off the modern world and to keep their minds calm and recharged for their duties, every member of the Eternal Order had their own created reality. A place that knew no time or space—a place they had conceived of from memory or fantasy or both—a place that could house events, crowds, one single being, or just the beauty of nature's elements.

In the reality of Order member number ten, Titus Evictus Roman, all four had been utilized.

It was his pleasure.

He sat now within the travertine walls of his reality—the Colosseum in Rome—on the podium overlooking the arena where so many of his brothers had battled. It was where he had been plucked from obscurity by one of the Order and taken with the other oversized Pureblood *paven* to an experimental facility in the North. He'd thought he was destined for great things, but instead had been turned into something horrible, unimaginable—a Breeding Male. But the hundreds of years he'd spent being poked, prodded, and surgically altered in that camp was not what he chose to remember—it was not part of the reality he'd created in his mind. Nor was it the decades of being held in a cage, only to be released whenever his masters wanted his cock inside the cold, dry body of one terrified female after the next.

No.

It was this—this place, the sounds, smells—the life of a gladiator.

He waved his hand over the empty ruins and brought to life the Colosseum of old, the roar of the crowds: knights, the common folk, even the beasts.

He laughed at the realness of it all, so thankful for the powers he now possessed. And they had only cost him his blood, his Breeding Male blood. Drained from his veins and used for a purpose he refused to question. The only one who knew what he was, what he had been, had granted him the tenth seat on the Order when it had been vacated by one who had ascended to the afterworld. The Order member who had once taken his life and turned it into that of a monster had given him a new path once again.

Of course, Titus was no fool. He knew Cruen couldn't be trusted, but the sacrifice had been worth it. He no longer had the unrelenting urge to breed. That alone was worth the move from tangible to transparent, but there were many other things; instead of being an empty vessel, his mind was now his own—and then there were the ones he'd left behind, the ones he'd created out of nothing but lust. His progeny. He could

watch them now, watch over them—protect them from
the ones who wished them harm—guide them if one
or more was gifted the cursed Breeding Male gene.

It is time to assemble, Ten.

Titus heard his brothers and sisters in robes calling
to him, as they too left their realties for the work of the
day. With one easy wave to the crowds, Titus pulled
away from the beauty of the Colosseum, farther and
farther until there was nothing left and he was standing before his chair at the table of justice and mercy, his
bare feet in the sand.

8

Still grinning, Ethan flashed to Washington Square Park. Seeing Nicholas Roman's face drop from shock and rage had been very satisfying. Not to mention, unexpected. What was the Roman brother doing on the train anyway, hanging out with the *veana* who had witnessed his true mate's death and had run with his *balas*?

The answers were somewhere hiding in the park, but Ethan would find them.

The Eyes' habitat was really hopping, the cover of night bringing out all the precious little drug addicts, their dealers and, of course, the skin sellers. Ethan walked toward the Arch, the rumored hangout for the Eyes. He knew the clan of trolls as well as anyone did, by reputation and whispers, even hooked up with them a time or two back when he was just a pathetic Impure looking for a good time at a decent price. The Eyes dealt in flesh, drugs, information, and getting permanently lost, but interestingly, they never dealt with the Order. In fact, they remained off the ancient ten's radar, and were notoriously suspicious of everything and everyone.

Ethan spotted one of them in the shadow of a tree several feet from the Arch, his greasy head lowered over whatever illegal substance he was hawking.

"Hello, Whistler," he said, his voice low. No need to draw attention.

The number-one flesh seller looked up and around, then nodded at Ethan, his staid grin a mismatch to his highly suspicious glare. "Need company, friend? Human or otherwise? I have anything you want."

"Information," Ethan said.

"I have more Impures unhappy in their communities, but it all comes at a price, friend."

Ethan reached in the pocket of his coat and tossed the Impure a wad of bills. "Where's Cambridge?"

Whistler grinned wider, showed off his worn-down fangs, compliments of too much *gravo*. "He's escorting two females to a private party for a very well-known, very dirty New York City ballplayer."

"You see him with a boy today?"

"We don't deal in *balas* flesh."

Ethan sniffed. "You and I both know that's total bullshit, but right now I'm not interested in a buy, or the list of Impures you have tucked away in that scavenger's mind of yours—the boy I seek came from a Pureblood female." He lowered his voice. "She was looking for his father."

The short, hairy bastard had the nerve to try and look innocent. "Nothing went to Cambridge today."

"You're sure about that?"

Whistler nodded distractedly. "Who's the boy's father?"

"Nicholas Roman."

That brought the head up and had the eyes going all buggy. "No shit!" Under his breath, he added, "Now, him I've seen."

"What's that?" Ethan said, moving in closer.

Realizing what he'd said, Whistler tried to blow the comment off. "Nothing, friend. Nothing at all."

But Ethan knew a juicy bit when he smelled one. He grabbed the Impure by the neck, forced him back, deeper into the shadows. "I can flash us both into the Dead Sea—the very center—and I can flash back out again. Alone." Ethan lifted him in the air with every bit of the strength the Supreme One had gifted him. "You thirsty, Whistler?"

The male swallowed hard. "A few days ago," he uttered, then stopped and gasped for air. "I referred a client to him."

"A client?" Ethan repeated. "Roman's buying blood? Tail?"

"Other way 'round."

"You lie."

"Believe it or not."

"Nicholas Roman has no need to sell himself. The Pureblood has more riches than Midas."

"Not my business."

Ethan narrowed his gaze. It made no sense. The troll had to be lying. "Are you saying Nicholas Roman is a whore? He sells his Pureblood cock for money?"

Whistler tried to nod. "Some habits are hard to break."

Ethan was hardly satisfied. It was like living on appetizers and never getting to the meal. "And what does that mean, *friend*?"

Ten minutes later, Ethan was flashing back to his enclave, his grin upgraded to full-on shit-eating.

Nicholas could've ended it.

Two seconds.

A quick twist of the neck and that waste-of-blood Impure would've been dead.

Nicholas stood in the same spot where Dare had flashed right out of his arms as though he had the power of a Pureblood *paven* within him. Snow pelted his face as shame swam in his blood. In his estimation, he had little worth, but saving his brother from morpho, and from the very real possibility of a life as a Breeding Male, was the one tangible way he could finally forget about Lucian's life-saving interference on the streets of Nice all those years ago—even if it ended with Nicholas in a body bag right alongside Dare.

He had to get home, strap up, get on the hunt, find that bastard, and gut him once and for all.

But what about her?

His gaze slipped to the *veana*—the *veana* who made

his body seize up with lust every time he was around her. She sat with her back against the railing, the wind whipping her blond hair in her face as she blew on the minor flesh wound on her hand. Things had certainly changed in the past fifteen minutes. She may be a felon, but she was no liar. Not to him at any rate. It was clear she knew Dare, but only because he was the one who had murdered Mirabelle.

Goddamn! Mirabelle. What was the connection there? Had she been just another Pureblood *veana* for the taking—and what? She'd fought back and Dare didn't like it?

He needed answers.

"How's the hand?" he asked.

The *veana's* chin came up and she shot him one hell of a fierce glare.

No, she wasn't forgiving or forgetting anytime soon. "You didn't know Dare," he said. "I get it. I apologize. Maybe I can help you—"

"You want to help me now?" she interrupted, cradling her injured hand to her chest.

He shrugged. "I figure I owe you that much."

"If you want to help me then turn around, walk away, and don't contact me ever again."

He wanted to tell her that was never going to happen, but instead he went over and helped her to her feet.

She pushed away from him the moment her boots hit metal, but not before he saw the shadow of heat in her eyes when she met his gaze. She may have hated him, may have wanted to break both his knees and trim his fangs with a pair of dirty hedge clippers, but there was no denying she was attracted to him.

"I'm not walking away, *veana*."

"Fine," she said. "Flashing works too."

"That Impure is after you."

"No, not me. The boy."

"But if he can't get to the boy, he'll force the answers out of you."

She looked away, her body all sorts of jumpy. "That Impure is the least of my worries."

"Someone else after you?" he asked, testing the waters as the train rocked like an angry sea.

She said nothing, just lifted her hand to her lips once again and blew on her wound. A Pureblood *veana*'s breath was an incredibly powerful healing device, and as the warm puffs of air circled in the cold air around them, the cut on her hand began to close.

All the blood in Nicholas's body headed south as he stared at her mouth and all it was doing. Goddamn, this *veana* was hot. Just a simple "O" with those pink lips and he was losing it.

There was a definite problem here—and Dare's "magic" had nothing to do with it.

"Are you running from the Order?" he asked, keeping his eyes off her mouth. "From Mondrar?"

"No. Actually, I'm running back to the Order, so unless you want to meet up with the ancient ten I suggest you take a hike."

Understanding hit like a slap to the face. It all made

sense now. Why she was running—and why so bloody fast. "You're on parole," he said.

"Work release," she corrected.

"How much longer?"

Her gaze slipped. "Two months."

"And you risked your freedom bringing the boy to me? Why? Why not bring him to the Order? Let them sort it out?"

She broke away from the railing, stuck a finger in his chest. "You know why, Son of the Breeding Male." She said the last part with a punctuated disgust.

Fuck. Mirabelle must've truly thought Ladd was his if she was so afraid of the Order taking and testing the *balas*. "What are you planning on telling the Order? Where are you going to tell them you've been?"

She lifted her chin, said confidently, "I took the boy to find his father—a *paven* by the name of Jon Halstrom—in the Manhattan *credenti*, but when I arrived a gang of thugs jumped us and the boy got away. I looked for him, couldn't find him, and came back to the *credenti* for further instructions."

She'd been practicing, but it was a wasted effort. "They'll look for this *paven*."

She shrugged. "Let them. You have your answers. Why don't you get the hell off this train and back to the boy?"

"Oh, I am getting off this train, but you're coming with me."

"Not a chance." She turned to go past him, but the train jerked to the right and she lost her balance.

He had her by the shoulders, held her firmly until she had her footing. "You seem a relatively intelligent *veana*."

Her brown eyes flashed with impatience. "Flattery will get you a knee to the balls, *paven*."

His mouth twitched. "The Order will find out—even if they have to torture you to get the truth, and then Ladd will be watched, stalked until they can get their hands on him. If they truly believe he is of Breeding Male blood, the Order will not rest until he is tested."

She stared up at him, chewed her lower lip, the tips of her fangs brushing back and forth over the wet, pink surface.

Christ.

"I'm not going with you," she said finally, shaking her head.

His hands, still gripping her shoulders as the train continued to rock, slipped down until he held both her hands in his. "Kate."

Her eyes that had followed the movement of his hands now flipped up to meet his. "You know my name."

"The boy."

"Right. Ladd told you." She nodded. "Listen, I have two months left on my sentence. Two months. After ten years." She slipped her hands from his and said, "I will have my freedom, and I'll beg for it if I have to."

"The moment Mirabelle told you about Ladd, the

moment you ran with him, your freedom ceased to exist. You need to accept that." This wasn't his truth, it was the Order—how they worked.

"I will not."

He inhaled the cold, snowy air, then blew it back out again. Stubborn *veana*. "Did all that time in Mondrar affect your sanity? Think. You really believe they will forgive you running, taking a *balas* away from the *credenti*—to a *paven* they cannot find?"

Her jaw tightened.

"They may forgive you," he continued, "but their forgiveness will come with a longer sentence."

She shook her head, laughed bitterly. "If I don't return, they'll find me anyway."

"Not if you have protection."

"Now whose sanity is in question here? I'm bugged, *paven*."

Nicholas took in her words, sat on them, digested them. Shit, of course she was. They were dealing with the ancient ten here. "Where?"

"Above my right knee."

"I'll remove it."

"Really," she said sarcastically. "How are you going to do that? Use a metal spike from the railing?"

"In-house hardware."

Her eyes dropped to his mouth, and as they lingered there Nicholas's fangs elongated, the ridges carved into the white enamel vibrating with a desire all their own.

Damn this *veana* and her effect on him. This was more than morpho, this was something altogether knew and worrisome, and if he could get the chance to search her skin, he was going to take it. He practically growled at her. "What say you, *veana*?"

She didn't answer, just kept staring at his mouth.

Again, he uttered, "I'll take it out and you're free."

A small, sad smile touched her lips and her eyes went dark with feeling. Nicholas couldn't tell if she was afraid to have him touch her or if she was just coming up with scenarios for what happened afterward if he did. Then, all of sudden, she lifted her eyes and said, "No."

He really hoped he hadn't heard her right.

"It stays," she said.

Nicholas dragged a hand through his hair. "You foolish, stubborn female. You want to be free and yet—"

"I'm not free until they say I am," she interrupted hotly. "They run the show—don't you get that?"

One moment she looked feisty as a cat, the next her entire self fell apart before his eyes. She shook her head, her eyes trained on something behind his left ear. "No."

"What?" Nicholas turned.

She whimpered, a soft, very sad sound that curled inside him. He knew that pain. He also knew who was the cause of it.

On the exterior of the train walls, the metal was bubbling, letters forming one by one until the message was revealed.

PRISONER 626—RETURN TO VERMONT CRE-DENTI FOR CONFESSION AND PUNISHMENT. BRING THE BALAS.

9

Marina Perez hovered near the packed bar, her hand around a half-empty Corona. As the punk band blasted their sound onstage, her green eyes trailed Gray Donohue as he slipped into a booth in the back of the club, Equinox.

He was so hot, his metal-gray eyes watchful, predatory, his face a mass of striking angles and ferocity, and his mouth—Jesus, the mouth—so cruel with its promise of delicious sex that Marina could barely look at him for longer than a moment without her legs starting to heat up.

Her fist tightened around the bottle. Problem was, she wasn't the only one who thought he was tasty—who wanted to jump his bones and hang on for the ride. Every club he went to, everywhere she looked, females were going out of their way to get to him.

And it wasn't just the way he looked, Marina thought. It was the attitude he was throwing off. No fear, no inhibition, just a desire to devour everything:

the air, the drinks, the music, the pussies of every female who sidled up to him—he wanted to get his
scarred, ravaged, extra-large hands into each of their
thongs, then send them on their way and drink until
he passed out.

Marina slid her gaze over him. Right now, tucked
into the booth, Gray Donohue whispered into the ear
of the redhead on his right, while his hand slipped
under the table and under the skirt of the female to
his left. As he whispered, the redhead lifted her heavy
lids, turned her gaze to wherever Gray's hand had
landed, and grinned.

Marina whirled back to the bar and drained her beer
to the very last bit of foam.

He was the best assignment she'd ever had.

Or he would be, if she could just get him to notice
her.

Prisoner 626.

Not Kate Everborne.

Not Pureblood *veana*.

Just Prisoner 626.

The shrunken heart in Kate's chest squeezed. Every
day for ten years, the Order had sent messages to the
walls of her cell, letting her know when it was time to
feed, to sleep, to hit the john. Letters had bubbled up
to make words; words made commands. When she'd
been transferred to the *credenti* to work at the elementary school a few months back, the absence of those

messages had been really difficult at first. All of a sudden, she was in charge of herself . . . for the most part. But it was strange how something you hated for so long became so familiar that it was hard to function without it.

As the train slowed and the snow fell harder, she gripped the railing and her gaze moved over each word, each letter, the spaces in between. "It's done," she said softly.

"Did you really expect anything else?" she heard Nicholas say, though his voice seemed far away.

She didn't answer him.

"Kate . . ."

"I'd thought they might show me a little mercy for coming in on my own, giving myself up, but this has changed everything. I go back now, after they've called me in—pretty much declared me a fugitive—and I'm as good as locked up again." She slid her gaze over to him. "Happy, Roman?"

"Don't do that."

"What? Be devastated or pissed off?"

"You're reacting like a *balas*."

No, she was reacting like a prisoner who'd seen and carried and held on to the light of freedom for ten long years only to have it stripped away in an instant.

But what did Nicholas Roman know about that?

She stood there, back against the railing as the train picked up speed once again and the winter wind tried to freeze her regret. Then she reached down, ripped one pant leg from ankle to knee, and met his gaze. "Do it."

*   *   *

Nicholas Roman had the control of a machine. He'd been bred for it, practiced it as a *balas* on his knees, then as a young vampire giving and taking in the alleyways of Nice. He could turn on the desire in seconds, then turn it off just as quickly.

As long as he was paid.

Currency had been a powerful motivator as a *balas*. It had kept his mother alive, then kept Nicholas in *gravo* when the pain of what he was doing to himself—what he was giving up to anything, anyone with the funds to buy him—became too much. Unfortunately, once he'd trained his cells to react to the exchange of goods for services, he couldn't stop it. Even if he needed a fuck. The parts wouldn't go to work without the bill being paid first.

But as the train slowed and the *veana* before him spread her legs and asked him to put his hands on her, the need to jump, to take, to consume flared to life.

"It's there." She pointed to a slight bump just above her knee, on the inside of her thigh.

Nicholas growled low in his chest at the thought of the Order placing the steel tracking device under her skin. Had those aged bastards enjoyed making her feel like a lab rat? Had they enjoyed touching her?

He ignored the momentary rush of aggression his query brought forward and dropped to his knees, spread the torn fabric back, and reached out for her. The second his hand touched her skin, he felt like he'd been shot by a barrage of bullets. Every inch of his flesh, his muscle, his bone went hot and electric, and his fangs dropped—even his cock pulsed. Jesus, the thing wanted out, wanted up, wanted inside.

He closed his eyes.

He needed to get this under control before he went savage—before he turned into his father.

He needed to search her skin.

Forcing his eyes open and on the task, he started below her knee and worked his way over the cap, his fingers probing for the hard little piece of metal as his gaze searched her skin. There was no mark, but damn he'd never felt skin so soft, so warm—like a feather bed calling him in for a nap. He pulled air into his lungs, her air, her scent, and said, "Ready?"

"Just be careful."

Damn right. His thumb brushed over the circular device. Too much of her blood in his system could trigger even more lust than was already coursing river-quick through him.

As the train slowed into the next station, Nicholas struck gently, his fangs easing their way through the muscle, careful not to take in too much blood along the way. His lips, fastened to her skin, wanted desperately to explore, to suckle—get his tongue in on the action—but he held himself in check. Had to. *Had to.* Christ, it was hard though. Starving *paven*, thirsty *paven*.

Finally one fang hit pay dirt, and slowly he guided the razor-sharp tip around the rim of the thing. Then, he tugged. Above him, Kate sucked in air. Nicholas made the foolish mistake of looking up. Her head was back, eyes closed, snow falling on her pale throat as she gripped the railing like she was climaxing.

Nicholas closed his eyes and tugged again until the tiny disk left her skin through one puncture wound and entered his mouth. He pulled back, but not as gently as he should have. He needed to get away, off her before he drank her dry like his body was screaming for him to do. Her skin was fine, no marks—just two small puncture wounds that were already healing, but inside his mouth, on his tongue, he tasted her.

Not just her blood, but her.

It slithered down his throat, a taste, an essence so delectably powerful it blossomed in his throat, his belly, and he wanted to rip her apart and consume her completely. The thought was both terrifying and deliriously hot. His body was tight as steel, his chest too, his cock . . . fuck. It was like they were lying in a cave filled with gardenia and honeysuckle, not on a moving train in the dead of winter with snow falling all around them.

He felt no cold. Only heat. Delicious, delectable heat.

God, he needed to strip her bare and find out what the hell was going on before he went insane. 'Course a move like that would need to come with some kind of explanation, and he wasn't about to reveal his suspicions regarding their true mate status. Not yet. Maybe not ever.

He slipped the bug from his tongue. "Here." He stood and handed it to her, then watched as she stared at it, her eyes wounded like a baby deer. He'd seen that look on many, had taken that look away for many. But on her . . . He seemed to be able to feel it inside his gut, his soul. It was one unwelcome burden.

"Fuck me." She stared at the tiny bug for one more second, then hauled back and threw it over the side of the moving train.

"We need to go, Kate."

She looked at him. "I need a place to crash."

Nicholas didn't say another word, just nodded and opened his arms to her. A flicker of trust registered in her eyes as she curled into his embrace. He tried not to think about that as they flashed off the train.

Or when they touched down on the hard ground of the mountaintop near the caves.

What he did, he had to do. For her as much as for himself.

Still in his arms, Kate glanced around, at the idyllic, overly serene setting: trees, rocks, a brook in the distance. Then she turned to look at him, her large brown eyes now wary under the light of the moon. "Where the hell are we?"

His expression grim, Nicholas didn't answer. Within seconds they were pulled from the mountaintop and thrust down into false daylight, their feet hitting sand with an audible crunch.

The table of the ancient ten spread out before them, and seated in the very center was Cruen, one thinning eyebrow lifted, red fangs flashing. "Not the Impure filth we were expecting you to deliver to us," he said to Nicholas, "but pleasing nonetheless."

10

It took a total of five seconds for Kate to know where she was and who she was standing before. But when the information registered, she whirled on Nicholas Roman and shouted, "You bastard! You motherfucking prick!"

He held her against him, trapped her in his massive frame like the prisoner she was. His gaze remained trained on the ten, but she saw his jaw flicker with tension. Her vision went scarlet and she yanked her arm loose, hauled back, and punched him in the face.

The Order reacted at once, members coming to their feet, a cacophony of concerned and angered voices. But Kate tuned them all out. She was waiting, waiting for him to look at her, react, say something to justify his unjustifiable move—at the very least, fight back. But he did nothing. It was almost as if he hadn't felt her fist at all.

"Take her," he commanded.

Two Impure guards rushed forward and grabbed Kate by the arms, pulled her away from Nicholas's embrace. In a way, she was glad to go, but she still fought, kicking her feet, looking for flesh to bite.

"You'll pay for this, Roman," she screamed at him as the guards hauled her past the Order and toward a small structure with a thatched roof. "I swear to God, whatever I have to do."

He didn't look at her, just kept his eyes on the ten red-robed bastards who were returning to their seats as if nothing had happened.

"You're a fucking coward, you know that!" she shouted at him—at them.

But she wasn't sure if anyone heard that last bit or not. The guards had shoved her inside the structure, tossed her into a room, and shut the door.

She lay there for a moment, her back to the sandy floor, her eyes on the ceiling.

WELCOME BACK, PRISONER 626

It wasn't Mondrar, but it may as well have been. No waves, no words coming together to create a command. It was already written, already done.

Hatred filled her every vein, every cell.

She was dead, and Nicholas Roman would pay.

Nicholas stood before the Order, forcing down his instinct to run after the guards who held the *veana* and drain them dry. Their hands on her flesh, their rough ways made him want to wage war against them all: the Order, the guards, even himself. But Lucian's future, his existence was the only concern he would allow himself now.

"Bringing back our prisoner without being asked. Your loyalty is appreciated, Nicholas Roman, and yet it's surprising."

Nicholas slid his gaze to Cruen. The oldest member of the Order was sitting forward, his merlot robes hanging off his thin frame, his gnarled hands resting on the ancient wood table, pale blue eyes lit up with delight.

"You mistake my motives in coming here, bringing the *veana*," Nicholas said with little emotion.

"Do we?"

"Kate Everborne is mine."

There was a rustle of robes amongst the ten, the black circles around each of their left eyes going glassy as they spoke to one another with their thoughts. But Cruen looked at no one save Nicholas, his eyes narrowing with distrust. "Prisoner 626 belongs to the Order."

"No," Nicholas said, walking toward the table. "She is my prisoner, and I intend to use her as bait."

"Bait?" The white-haired *veana* next to Cruen raised her snowy eyebrows. "Explain yourself, Son of the Breeding Male."

"You want Dare. Dare wants her."

"Why would Dare want her?" asked the white-haired *veana*. "Not simply because she is a *veana*?"

"No. He wants the *balas*, and he thinks Kate knows where the child is."

A *paven* on the end with a black beard tapered to a

point called out, "You are speaking of Mirabelle Letts's *balas*?"

Nicholas nodded.

"But why?" the white-haired *veana* asked. "Why would Dare want the boy?"

"I don't know."

Cruen cocked his head to one side, studied Nicholas. "You don't."

"No," Nicholas said easily. "But perhaps for the same reason the Order wants him."

Cruen's eyes narrowed.

"The Order wants the boy back because he belongs in his *credenti*," the *veana* said quickly. "Wherever it is that Prisoner 626 took him he will be discovered and returned to his *credenti*."

Nicholas shrugged. "I hope so, but in the meantime, Dare searches for him too—and for Kate Everborne. We would all be fools not to use this opportunity, not to use her."

"What are you asking for, Son of the Breeding Male?" Cruen said, scowling.

"I'm not asking. I want Dare and she is the key."

Cruen's scowl deepened. "No."

"You want Dare dead before he takes another *veana*, before he recruits another Impure, do you not?"

Many seated at the table nodded, but the *veana* with the white hair asked, "And when Prisoner 626 is done assisting you? What then?"

"I will return her to you." The words were easy enough to say, and yet there was something within

Nicholas that stumbled. As it was with all Pureblood *pavens*, he didn't possess a beating heart, so perhaps it was the concern he had regarding her hold on him, or a moral compass he had no idea he possessed, one that was trying to direct him back to what was good, what was right.

Either way he wasn't listening.

"If we agree to this," the white-haired *veana* said, "Prisoner 626 must have the tracking chip replaced."

"No."

Cruen hissed. "We grow tired of your obstinate manner, Son of the Breeding Male."

"She will be with me always. A morphed Pureblood. Tracked by the Order for eternity. You want her, just look for me."

Cruen grinned at him, flashing his red fangs. "You wish to take full responsibility for her, then?"

Nicholas nodded.

"Fine."

The *veana* lifted a hand. "And the *balas*—"

Nicholas didn't even let her finish. "If I find the *balas*, I'll bring him back with the *veana*."

"We have a deal, Son of the Breeding Male," Cruen said, leaning forward over the table. "But if you do not return the *veana*—for whatever reason—Lucian Roman will be morphed. Even with Dare's body at our feet."

The odd feeling inside Nicholas stumbled again, but he ignored it. All that mattered was his brother, and keeping him from morpho—keeping him protected until Nicholas could do it no longer. And after what

Lucian had sacrificed for him so long ago, his very life in the face of seven males who had tried to bleed Nicholas dry, this *veana* and the chance she might be his true mate was a blip in his long existence. He refused to be responsible for her future—he owed her nothing.

"Do I have your word?" Nicholas said gruffly.

Down the row, each member of the Order nodded. Though when Nicholas got to Cruen, the *paven*'s eyes burned blue fire before he dropped his chin.

11

They'd done something to her.

The Order had screwed with her brain.

Again.

Lying on her back, she turned over to her belly and executed twenty wide-grip push-ups, nose to the sand floor and back again. The exercise stopped the little electric shocks that were flickering within her mind, showing up on the lids of her eyes when she was lying prostrate.

Life had just become unbearable again, but giving up breathing wasn't an option—even if she was headed back to Mondrar. That dark hole she'd allowed herself to sit in just moments after the guards had dumped her ass in there had lasted only a few minutes. The Order loved to see her kind suffer, but fuck them if they thought she was going to feel sorry for herself.

Twenty more.

Wider with the hands this time—make it hurt like hell.

She grunted her way down, going real slow, feeling every bit of the strain in her shoulders, back, elbows—

"Get up!"

Kate paused, her nose inches from the pale sand. Huh. Interesting. *Similis* coming for her already. The Order must be real excited to see her, all hot and heavy about getting her ass back in a cell.

"Get up, *sacro* Pureblood," the Mondrar guard said again.

She lifted her eyes, grinned. They could call her dirty, try to intimidate her, but she knew who they were—what they were. "Make me," she uttered.

Without an answer, the guard, followed by a second, pushed into the cell.

Kate jumped to her feet and met them halfway with hard eyes and a vicious attitude. "What do you want from me, Impures? I know it's not my body—that urge got cut off a long time ago."

The guard's nostrils flared. "You are being released, 626."

She chuckled. "Really?" What kind of game was this? "The Order has set me free and I can just walk out of here with no assistance from either one of you?"

They nodded, their expressions grim.

"Fine. I'll play." She started toward the door, all casual, waiting for the two impotent bastards to call her bluff, grab her by the arms and haul her back. Maybe stand over her for a few seconds, laughing their collective asses off.

But they didn't. Instead they called at her back, "You are being released into another's custody."

Kate stopped a few feet from the door, her mind shifting gears, her lungs working with the heavy breathing and the nerves. "Whose custody?"

The Impures didn't answer. Hell, they didn't have to. Standing at the open door of her cell, looking all savior to her sacrifice, was Nicholas Roman.

Damn, she looked angry, and murderous—and like she wanted to cut his balls off. And if Nicholas was into that kind of thing he may have let her try just to have her hands on him.

She'd been stripped of her coat and long tunic and was wearing just the ripped jeans and a white tank. He knew she was tall for a *veana*, up to his neck in fact, but he'd never guessed her body would look like that: long and lean with curves in the back and front, and muscles down the sides.

He itched to take her hands, pull her into the protection of his chest and shoulders. But they would both know what a lie that was. Protection and kindness were the last things in the world he was going to give her.

"Where to, *paven*?" She walked out the door, passed him, and headed down the hall. "Got a cell for me somewhere in your house?"

As a matter of fact, he did. 'Course it was Alexander's, and was in use by the brother and his mate for things not related to confinement—gentle torture perhaps—but that was none of Nicholas's business.

Kate pushed open the stone doors of the small detention center and headed for the Order's table. Nicholas followed, knowing damn well that the ancient ten were gone now, spreading their particular brand of misery somewhere else.

"Anytime you're ready, Kate," he said, following her at a leisurely pace. She was still pretty pissed off at him, but soon she was going to realize that although he'd been the one to bring her before the Order, he was the only one to get her out again.

But not only did she not turn around, she walked faster, kicking up sand as she hustled toward the empty wood table. When she got there, she cupped her hands around her mouth and shouted, "Where are you? You cowards! I don't want a fucking babysitter! Deal with me. Only me!"

Christ. He didn't want them back here—and no matter how she was acting, she didn't want them either. He flashed directly in front of her and took her arm. "Let's go."

She yanked it back and changed direction. "Fuck you."

Again he flashed in front of her. "Take my hand and let's go."

She turned and slammed her gaze into his. "Fuck. You."

"Don't you get it? I got the Order off your back."

"Are we really going to pretend I'm listening to you?" Again she cupped her hands. "I will be heard! Before you strike a bargain for my life, I will be heard!"

Nicholas cursed, and before she could say another word, he hauled her against him and flashed out of the Order's reality and onto the mountaintop, near the caves.

Above them, the moon was full and round and spitting off yellow rays through the treetops, turning the long hair of the *veana* in his arms an almost mystic white.

He whirled her to face him, his fingers curling around her biceps. "Listen to me."

"Do I have a choice?" she said viciously. "I think I may be your property now. Word to the wise, I'm lazy, I snore, and my table manners are atrocious—think wolf on a deer carcass."

He tried not to stare at her mouth. But it wasn't easy. "I'm a morphed *paven*, sweetheart. Which means the Order can track me. They knew we were together on the train. If we'd gone back to my house, they would've been on us in minutes."

"Damn right!" she shouted. "I'd told you I wanted to be alone. I told you to get off the train and leave me alone. But you had to have your answers and now I'm screwed. This is all your fault!"

"I believed you were working with Dare," he said, this time with a sharp edge. "It was a fuckup, okay? But what's done is done. And when that message came through from the Order, I knew there was no other way—not if we wanted to keep them away from the boy."

That stopped her, had her shutting off the slash,

burn, and blame for a moment. Her gaze flickered—
the ground, a rock, his chest. "If that's true, why
didn't you tell me before we flashed there, before I got
dragged off and thrown in a cell?"

"I needed it to look like you were surprised, pissed
off."

"Humiliated."

"Devastated." His fingers dug into her skin, and he
leaned in closer. "I needed them to see you fight."

She tilted her head, locked eyes with him. "You sure?
Because I think you get off on making *veanas* struggle."

"And I think you get off *on* the struggle."

"You'll never know," she whispered, then tipped
her chin. "*Sweetheart.*"

Her blood scent, brought on by her ire no doubt,
shot forward like a bullet. He released her, took a step
back—and tried to gain control of his body. "The Order
needed to think I was doing something out of loyalty
to them to get them to agree to my terms."

"Terms?" she repeated with a sniff of derision. "I'm
intrigued."

"They want me to find and kill Ethan Dare, and
you'll draw him in."

"Worm on the hook, huh?"

Nicholas nodded.

"And he's coming after me because of the boy," she
said. "He'll steal me away, torture me until I give up
the kid's location."

"He won't get that far. He'll be dead before he even
has a chance to touch you."

"You hope." She leaned back against the exterior of the cave, crossed her arms over her chest. "If the Order wants Dare why can't they just go and get him? He's an Impure, for Christ's sake."

"Not that simple. As you saw on the train, he's not your ordinary Impure."

"How can that be?"

"No idea."

She was quiet for a moment, her gaze swimming laps across his face. "Why is the Order making *you* find Dare? They holding something over your head?"

"Why would you think that?" he said, impassive.

She rolled her eyes. "Please."

"It's a family matter."

She nodded, her mouth lifting at the corners. "Secrets and lies . . ."

"Are what?" he said, shrugging. "Bad for the environment?"

She looked down, chuckled softly. "So what now, Mr. Roman?" Her pale brows lifted. "I become your bait, you get Dare, then what? You deposit me back at the Order?"

"That is what I told them." Brothers before others. In this case, one brother in particular.

She flashed her fangs, white as snow and sharp enough to cut through Nicholas's thick skin.

"You're a real prince among vampires, you know that?" she uttered tersely.

Oh, he knew. And worse. Hell, even at the moment, unsympathetic to her plight, all he wanted to do was get her clothes off, her back to the dirt, and her legs spread.

His nostrils flared as he pulled in a breath. "You work with me to bring in Dare, and when it's time to drop you off at Mondrar and you're not around—you've disappeared—I'll shrug and act surprised. How about that?"

She sniffed. "Try again, because we both know the Order isn't going to let you get away with that."

"What do you want me to say? That I'll guard you with my life?"

"Yes."

Her chin was lifted, brown eyes flashing twin "buyer beware" signs. She wasn't going to believe him either way, but he needed her to go with him, easy and smooth. "Fine. I'll guard you with my life."

She was staring at him, trying to read him—and no doubt coming up with several ways she was going to attempt to escape him during their time together.

Go ahead and try, veana. *Might be fun to chase you . . .*

"How about we agree," she began, "that I don't trust you and you don't trust me?"

He grinned. "Sounds about right." Shrugged. "Sounds perfect, in fact. A match made in—"

"Hell," she finished for him.

Her eyes flared dark as chocolate, and she pushed away from the cave wall and sidled up to him, curled into the groove between his shoulder and his chest and waited.

Nicholas breathed her in, tasted her scent on his

tongue and felt his cock get stiff. No doubt she felt it too, his erection pressing into her lower back like a hungry animal all its own, but she said nothing. Clearly, he couldn't control that one part of his anatomy. Good thing he had control over the rest.

They flashed from the mountain and took form in front of the SoHo compound. Without a word, Kate left the shelter of his arms and walked ahead, getting a good look at her surroundings. She looked up, around, took in the brick and mortar. "This your place?"

"Yes."

She turned to face him. "Good. I need a room and a shower. Then I'm all yours." She lifted one pale brow, but her eyes flickered down to his crotch. "Just let woody there know I'm not interested. Now or ever."

12

Their thoughts were only whispers inside the tunnel of punk and heavy metal. Whispers like *"Scars . . . alone . . . Get me off . . . A freak but . . ."* And after a day in the city, trying to hide out in the park with his headphones, inanimate whispers were nothing. He could lose himself and his mind in the feeling, in the soft, wet bodies of the two women who bracketed him. They didn't need conversation, didn't require dinner first. Just like everyone else at Equinox, they came for the music, the darkness, the anonymity—the sex. And sex was happening all around. Singles, doubles, hell, even triples. No sound track but the music.

This was his life. Hide and keep his ears covered during the day, hang out in the club all night.

Once an empty shell who took up nothing but air. Now a half vampire–half human who belonged nowhere and to no one.

Shit, he wasn't long for this earth, he mused as he let his fire-ravaged hands sink beneath the table, beneath a strip of smooth, wet silk.

And that was just fine by him.

The moan that came loud and strong wasn't inside his head this time, but rushed from the mouth of the female to his left.

"Yes. Oh fuck, yes," she cried, arching her back as he spread her pussy with his fingers and began stroking her clit.

"Faster. . . . God. . . . Going to come."

Gray watched her, watched the rush of pink travel up from her chest to her neck and out her throat. It was beautiful. Stunning.

He turned. To his right, another female, one who had been shadowing him all night, had her hands on him, trying to stroke him through his jeans.

"What's your name?" he shouted.

She smiled. "Marina."

"You have a very pretty mouth, Marina."

"So do you."

His turn. He smiled too. "Would you like to use it?"

"Gotcha, baby," she thought, then let her tongue flicker out to swipe at her lower lip. Grinning, she unzipped his fly and released his straining prick.

Gray's nostrils flared as she wrapped her soft hand around him, then lowered her head and took him into her mouth.

The band screamed, the crowd cheered, and as Gray slipped three fingers inside the wet heat of the woman to his left, he let the whispers of both lull him into a rare state of euphoria.

"Deeper . . ."

"Fuck . . ."
"Tastes like . . ."
"He's mine . . ."

Kate stood inside her newest prison. It wasn't tiny and cramped and stinking of ammonia. In fact, it was pretty damn lovely—white and pale blue with a fireplace, and the kind of carpets toes had orgasms over. But it was a holding cell nonetheless.

Standing at the door, she and Nicholas eyeballed each other like a first date gone bad. He had her in his fancy mansion, locked up in the tower, waiting for his next move, and all she wanted to do was be alone, get her mind working on a plan to disappear.

"If there's anything you need just use the phone by the bed," he said, his hands gripping the sides of the doorframe, the stance accentuating the width of his chest.

Not that she was noticing or caring—or admiring.

"If I'm not here, Evans will get you whatever you need."

"Who's Evans? A servant? True mate? Geisha?"

His mouth twitched with humor. "Evans handles the household. He takes care of the guests."

"Great. Thanks."

He raised a brow. "That almost sounded like you meant it."

"Did it?" she said, making her eyes wide with false surprise. "Well, I can fake it when I have to."

"That's unfortunate. A *veana* should never have to fake anything."

"Sometimes, with certain individuals, it's a necessity."

"Clearly you're hanging out with the wrong individuals."

"Don't think I have a choice."

His eyes narrowed and he leaned in, his mouth dangerously close to hers. "As a morphed *paven* my senses are highly acute. They can not only pick up the scent of location, fear, and anger, but lust as well." He laughed. "And your scent, my stunning houseguest, is so vast and heavy with desire I could drown in it."

"Stop it," she said, stepping back.

"In fact, the only thing you're faking is that you're not attracted to me."

"Get out of here."

He grinned. "I am. I have a meet with my brothers, but I'll be back in a few hours."

"Bated breath, *paven*," she muttered, hand on the door ready to close it—shut him off, out, and her unfortunate reaction to him as well, but the sudden pain in her chest stopped her, had her lunging forward. She felt the breath leave her body, her lungs, and tried to swallow, tried to keep what was left of the air inside, but it was no use.

"You okay?"

Sounding annoyingly concerned now, Nicholas put his hand on her shoulder.

She brushed it off. "I'm fine. Just tired."

"You sure?"

She took a deep breath, tried to refill her lungs, but it was no use. What the hell? She forced herself to straighten up, face him. Maybe she needed to feed.

Hunger.

Yes, that would explain why she had the urge to grab the back of Nicholas Roman's head every time he was near, pull him toward her and suckle the thick vein pulsing on his neck.

"You can go," she told him, acting as though the episode was over, gone now. Poof. But as she stared at him, chin up, she couldn't shake the breathless feeling inside her, and the dizziness, the sparks shooting off in her mind.

He looked less than convinced, but he nodded. "Get some rest, then. We have work ahead of us."

"Can't wait," she muttered.

"And, by the way," he said, backing up and out the door. "The *balas* is next door."

Another wave of dizziness hit her, but she managed to close the door on his retreating frame and lean against the wood. Where was she going to get blood? she thought, trying to regulate her breathing. As was her way in Mondrar and in the *credenti*, she could eat berries and grains, nuts and seeds—but her body also needed the blood rations that the Order, in their eternal attempt to control both the purity and whereabouts of their flock, had provided.

As her breathing started to return to normal, the spot where her tracking device used to be, where Nicholas's fangs had penetrated her skin, started to pulse, to hum. It knew what she needed, what she craved.

His blood.

Nicholas's blood—pure, strong . . . delectable. And straight from the source. Goddamn, that would be wonderful. She could almost scent it, feel it rushing down her throat, coating all the right spots.

"You are in heat, *veana*!" She pushed away from the door. Maybe she could scrub the shit out of that spot, get rid of it all—the hunger, the lust, the thoughts, the asinine desires—drown it out, send it through the pipes to the sewer where it belonged.

Just as she was heading to the bathroom, there was a knock on her door. He was back. And that meant his blood scent, his devil eyes, and his dangerous hands were back too. Shit. Maybe if she backed off the bitchy *veana* thing for a minute, she might be able to get him to offer up a little O Positive—just enough to get her through a couple of days. Hell, he owed her a pint or two after dragging her in front of the Order like that.

She was on her way to the door when she heard a female's voice call through the wood, "Kate?"

Disappointment washed over her. Satisfying her hunger was going to have to wait.

"Who is it?" she asked.

"Sara Donohue. I'm Alexander's mate. Could I talk to you for a minute?"

Gripping the knob, Kate drew back the wood to reveal an incredibly beautiful *veana* with long dark hair that was piled loosely on top of her head, and a pair of the most incredible blue eyes she'd ever seen. "I'm sorry—who are you?"

"Alexander is Nicholas's brother," she said, her tone impressively gentle and soothing. "I'm his true mate."

Kate remembered what Nicholas had said on the train. "You've been watching Ladd."

"Yes."

She softened slightly. "How is he?"

"Okay. Sleeping now."

"Good. That's good."

"He's a tough one," Sara confided. "But who can blame him, right? He's experienced a significant loss."

The grounds of the Vermont elementary school popped up in Kate's mind along with Mirabelle's face as she lay dying in the snow—her fear, not for herself, but for the boy, paramount in her gaze.

"He's experienced a lot," Sara added.

"More than any *balas* should," Kate said with more passion that she'd meant to, or wanted to.

Her tone wasn't lost on Sara, and the *veana* gave her an easy, pleasant smile. "I thought you might like some company."

"That's really nice," Kate said—and she meant it. "Thoughtful."

"But you want to be alone."

Actually, she'd like to be in Fiji. Or Crested Butte. She gave the *veana* a small shrug. "You know what I'd really like is to feed. At the *credenti*, the Order supplies our rations, but here . . ."

"Of course," Sara said. "I'll see what I can do, have something brought to your room."

"Thank you."

"Sure." With a quick inhale, Sara lifted her chin and looked past Kate. "You know, I used to stay in this room once upon a time."

"Really? When you were abducted by a Roman brother?"

Sara laughed. "Kind of."

Kate's brows drew together. "Worked out well for you, then."

"It was for my own good."

"Your *paven* sold you that story, huh?"

A blush spread from Sara's cheeks to her neck, making the blue in her eyes pop with intensity. "My mate has a way with words. His mouth is quite a persuasive tool."

Okaaayyy. Kate raised her brows. "That's a lot of info for a first meet, *veana*."

Sara laughed, shrugged. "Sorry. I'm a bonder."

It was Kate's turn to laugh, the sound dry and hoarse as it exited her throat. She liked this one. Not sure how much she could trust her—but Sara Donohue was definitely a funny, intelligent female.

Sara popped up a finger. "And I'm not a *veana*, by the way."

"But you're mated to a Pureblood?"

"It's a good story. Maybe I can tell it to you sometime."

"Maybe."

"But not tonight," Sara said, her understanding smile easy and no-pressure. She gave Kate a little wave as she backed up. "I'll see you later, and I'll make sure you get a feed, okay?"

"Okay," Kate said. "Thanks."

She closed the door and waited for several seconds to hear the sound of the female's retreating heels. It had been a nice gesture, coming to her room like that, trying to do the make-the-captive-feel-at-home thing. She wondered if Nicholas had anything to do with it. Had he asked Sara to check in on her?

Ditching the shower she'd been so keen on jumping into a few minutes ago, she slipped out of the room and walked the six or so feet down the hall to the room next door. A nervous energy bubbled in her stomach, and she hoped Ladd was asleep when she walked in there so she wouldn't have to face him, explain herself and the run back to her *credenti*—or talk about what had happened to his mother and, God help her, about what would happen next.

Because . . . she had nothing.

Shaking off her nerves, she opened the door, saw the *balas* asleep on the bed, his small body curled into a pillow, and gratefully released a breath as she went in and sat down on the bed.

A garden of emotions ran through her as she watched him slumber. She was envious of his peaceful, calm state of being. She was angry with his mother for having been late to pick him up yesterday, angry that she showed up at all, and brokenhearted that she'd ended up dead and leaving her son and some random *veana* who happened to be on parole, up shit creek without a paddle.

She inched her hand closer to Ladd's small one, stopped before her fingers touched his. She was covetous of the fact that he had a father who didn't even know him but seemed moderately interested in his welfare. And she was grateful for the closeness and protectiveness and kinship she felt when she was around him. He may have been a *balas* and she a grown *veana*, but they were forever connected by tragedy.

"I'm sorry." She whispered the all-encompassing apology into the darkness.

And in his sleep, Ladd reached out and placed his small hand over hers.

Nice, France
1899

Nicholas could barely move. On the bed that had once been his mother's, he lay curled up in a ball, whimpering softly. He had been worked over well and good by both a veana and a paven, who had called him their grand chien, their big dog, as they wrapped his neck in a collar and proceeded to beat him with a stick as the male screwed him at one end and the female knelt before him, her legs spread. It wasn't always this way. He also serviced many who gave him a modicum of pleasure, who were kind to him. In fact, there was a veana who had lost her child to sickness and had wanted only to be held, kissed sweetly on the cheek.

Nicholas lived for those days.

"Nichola."

Nicholas heard the familiar sound, the raspy call from the other room. She never called to him while he was servicing, but he knew she must have listened. Was she proud of her balas? *At fifteen, he earned twice what she had per week. It kept her in blood and* gravo.

"Nichola, please."

He didn't want to go, didn't want to see her or hear her anymore. But she was his mama, and to deny her would be his end.

He pushed himself off the bed and limped into the front room, feeling as though the male's stick was still lodged inside him. His mother lay on the canapé, *terrifyingly thin, her eyes hollow and emotionless, her short hair dirty from a continuous refusal to wash. "I need my medicine,* mon petit. *The pain is desperate today."*

As a balas, *Nicholas could do nothing but love her, but as a young* paven *he had begun to resent her. "The gravo is killing you, Mama."*

She attempted a laugh, her fangs black and completely worn down. "I was dead long ago, Nichola. The moment I sent you to your knees."

She looked almost regretful. It was rare to see her in any real way, and it touched his unbeating heart. "Let me take you away," he said as he had so many times before. "We will go, find another life."

"Go where?" she said bitterly. "There is nothing but this." Her eyes were hooded and tired. "You want to quit, do you not? Run away from here and from your mama?"

Oui. Mais oui. Nicholas looked away. "*I will not leave you.*"

"*Of course you won't,* mon petit." *The momentary expression of regret evaporated and the familiar mask of self-pity returned. "Where would you go? You can do nothing but this. You are a* putan. *It is what you are, all that you are.*"

Her words cut into him more than any stick or fang or blade, but he forced himself to believe it was the pain that made her speak so, not her lack of love for her balas.

He stumbled back into his room and dressed, his clothing scraping against the cuts and bruises on his skin. Even now, even as his body pained him so, he would go out into the streets and bring her back her gravo.

13

Dillon looked up from the computer she was sharing with Alexander and eyed Nicholas with a concerned expression. "The Order agreed to that?"

"They had little choice," Nicholas said, joining Lucian at the table as he cleaned weapons. "Dare's demise is the key to everything."

"Yes," Alexander put in, "but using her as bait . . ."

"What?" Nicholas said with a shrug. "It's shitty? Low rent? The act of a true bastard?"

"Pretty much."

"Don't listen to him, Nicky," Lucian put in, his nostrils flaring with annoyance. "He's become one of those sensitive males. It's the mating—it's made every inch of him soft."

Alexander chuckled dryly. "Not every inch."

"No," Dillon said, shaking her head. "Hell no."

"Oh right," Lucian said, dropping one cleaned Glock on the table. "Forgot about those incredibly important six you got under your fly."

"Try nine"—Alexander's merlot eyes shot up and he grinned—"and a half."

Dillon cursed. "Want to be anywhere but here . . ."

"And every female needs a half." Alexander pointed at his little brother. "Remember that."

A snarl formed on Lucian's mouth. "You wanna go there? Do you really?"

"I know I don't," Dillon said, typing furiously on the keyboard.

Nicholas jumped in. "Before one of you calls Evans to bring a ruler, let's talk plan."

"Fine," Lucian said, dropping into a chair. "But just to clarify. You're keeping your bait until Dare is dust and then she's out of here, right?"

Nicholas said nothing. Not because he didn't have an answer, but because he didn't think Lucian would appreciate the one he had. At this point, all he was willing to acknowledge was that he needed Kate— they needed her.

Lucian cursed, glanced at Alexander. "He gives us nothing."

"Looks like I'm not the only soft *paven*," Alexander said with a grin.

"Dare keeps running and the females keep coming," Lucian muttered, grabbing another weapon.

"Nice," Dillon said, her eyes still focused on the screen. "You got some talent there, Luca. A regular Dr. Seuss with fangs."

"Two *veanas* and a *balas*." He brought a sniper rifle

up and looked through the scope. "In this house. Not what I signed up for."

"We hear you, brother," Alexander said.

"But you don't give a shit."

"Not so much."

Lucian pointed the rifle at each of them. "Females will be our downfall. Mark my words."

"Our downfall will be the Order," Nicholas corrected, palming two Glocks, the cool, deadly metal reminding him of all that lay ahead—all that was at stake. "If they succeed in having all three of us under their control. We can't let that happen."

The room grew still and heavy. Putting down his weapon, Lucian nodded, as did Alexander.

"It's nearly dawn," Nicholas said. "Tomorrow night we take the bait and go fishing. In the meantime, we train and gather all the information we can on sightings, and Impures and *veanas* who've gone missing."

"Nearly there," Alexander put in, his eyes on the computer screen now. "Should we bring Gray in on this?"

Lucian sneered. "Please."

"What?"

"Are you seriously asking that?"

"The boy been out again?" Dillon asked, standing, heading over to the weapons table.

"And again and again," Lucian said fiercely. "He wants none of this. Clearly, the blood in his veins has spoken."

A growl came from behind the computer monitor. "His Impure blood, you mean—"

"No," Lucian said, his gaze steady on Alexander. "I'm talking warrior blood. He has none. He's useless."

A snarl lifted Alexander's top lip. "He is a part of this family."

"Only when you're running after him, begging him to come home."

Alexander stood, his shoulders hunched like a predatory beast.

"Enough," Nicholas said, eyeing both *pavens*, deadly serious in his tone. "We have work to do, and a battle to prepare for. One that will be fought out there, *not* in here."

Nicholas took the stairs three at a time, adrenaline mixing with desire in his blood to create a perfect Molotov cocktail of predatory male.

It had been his plan to leave the *veana* alone, let her rest for one solid night before he brought her out, set his trap for Dare. But there was something in him, something built out of a natural mistrust of everything and everyone that made him need to see for himself that she was where he had left her. And perhaps he wanted to take another look at her skin.

He pushed off the last step and rounded the corner. When he hit the hallway, Kate's blood scent rose up and smacked him in the face—a warning, an omen.

When he reached her door, he knocked once. But after five seconds of no answer, he opened the door and went in. Her scent was actually weaker in there and his gaze shot to the bed. Still made.

Heat started in his feet and spread upward as he stared at the empty bed. If she had escaped, he would first break Evans's thin, Impure neck for allowing her to get away, then head out into the night and go feral vampire until he tracked her down.

He wouldn't lose. Not her, not Lucian's future.

Not to the motherfucking Order.

He headed out the door into the hall. Bam—into his nostrils again. His skin prickled. She was near. Not in her room, but close by.

He whirled around, his eyes narrowing in on another door. He stalked over to it and had to stop himself from pulling the thing off its hinges. Breathe, asshole, he chided himself. Breathe and get control over yourself.

All he could spare were twenty seconds of in and out; then he opened the door and went inside. It was black as pitch, but the shades were drawn back on one window, letting in one hazy shower of moonlight. His eyes went looking, searching. Kate was nowhere in sight, but her scent was all over the place. He zeroed in on the bed. Asleep on the plush queen, curled up with a pillow in his gut, was the boy. Nicholas had a moment of shock and sentiment.

When he slept, which wasn't all that much—but when he did, he slept just like that.

The aggression inside him melted a fraction as he gazed down at the *balas*. Had he really created some-

thing like this? Something so perfect, so small? *Jesus.*
The very last thing he ever considered—ever thought
about—ever wanted was a child. He was no *father.*
He was an introvert, a liar, a whore—but he was not a
father.

Poor Mirabelle. If this was true and she'd made a
child with him—poor, sad Mirabelle. Why hadn't she
just found a lover—a real lover she didn't have to pay?
A stand-up *paven* who would be worthy of a *balas.*

Poor Mirabelle.

They had lain together many times, had talked
about her mate and the ceremony that had ended the
life she'd hoped for, had thought she would have, that
she'd been so looking forward to. He'd known exactly
what she'd meant by that.

Nicholas's eyes moved over the little face, little
hands, little body.

He couldn't—but he had to . . .

On impulse, he slipped a knife from his pocket and
went over to the bed, knelt down. "Be still, little one,"
he whispered to the sleeping child.

When he felt the blade of a sharp-as-shit Combat
Bowie at his throat, he grinned. "Shouldn't you be
sleeping too, Kate?"

"Drop the knife."

He chuckled low.

She pressed it closer to his neck. "Drop the knife or
your head will be severed from your body."

"You need to calm down."

"Oh, I'm very calm," she replied. "If I wasn't, you'd

have blood spurting out of your neck in a zigzag pattern right now."

"What exactly do you think is going on here?"

He heard her release a breath, almost a whisper of a laugh. "If you don't want the boy, I'll take him—far away from here and from you."

"Easy, mama bear," he muttered.

"I'm no one's mama, just won't have you ending this life before it's even begun."

Nicholas moved lightning quick. He was up, had Kate's arm wrapped around her back and her back pressed against the wall by the door before she even had the chance to exhale.

Kate's blade was on the floor, rocking back and forth against the wood, the clicking sound echoing throughout the room.

Oh shit. What now?

Running on instinct, hunger, desire, and stupidity, she arched her back and pressed her hips forward, desperate to make contact with the hard bulge in his jeans. Her heart rapped against its prison of ribs, and her eyes combed over his face. The flecks of green in his black eyes held a stark intelligence she hadn't noticed before, and the brands on his cheeks, the circles with some kind of smudge markings inside, screamed that he too was under the thumb of a force he despised.

As she stood there, took in his scent, felt the warmth of his breath against her mouth, she fought the urge to dive into the curve of his neck and drink.

God, her throat was dry.

Her stomach, too.

The blood Evans had brought for her, per Sara's request, had been animal blood. She'd tried like hell, but hadn't been able to get it down.

Nicholas's lips moved then, forming words. "I may be many things, *veana*," he uttered, his gaze fierce, "but a *balas* killer isn't one of them."

He was so close, her tongue could dart out and taste him. "And yet you had a knife to his throat," she said breathlessly.

"To his hair," he corrected, his fangs dropping as his cock pulsed against her belly. "I need a sample of his DNA, and I didn't want to take his blood."

Blood.

She shivered, and the muscles inside her cunt contracted. God, she could practically hear the blood rushing inside his veins, calling to her. And what was that? His fangs—his brilliantly white fangs—they pressed against his full bottom lip, the ridges carved into them a leg-shaking surprise.

"What's wrong with you?" he asked, his nostrils flaring as he narrowed his eyes.

She swallowed, saliva hitting the back of her throat, but doing little to curb the dry sensation. "What are you talking about?"

"Your eyes are glowing. Shit, they're nearly gold." His hands gripped her wrists behind her back, inching them forward into the small of her back until her breasts jutted forward, until she sucked air between her teeth. "You're hungry."

"And you really enjoy the rough stuff, don't you?"

He growled low. "Only with you, it seems."

"I doubt that," she said, hoping he couldn't scent the wet heat that was building inside her.

"The Order rations their illustrious blood at the *credenti*. A cup every other day."

It wasn't a question, but she nodded anyway. "Keeps us perpetually hungry—not starving, but always looking to our lords and masters to care for us. Brilliant way to keep us tethered to home."

"They are nothing if not calculated in their motives," he said. "We'll have to see about getting you fed. After all, you are a guest here. We feed from animals when we can't get—"

"I can't drink animal blood," she said quickly.

His jaw was set into a hard line. "Why not?"

"Evans brought me some earlier. It made me ill."

His head moved in, closer, until their lips touched. His were soft, full, and with a pained groan he tipped up his chin and licked her with the tip of his tongue. "I won't have you ill," he murmured. "I need you too much."

"Keep the bait breathing?" she whispered, her legs trembling.

"In and out, *veana*."

She followed his example and traced his lips with her tongue. "Perhaps one of your brothers would allow—"

"No!" His feral growl stopped her, and she pulled her mouth away from his, just a few centimeters.

He slipped his hands from her back and circled her waist, pulled her impossibly closer against his chest, against his arousal. "No one feeds you . . ." He scraped the tips of his fangs gently against her top lip.

But him? No one feeds her but him?

She couldn't help herself. The pain in her belly, the crushing, aching heat in her cunt was too much. Her fangs elongated and she pierced the flesh of his lower lip.

Nicholas came alive at her sweet assault, felt air rush into his lungs, but he didn't draw back. His cock pulsing like a heartbeat against her belly, he tipped his chin and allowed her fangs to delve even deeper. He didn't know how much blood she could consume this way, but he was willing to give for as long as she suckled.

"Oh God," Kate moaned, her fingers getting tangled in his hair. "You taste—"

"Tell me."

"Warm."

He growled.

"Sweet."

She stopped speaking then and just drank, fed, suckled, deep pulls until his lip ached—along with his throat, his cock.

"Need a third?" A male voice registered in Nicholas's brain, and he felt Kate break from his embrace, felt her fangs retracting back.

"Shit," he uttered, his eyes at half-mast as he moved in front of her, blocking her from his brother's view.

Kate stared at the *paven* in the hall outside the door. He was incredibly tall and broad like Nicholas, but that's where the comparison ended. His jaw-length white hair was a stark contrast to his piercing light brown eyes and black lashes. And though he was alarmingly, almost shockingly good-looking, everything about him, every intake of breath, every movement of his gaze, his chin, his mouth fairly screamed hostility. Like an animal who'd been tortured over and over and knew only biting as a response to anything.

"What the hell, Nicky?" the *paven* said with true disgust. "Training? Remember? You called it, and we've been waiting for your sorry ass for over twenty minutes." His intimidating gaze moved over Kate nice and slow. "Of course, if you share your sweet little bait with me, I may be inclined to forgive you. Let me take her first, warm up that cold blood for you."

"Get lost, Luca," Nicholas snarled, then promptly kicked the door closed.

Under the splintered light of the waning moon, Kate watched Nicholas step back and assess what had just gone down between them.

"He's charming," she said dryly.

"He's the devil. Stay away from him."

"Maybe I should stay away from all the Romans."

"Yes, perhaps you should."

Frustrated at herself for allowing things to get so out of control, and wanting the uncomfortable moment between them to end, Kate said, "I was hungry. You were available. Let's just call it a mercy feed and forget it ever happened."

"You can do that?"

"Sure." God, she was good at lying.

His jaw went rigid with tension. "I will get you the blood you require so that this doesn't become a . . . problem."

"Great." But it was already a problem. A huge problem, in fact. Right now, his life's blood was running through her veins, attaching itself to her life's blood. In the *credentis* what had just happened between them would make her a dirty *veana*—a *sacro*—used, unable to give herself honorably to her true mate someday. It was one of the reasons why the Order gave their own blood to the unmated—to keep them pure, chaste and satiated, until their time came.

But Kate didn't give a shit about that kind of thing, about saving herself for her true mate. What she was worried about was the connection she'd just forged with this *paven*—this *paven* she despised and didn't trust for a second, yet couldn't seem to resist.

Nicholas glanced down at the boy then, still sleeping so peacefully despite the insanity that had occurred around him. "Are you going to stop me again?"

"If it's really a hair sample you want, then do it," she told him.

"What are you going to do?"

"Watch."

His gaze slid over to her and the wolfish look in his eyes made her pulse jump in her throat.

"Get it done," she said, needing to get the hell out of his air space for a while. "We should go, let the child rest undisturbed."

With the utmost gentleness, Nicholas leaned over and cut a few strands of the boy's hair. When he left the room, Kate followed, then stood there waiting for him to head down the hall and down the stairs.

He observed her for a moment. "For someone who claims to not give a shit about this *balas*, you're sure keeping a close watch."

She shrugged. "Never said I didn't care about the boy."

"What did you say, then?"

"Just that I care about me more."

"And yet you risked your freedom to bring him to his father."

"I'm not debating my motives with you. So I took care of the kid for a moment in time—anyone would've done as much."

"No." The word was tight and pained, and all he said before walking past her down the hall, the electric shades on all the windows beginning their descent.

14

Sun.
   Another day.

Everlasting noise.

Gray pressed the earbuds deeper into his ears, pressed play, and walked out of the club. Hustling past him as Metallica wailed into his head, ladies and gents in their evening wear kept their heads low, their hickeys hidden as they scattered into the streets like roaches—the six a.m. walk of shame.

All but one.

The dark-haired woman Marina kept pace with him as he moved down the street. Her eyes up and wary, she looked real fresh, as though she hadn't been out all night. Gray picked up the pace. He didn't want anything to do with that, hearing what was going on in that pretty head of hers—not in the daylight.

He waved her off and headed down the alley. Just wanted to get to the park, sleep a little near the fountain before he thought about heading to SoHo for a shower.

Suddenly, he felt a hand on his shoulder, yanking him back. He whirled around, his instincts and all the combat he'd been forced to participate in over that past couple months rising to the surface of his skin.

But it was just the woman. Marina. Gray stared at her. Breathing easy and looking interested in more of what she'd had in the club.

What the hell?

Smiling, she tapped her ears, then lifted her hands. She wanted to talk.

Fuck.

Gray turned down the music. Just a thread, just so he could hear her. "What's up? Need something?"

She moved closer to him, catlike, her eyes heavy with flirtatious energy. "I don't live far," she called over the din of street traffic.

Gray shook his head. "Another time."

"Why? You have somewhere to be? A *veana* to get back to?"

"Yeah, and her name is *Death Magnetic*," he said, then palmed his iPod and cranked up the sound on Metallica's best album.

He left the woman standing there, her hands on her hips, lips pushed out into a pretty pout. He was half-way down the alley when he realized what she'd said, what she'd called a woman.

Veana.

He whirled around, his eyes locking on the woman's. She grinned at him, real wide this time, showing off a set of bride-white fangs.

Before Gray could move, before he could use any part of himself as a weapon, he was grabbed from behind. Steel arms had his shoulders locked in place and his head yanked back. His earbuds dropped out of his ears and the New York City streets rushed in, sounding like a low-grade cocktail party in his mind. Then two sets of fangs drove into either side of his neck like hot needles, and in seconds he could hardly see, much less hear, and liquid black swallowed up the day.

Nicholas walked into the library and dropped into the chair opposite Lucian. He had just left Kate in the hallway upstairs and all he could think about was getting back up there, inside her room—inside of her. He pointed his finger at the near-albino and said, "I really don't need a ball-busting session from you right now."

Lucian lifted his brows. "The *veana* taking care of that? No, on second thought, that would be a blue-ball session."

"Watch yourself," Nicholas warned.

"I can see why you lost track of the time. She's one hot piece of—"

Nicholas shot out of his seat and had his fangs extended over his lower lip and his hands plastered onto either side of his brother's face. His little brother, his *duro*, his savior from a time when he'd thought his body would be ripped apart by a gang of tricks in the back alley behind his house when he was barely out of short pants.

"Easy, Nicky," Lucian said grinning, his lip curling

back. The near-albino welcomed the fight, got off on the fight.

Nicholas shook his head slowly, his hands trembling on his brother's cheeks. "I love you more than my own life, would do anything for you—you know that. But speak of her again like that and I won't be able to control myself. Do you understand?"

Lucian's eyes grew curiously amused. "Question is, do you understand?"

Nicholas released the *paven* and dropped back into the chair, his chest heaving as he tried to calm the fuck down. This was misery. Or just plain old-fashioned stupidity.

"Did you take her blood?" Lucian asked, his nostrils flaring.

"No."

"She took yours."

"Yes."

"That shouldn't bond you." He gestured to Nicholas with his hand. "Not like this. Maybe you need to stay away from her."

Maybe I need to see her skin, run my tongue over every inch until I find that mark. Nicholas shook his head, against the words, the feelings, the images running through his brain. "I need her," he said, and when Lucian cursed, he clarified. "I need her to bring in Dare."

"Just watch your back, *Duro*."

Right. Reaching into his pocket, Nicholas took out Ladd's sample and thrust it at his brother. "Here."

"What is it?"

"Hair sample."

"The *balas*?"

Nicholas nodded.

"What do you want me to do with it? Build a nest?"

"Just take it."

"Take it where?" Lucian asked, palming the sample, staring down at the pale strands that were so like his own.

"Only one vampire I know who handles DNA," Nicholas said slowly, knowing what kind of reaction he was about to get.

Realization dawned quickly and Lucian shook his head. "Hell no."

"Lucian—"

"Fuck no."

Nicholas laughed, releasing some of the tension inside his body. "Are you scared of the beautiful and brilliant genealogist?"

"Yes, that's right. Shaking in my shit-kickers."

"Whatever it is, I need you to do this."

"Send Evans."

"He can't go into the *credenti*."

Lucian rolled his eyes. "I'm not going to be your errand boy."

Nicholas grinned. "Yes, you are."

"It's in Boston."

"Nice town," he said, feeling lighter and more like himself every second. Every second he was away from her . . . "Good chowder."

"I hate fish."

"Luca . . ."

"Sun's out."

"Yes, and you can still walk in it with no trouble." Nicholas popped an eyebrow. "For now."

Lucian growled. "Fine."

"Tell her to compare my markers with the *balas*. Tell her I need this ASAP. Tell her the Roman brothers owe her for this."

"Bullshit," Lucian said, this time the one to point an accusatory finger in his brother's direction. "Nicholas Roman owes her."

"Just try and act like a gentleman."

Lucian snorted his response as he stood up and walked out of the room.

On the long mahogany desk her father had built for her, Bronwyn Kettler typed furiously on her laptop before a picture window overlooking the snowy streets of her *credenti*. For most in the Boston *credenti*—any *credenti* really—outside technology was frowned upon. Believing that electronics destroyed the dialogue and closeness of a community's membership, the Order had long ago placed a ban on any technological advances made after the telephone.

However, they'd allowed an exception in Bronwyn's case. Her work was incredibly important to the breed, so important, in fact, that they allowed her free rein. And a good thing, too. Though she loved her home and family and her community, she was a mod-

ern *veana* at heart, and if she'd been pushed to reject
her professional life and its trappings, she may have
had to push back.

The nine-generation genealogy chart she was as-
sembling for a private client, a very demanding client
whom she'd yet to actually meet, sat on the screen before her. It was still missing several names. She was
tired and not feeling herself as of late, and the work
was coming too slowly. She had covered the Romans,
of course, and their possible true mates, but she had
yet to find the final three females who'd lain with the
Breeding Male, and their supposed six offspring.

But she would.

Her own fascination with the subject, not to mention her constant confusion over who her future mate
was, and if he belonged to the Breeding Male family,
spurred her on. As her time grew nearer, the year of
fifty, when meta would reveal the mark of her vampire, she grew more wary of her romantic future—and
there was nothing she wanted less than to be forever
connected to a Son of a Breeding Male; her own sister had been forced to lie with one twenty years before
and had died just months into her *swell*.

A sudden growth of sound in the *credenti* street outside her window jerked her attention from the computer
and she looked up and out. The afternoon's sunlight
seemed to be everywhere at once, changing the colors
of the leaves to pale yellow, making the snowy ground
glitter like diamonds—and keeping all morphed Pureblood *pavens* inside their homes for respite.

Unclear as to what was making the others gathered on the street point and bustle so vociferously, Bronwyn stood and leaned nearer to the glass.

Several yards away, a *paven* with hair the color of the snow at his feet was walking in healthy strides down the main road. He was tall, broad in the shoulders, and dressed in a long dark gray coat with black boots to match his even blacker expression.

As he walked, he stared straight ahead, acknowledging no one. He was so imposing, so terrifying, so undeniably beautiful that the *credenti* members who spied him were split in their decisions to run away or move in closer to get a better look.

Beneath the binds at her wrists and neck, Bronwyn's blood sped up with equal parts revulsion and excitement.

Lucian Roman. The terrifying angel.

Why was he here?

When a knock sounded on the door belowstairs, she knew she was about to find out.

15

Their blood, his and hers, ran an unending race inside Kate's veins as she switched her hand position and pressed down into another set of twenty push-ups. It was how she'd coped inside Mondrar for so long—switching off the brain and turning up the volume of her body.

"How many can you do?" Ladd asked her, lying on his belly, palms on his chin as he watched her.

After an entire morning cooped up inside their rooms, she and Ladd had escaped downstairs. Exploring the various rooms on the main floor had gotten pretty dull until they'd come across a door leading down another set of stairs to what Kate had thought would be a basement or cellar. But instead, there had been tunnels, several of them, running in all directions. She was dying to know what they were used for. However, she'd wait on asking the master of the house. For now.

"I can handle about seventy-five before I shut down," she told him in between breaths. "But I did a hundred once."

"Wow," he said, his eyes huge. "Can I try?"

"Sure." Kate sat up and helped him into a basic position, knees on the stone floor, palms even with his shoulders. "You want me to help you?"

"I can do it myself."

"Oh, sure you can."

"I have extra-big beeceps."

Kate bit her lip to keep from laughing. "I bet you do."

"My father has big beeceps, too."

"Does he?"

"Sure. Haven't you looked?"

Jeez, kid, she thought. Didn't he know she was trying her damnedest not to bring up images of that *paven* and his extraordinary physical gifts? Not that her trying was working all that well. She'd spent thirty minutes in the shower this morning with a loofah, trying to scrub away the scent of him on her skin.

No dice. He was in her blood now.

"Come on," she said to Ladd. "Let's see what you got."

She watched him as he grunted his way down on his first push-up, then grunted his way back up. Bending and straightening like a real champ.

Four push-ups in, he settled back on his feet and announced, "That's hard."

"Takes some practice," she said, then wondered if maybe she ought to add a little encouragement to the statement. "But you did pretty damn well."

He looked at her with reproving eyes. "That's not a nice word, Kate."

She nodded grimly. "You're right. Sorry."

"It's okay." Suddenly, his face lit up like twin stars and he jumped to his feet. "I know what I'm really good at. Racing. Do you want to race me? I have very fast legs."

"Let's do it." She stood too. "But I need to warn you, I have pretty fast legs, too."

He smiled real wide, real sweet, and she kind of felt like maybe she'd won a prize or something.

They walked down the center tunnel together, stopping once they'd reached a decent enough racing distance. Kate sank into a starter position. Ladd followed.

"To the stairs?" she asked him.

He nodded.

"On your mark," she called out, her gaze shifting to the finish line, "get set—GO!"

Ladd took off like a bullet, all arms and legs pumping, and Kate followed at half speed, feeling lighter than she had in days.

"I'm going to beat you," Ladd shouted back, making Kate laugh as she sped up after him.

"No, you're not! I'm coming for you! I'm going to beat—"

Ladd hit the bottom step of the finish line just as Nicholas Roman did. The *paven* stood there, arms crossed over his chest, looking furious.

"Ah, shit," Kate muttered to herself as she came to a stop in front of him.

But Ladd had bat ears and made a face at her. "That's not a nice word, Kate."

"You're right. Sorry."

"I won, right? I won?"

"You did. Congratulations."

Clearly having little patience for their post-chase chat, Nicholas got to barking. "What are you doing down here?"

Kate shrugged. "Racing."

"You're not supposed to be here. This section of the house is off-limits."

"Says who?"

Nicholas inhaled deeply, then spoke calmly. "Ladd, Sara's waiting for you upstairs. She has a game she wants to show you."

The boy glanced over at Kate. She nodded. Fine, he didn't need to be around when his potential father was bawling her out.

She waited for the boy to head up the stairs and out of sight before throwing her hands up and asking the black-eyed *paven*, "What's your damage?"

"I instructed you to stay in your room," he said, coming to stand before her.

"No, you didn't."

"Of course I did."

She wasn't about to keep that argument going—they'd be down here all day. "Listen, the kid and I got bored. We went in search of somewhere to hang out, let loose, and we found this. No harm done."

His eyes moved over her then, from bare feet to ripped jeans, to her soaking-wet tank top.

"What?" she said, unnerved by his leisurely perusal.

"You're wet."

"Sweaty," she corrected.

Again, his gaze moved over her arms, her stomach. "You work your body like an athlete."

"I do."

"Why?"

She shrugged. "Keeps the demons at bay."

"Not this demon," he growled, reaching out and brushing a bead of sweat off her temple.

She eased back. "What are you doing?"

"Foolish, foolish things," he uttered before bringing the fingertip to his lips, lapping at the minuscule drop of sweat with his tongue.

Kate's insides went liquid. "I thought we weren't going to do this again."

He lifted his black eyes to her. "What?"

"Taste each other."

"I never said that."

"Of course you did."

He grinned, nice and slow, showing off those spectacular ribbed fangs.

Asshole. She grinned, too.

"Come on, *veana*. We're going out tonight and you need a shower."

She sobered. "Bait and switch time?"

"Ticktock."

"I'll need something to wear, unless you don't mind these old things. I know I don't."

His eyes swept over her hungrily. "You and Sara will go shopping."

"I hate shopping. You want me out there, why don't you find me something to wear?"

"I can't go until the sun's down, and if I did you'd probably end up with a lime green potato sack."

"Perfect. Sounds lovely."

He shook his head.

"Dare's not going to care what I have on."

"No, but I do."

"Fine." Kate raised a brow. "I'll race you to decide."

"What?"

"Down and back again. You make it to the steps first and I'll do the shopping thing. I make it to the steps first, you're heading to the women's department at BG."

"BG. Unless that stands for Blood Giver, I'm not interested."

"Bergdorf Goodman."

He looked down his nose at her. "Did you not hear the lime green potato sack example?"

"You afraid, *paven*?"

He grinned. "I'm a morphed male. You'll lose."

God, she'd never seen anyone so sexy. She hated herself for the thought, for wishing he would lay her down on the stone floor and lick the sweat off of every inch of her body. She pointed a finger at him. "There's no flashing."

"Not possible. We're inside."

"Right. Let's do this."

They walked all the way down the center tunnel, farther than she had with Ladd. When they turned and dropped into starting stance, Kate chided him. "Just so you know, I look terrible in green."

He shot her a half smile. "Yeah? Me too."

The older *veana* who led Lucian through the house with an irritated puss on her face was the very same one who'd been to his home in SoHo a few months back. Edel, the nursemaid, the *tegga*. Or who Lucian had assumed was Bronwyn's *tegga* at the time. Turned out she was just a business associate.

Business. How was Bronwyn running a business inside a *credenti* anyway? In the home she shared with her parents, no less. Parents who were thankfully not at home. No telling how two upstanding Purebloods would react to a Son of a Breeding Male visiting their home, and their very precious, very pure daughter.

Not that he cared. Just didn't need the drama and the bloodshed right now.

Edel kept glancing back at him as they climbed the stairs, shooting him looks of warning.

"Not to worry, love," he said casually. "Your mistress and her chastity are safe from me."

She turned around and muttered a terse, "Disgusting Breeding male *witte*."

The *witte*, the animal, in him snarled playfully. "You know I can hear you."

"Yes, I know!" she nearly shouted.

Lucian laughed.

When they reached the top of the stairs, Edel led him down a long corridor, then stopped in front of a white door. She knocked once, then said, "Lucian Roman is here to see you. Shall I send him away?"

"No, Edel." Bronwyn's light, lovely voice. "Send him in."

"Subtle," Lucian said to the older *veana* as he walked past her.

She narrowed her eyes and kept her hand on the knob. "The door remains open," she hissed.

"Yes, that will stop me from ravaging her." Lucian walked into the room and found Bronwyn seated at her desk, her back to him, long silky black hair hanging down over the chair. His hands twitched at his sides. "I see you still employ your *tegga*."

"And I see you're still a gigantic ass." She turned around and gave him a wide, distrusting smile. He liked that she wasn't afraid of him. Too bad she lived in a *credenti*, had an interest in following the rules of the Order, and was way too beautiful for her own good.

She would've been fun to play with.

Her leaf-green eyes appeared a bit more fatigued than usual, but her pale beauty remained constant. "Hello, Lucian."

"Princess."

She rolled her eyes. She was dressed simply in a black sweater and a black skirt, but on that body nothing was simple and everything looked like lingerie.

She crossed her arms over her perfect chest and said, "Not that having you here isn't an interesting turn of events, but I'm willing to bet you were coerced by one of your brothers into coming for a specific purpose."

Brains, beauty, and body—and only able to use one—what a waste. "Nicholas may have a *balas*."

"May have?" This changed her mood altogether and she gestured to the chair opposite her.

"A *veana*," Lucian explained, dropping into the handmade leather armchair, "the mother of the boy, has claimed that Nicholas is the father. He needs to know if it's true." He leaned over and dropped the bag with Ladd's hair in it on her desk.

She barely glanced at it. "You are aware that I'm a genealogist, not a DNA lab tech?"

"But you have the equipment here to perform the testing, don't you?"

"Maybe." She picked up the bag, examined the sample. "Sure this *balas* isn't yours, Lucian?"

"Never can be one hundred percent sure of anything. I do get around. Wouldn't know if I were going to town on top of one of Nicholas's castoffs or not."

"Delightful." She tossed the bag back on her desk. "I'm guessing he wants the results yesterday."

"You really are brilliant."

"You had doubts?"

He grinned.

"Now," she said, sitting up straight, crossing her legs. "Why should I help the Roman brothers? Seems to me I wasn't treated very well in their household."

"Only by me." He had a hard time keeping his eyes up and off her legs. Pale and deliciously formed, they could be used as weapons, or at the very least, wrapped around a *paven*'s waist, squeezing until he came. "Alexander and Nicholas were gracious as fuck to you, princess—especially Nicky—and you know it."

She didn't disagree, just cocked her head to the side and watched him.

He growled at her. "You aren't doing me the favor."

"That does make it far more agreeable," she said. She inhaled deeply. "All right. Give me a few days."

"You can't just knock it out right now? Few minutes' work?"

"Oh, Lucian," she said with a sardonic smile. "This is science, not a female you're just—what was it again—lying on top of, going to town on?"

"Sometimes that's all it takes."

"A few days, *paven*," she said, turning her chair around and facing her desk again. "I'll send word."

"Peachy," he grumbled.

Edel poked her head in the open door. "Your client is here."

"Very good. Send him in, Edel." She glanced over her shoulder at Lucian. "We're done here, yes?"

"For now," he uttered.

A Pureblood and morphed *paven* stepped into the room, his blue eyes searching out the space until they landed on the *veana* he sought.

Standing, Bronwyn went over to him and shook his hand. "Hello, Mr. Wade, it's nice to see you."

He nodded. "Mistress Kettler."

"Bronwyn, please. You may have a seat . . . when Lucian Roman has dislodged his backside from it, of course."

Lucian stood. "Fine. I'm going." But as he passed her, he leaned into her ear and whispered, "Remember, princess, Roman work comes before this clown."

She moved away from him. "Goodbye, Lucian."

He walked out, attempting to tune out her voice as she spoke to the *credenti paven*, pretty little trills and frills in her tone. Maybe he'd wait outside and break the asshole's neck, he thought as he headed down the stairs and toward the door. Or maybe he'd just get the fuck home and pray this was the last time he'd have to see Bronwyn Kettler's face, and eyes, and hair, and legs.

16

"If you lost, why are you still here?" Alexander stood dead center in the workout room Lucian had put together a few months back, holding a heavy canvas bag while Nicholas punched the shit out of it. "Why aren't you out looking for a nice dress and clutch."

Nicholas paused midjab, and glanced up at his brother. "What the hell's a clutch?"

"It's a purse." His brows knit together thoughtfully. "At least I think it's a purse."

Nicholas shot the *paven* a troubled glare. "Maybe you should ask yourself if that's something a Pure-blood *paven* needs to know."

"I have a mate, asshole."

"And she has a clutch?"

Alexander grinned, flashed his white fangs. "Several of them."

"And I didn't lose." Sans gloves, Nicholas hauled back and smashed his bloody knuckles into the bag. "It was a draw."

"Wow. She's either extraordinarily fast or you're—"

"A *gentlepaven*," Nicholas finished for him. To be honest, he wasn't sure what had happened down there in the tunnels, from the moment he'd tasted her all the way to the end of the race. He wasn't about to share his lack of clarity with his big brother. "I don't need to prove myself."

"So you let her win."

"It was a draw," Nicholas said again, showing his annoyance with a fast six-punch combination.

Jacked backward with the bag, Alexander asked, "Then why aren't you together right now instead of hanging here, mucking up this bag with your O Negative?"

"Because I don't have any SPF 1000."

"Right. The crispy bacon excuse."

Nicholas grinned. "Gotta keep myself pretty for tonight."

"Hot date with your bait?"

Nicholas jacked up an eyebrow. "How long have you been waiting to say that?"

"Just came to me on the fly," Alexander said, grinning, displaying his pearly white fangs. "Dare doesn't need sunscreen, so what's going to stop him from going after your girl while she's trying on shit?"

"Dillon," Nicholas said, accentuating the name with a hard jab to the bag's belly.

Alexander laughed. "No shit. Didn't she have to go back to the office?"

"She made it happen."

"Oh my God, that's priceless. How did you get her to agree to it?"

"I didn't, Sara did."

"Figures." Alexander shook his head. "What I wouldn't give to see that hard-ass *veana* hanging out in the dressing room at BG."

Nicholas stopped and hugged the bag, his breathing heavy. "If you didn't have a mate I swear to God . . . You know what BG stands for, right?"

"Of course."

"It's not 'Blood Giver.'"

Alexander shrugged. "Bergdorf Goodman."

"Christ." Wiping the sweat from his eyes, Nicholas started again, started over with a right uppercut to the "head." "Has Sara spoken with Pearl McClean's mother yet? Any word on the location of Dare's human incubator?"

Alexander laughed darkly. "Interesting segue, *Duro*. Of course we don't have to talk about your *veana* anymore."

"She's not my *veana*. She's not my anything." But even as he said the words his body rebelled against him, sending all kinds of electric shocks into the back of his throat. So. What? Did he tell Alex about his suspicions? Did he tell him that Kate Everborne might be the catalyst to his aggressive mood as of late? That she may be sporting his mark on her skin at that very moment? Or did he keep it to himself?

"Sara spoke to the girl's mother twice over Christmas," Alexander said, pulling Nicholas from his thoughts and his questions. "But every time she's tried to get in contact since, nothing."

"No matter," Nicholas said. "We'll get to Dare without the help of his female." Suddenly there was no bag in front of Nicholas, just Dare, and he crouched down and hit the 1, 2, 3—head, chin, temple—with every ounce of muscle, every thread of hate he possessed. "Fuck!" he roared.

When he pulled back, breathing heavy and up to his eyeballs in hostility, he felt the marks on his cheeks tremble. "With the magic we have surrounding this place, Dare can't get to Kate, but he seems to be able to scent her everywhere else. The club is the way to go— dark, packed, easy to get her lost while we surround and take him out."

"Too bad we can't ask Gray to handle another look-out for us," Alexander said. "Club scene's been his home away from home lately."

"We can always ask, *Duro*," Nicholas said. "The boy will come around eventually."

Alexander shook his head. "The boy didn't come home last night." His nostrils flared. "Don't tell Sara. She doesn't need to know."

"Not a word." About anything, he thought. And this time it was Nicholas who held the bag as his brother gave it a good beating.

This was so not her scene.

Kate walked out of the dressing room in Bergdorf

Goodman and stood awkwardly in front of Sara and Dillon—the two couldn't have been more different in the whole shopping-for-clothes department. While one was nearly giddy, the other looked like she wanted to ram a sharp object through her unbeating heart.

"I love that on you," Sara declared from her post, seated deep within a lovely gold plush chair.

Kate shrugged. "Great. First one out of the hatch. I'll get it."

"And more importantly," Sara said, her blue eyes annoyingly endearing, "Nicholas will love it. Don't you think so, Dillon?"

Leaning against the wall, the cat-eyed *veana* who wore a black pantsuit and a bored expression muttered a terse, "Don't know. Don't care."

Sara tossed the bodyguard a frustrated glare. "Fine. Just stand there."

"That's the plan," Dillon said.

Feeling a bit like a mermaid in the tight-fitting black silk gown with a metallic panel running down one side, Kate headed over to the massive framed mirror where Sara was holding court in her gold chair. "I'm not trying to impress Nicholas. In fact, I'm here in this ridiculously expensive store only because he wants me to get something for my debut tonight."

"Debut?"

"Yes." Kate crossed her arms over her chest. "I'm playing the role of 'Bait' in the new production of 'Capture and Kill Ethan Dare.'"

Holding up the wall in the corner, Dillon snorted.

"What?" Sara came forward in her chair. "He's using you?"

"Don't look so shocked," Kate said.

"How about pissed off?" Sara returned. "Can I look pissed off?"

"Yes. You can." Kate smiled, tried to lighten the mood.

But it didn't work.

The female was up now, pacing in front of the mirror, her ire palpable now. "You don't have to do this. I'll talk to Alexander." She started shaking her head. "I swear to God, if he knows about this . . ."

"Stop," Kate urged. This wasn't anybody's business but hers. "Sara. Please, stop."

"Yes, Sara," Dillon agreed sarcastically. "Please stop."

Sara came to a halt and breathed out a frustrated, "What?"

"I *have* to do this." Cocking her head to the side, Kate eyeballed the pretty doctor, hoping that her expression and body language said it all—"I don't want to discuss it."

Sara bit her lip, the tips of her fangs showing. Then she sighed. "Well, if you have to, then I say we don't make it easy on him."

"What do you have in mind, Doc?" Kate asked, jumping on the playful wagon again. Anything not to have to explain her history with Nicholas and the Order, and Mirabelle.

"I'm thinking . . . torture."

Kate's eyebrows shot up. "What does that mean?"

"That means," Dillon jumped in, crossing her arms over her chest, "that Dr. Interference here doesn't know how to mind her own business."

Sara glared at the *veana*. "I thought you weren't going to talk." When she turned back to Kate, her expression softened. "Nicholas likes you. No, he wants you. More than he even realizes." She went over to the rack that held an arm's-length worth of dresses and grabbed a stunning red strapless bandage dress. "I think this will do the job quite nicely."

Kate exhaled and took the dress. "I'll try it on."

"Good." Sara dropped into her chair again, gave Dillon an exaggerated wink and announced brightly, "Then we need to get the shoes. I'm thinking some four-inch crystal-studded Louboutins should do it."

To which, Dillon, true to form, rolled her eyes and cursed.

17

"When is he coming back?"

"Where am I? I can't breathe . . ."

"Please. Please. I want to go home."

Strapped into a chair, gagged and blindfolded, Gray's heart pumped wildly, desperate to get out of his chest. He wasn't scared of much, barely feared death. But this—this not being able to move, not being able to feel, speak, or see—while his ears and mind were being bombarded with the silent screams of the strangers all around him was pure nightmare.

He'd come to only moments ago, fighting against his binds as he tried to figure out where he was, tried to recall how he'd gotten there, tried to calm his brain and ready his mind for the onslaught of sound.

"He's going to kill us! I know he's going to kill us!"

"Who else is here? Maybe someone will help me."

Shit! They were terrified; maybe three or four men. They seemed pretty young, college age maybe. Where the hell were they? The club? House? Why were they bound and gagged?

The alley near Equinox flashed in his memory—and that woman. No . . . that *female* with *fangs*.

Gray lifted his chin, scenting something. Ever since Alexander had gone into his brain, his senses had improved—gone from barely human to newly birthed animal.

"Oh God. He's back. He's back."

"We're just Impures. Nothing. We mean nothing."

Oh, shit. Impures—half vampires like himself. What the hell was this?

Then he heard something strange—soft male laughter in his mind. It was the sound of enjoyment, pleasure, even pride.

And it was coming toward him.

He fought the binds at his chest and wrists. He grunted, growled.

"I know this must be unpleasant for you, Gray."

A male voice. Unfamiliar, yet unmistakably deadly.

"Gray?"

"Who's Gray?"

"Not from my Credenti. Please . . ."

"It won't be for long," the male continued as the panicked thoughts in the room shot off like fireworks into the air. "Just until I know I have your understanding and allegiance."

"Please, Master. Come and get me. Find me."

Crying now . . . inside his mind. Splintered glass being tossed around near his brain stem.

Sweat broke on Gray's forehead. There was enough rage in him at that moment to kill the male in front of him, and yet he could do nothing but fight the binds and let the terrified voices, the screams, the desperate cries continue.

"Do you know who I am?" the male said.

Gray shook his head.

"My name is Ethan Dare."

"Oh God. Oh God."

"Ethan Dare!"

"The Impure who takes veanas, who builds an army against my master."

Gray's skin went hot and his mind warred with the sound, the panic. He knew that name, knew all about that name.

"And I want you to tell me if your new brothers hold a *balas* in their compound."

"Balas? *A child?*".

"Is there a balas *here?"*

This was insane—held captive by Ethan Dare. And a *balas* in his house? Gray racked his brain for some clue about what Dare was talking about. There was no *balas*—not unless a child had come while he was out.

"Thinking is good," Dare said, a smile in his voice. "Now all you need to do is nod your head for yes or shake your head—"

A door opened, maybe ten feet away. And another male called out, "Sir, we have someone on the house. Town car's parked out front. Looks like they're going out."

The silent cries began filling up Gray's mind, drowning him in despair and heart-stopping fear.

"Thank you, Mear."

Gray felt Dare move closer to him, felt his breath near his cheek. "You have been very helpful in tracking down the Romans' compound." He laughed. "You and Marina. She's been watching you, poor creature couldn't keep her hands off you. Just follow the club rat home and he leads you to all the other rats."

Oh God, he'd led Dare not only to the Romans, but to his sister . . .

"Perhaps Dare has what he wants now. Perhaps he'll let me go."

"Recruits. I can't be a recruit."

"Now, Impure," Ethan continued, the metallic scent of blood emanating from his skin. "Is there a *balas* at the Romans'?"

Gray shook his head. *No. No, you piece of shit.*

Dare grunted. "For your sake, I hope you're right."

"Fuck. The Supreme One will have my head."

As Ethan Dare left Gray's side and walked out of the room, as the sounds and screams of panic and despair swelled inside Gray's mind, a small grain of truth—of hope—of possibility began to take shape.

Ethan Dare held him hostage, yes. But for now.

And Gray could hear every thought inside his head.

She wasn't a date.

She was bait.

Nicholas left his rooms on the third floor and headed down the stairs. He'd sent a note through Evans about an hour ago letting Kate know that he'd be by to pick her up at nine.

That shopping spree at the store he now refused to name had better have landed her something appropriate for a night out in Manhattan. Classy and sexy. Dillon wasn't talking, and Sara seemed angry with him all of a sudden, so who knew what Kate had picked up—or hadn't. He wouldn't have put it past her to answer the door in her ripped jeans and sweaty tank just to piss him off.

Hell, even he'd fished something club friendly out of his closet—black and more black. Even spent more than a minute in front of the mirror. All in the pursuit of an Impure. What bullshit.

He came to her door on the second floor and knocked. "Let's go, Cinderella," he called through the wood.

"Keep your shirt on, Prince Not-so Charming," she called back.

Nicholas chuckled. Yes, this was going to be an interesting—

His words, thoughts, brain, all went to shit when she opened the door. It was like suddenly finding yourself in front of the sun without even a napkin for cover. He couldn't move, run—he had to stand there and stare at the most beautiful creature he'd ever seen and not be able to touch her. Her blond hair was parted in the middle and swept back in an easy bun at the nape of her long neck, which only proved to accentuate the ethereal beauty of her face. There was barely any makeup on her skin, but her eyes—her devastating, soul-crushing eyes—were lined with black, making the brown irises glow a deep chocolate.

And then there was the dress.

"The dress . . ." he muttered out loud. What an asshole. He could barely talk. Shit, he could barely think.

"It's Hervé Léger," she said, doing a quick three sixty. "I don't have a clue who that is, but I have to admit, the male makes one comfortable dress."

"You look . . ." Jesus Christ! What the hell was going on with his vocal cords? Something was sitting on them . . .

"How do I look?" she said, smiling a little uneasily.

"Well . . ." Shit.

"Like perfect bait?"

Yes, he realized. Yes, she did, and there was nothing he hated more in that moment. Nothing he wanted more than to take her hand and pull her back into the bedroom. She was bait to the whole fucking male population, and he didn't want anyone looking at her in that red strapless thing but him. He didn't want anyone's hands itching to move over her intensely erotic curves but him.

His fangs started to jut forward in his mouth. Was he going to be able to do this? Walk through club after club with her, waiting on Dare, wanting to rip out the retinas from every male who looked at her?

"Should we go?" she asked, her perfectly arched brow lifting. "Or are you having second thoughts?"

You have no idea, sweetheart. "Car's waiting out front."

"To take us to the ball?" she said dryly, but there was an edge to her voice.

"Wasn't that a pumpkin?"

She laughed softly. "Whatever."

He followed her down the hall to the stairs, his gaze traveling from pale neck to graceful back to tight ass to—

Holy shit.

His entire body went into overdrive. *The shoes.* Christ, four inches of sparkling, "push me up against the wall and fuck me now." They made her legs—her luminous stems—look like they went on for days.

He'd touched those legs. Wanted to again. But this time he wouldn't stop at the knee. He'd travel up, his fingers investigating every soft, pale inch, every warm, wet curve until he found his way home.

The blast of cold night air did nothing to kill his hard-on. Good thing he was wearing a jacket because with her looking like she did, he was bound to remain in that state until he dropped her back at her room at the end of the night.

He led her down the walk, keeping his hands to himself as much as possible, until they reached the limo.

"Nice touch," she said, giving the driver a polite smile.

"Easier to get around," Nicholas said, slipping inside the black stretch after her, hating how the rush of aggression was already inside his chest and wanting to claw its way out.

"Where to, sir?" the driver, who was now in the front seat, asked him.

"The Abbey." Feeling large brown eyes on him, Nicholas turned. Kate was looking at him—assessing him was more like it. "What? What's wrong?" He suddenly felt as though he should've asked one of his brothers for a quick style critique. Of course, those two bloodsucking apes knew nothing either.

"I didn't say it before . . ." she began, her tongue darting out to wet her top lip.

"What?" he asked, panicked like a fricking teenage human boy. Jesus Christ, she was making him—

"You look hot," she said quickly.

Oh.

Okay.

He turned to the window, looked out, and tried to suppress the shit-eating grin pulling at his lips.

The Abbey was loud, raucous, and sported hundreds of well-dressed, heavily scented men and women writhing to music with a beat Kate could feel deep within her belly.

God, she loved it.

Beside her, Nicholas scanned the area looking for signs of Ethan Dare, completely unaware of the females who were staring at him like he was a celebrity, or something to consume with a spoon. Not that she blamed them. He was something to see. Tall, trim, and clad in black from suit to dress shirt to tie. The only splash of color was a purple cashmere scarf that hung down both sides of his lapels.

"Do you and your brothers go out often?" she asked, looking up into his striking face, the jaw that was firm enough to crack nuts.

He continued to scan the room. "We don't drink and we don't dance."

She laughed. "There are other reasons to go."

"Like what?"

She gestured around herself. "A hundred or so reasons, and they're all very pretty and clearly available."

"I don't appreciate availability."

"What does that mean?" Odds were he was going to say he liked the chase, the catch—the release. But she asked anyway. "What do you appreciate, Nicholas Roman?"

His head turned and he looked down at her with dark, hungry eyes. "Someone who needs me. Really needs me. Someone who isn't afraid to ask for what they want and be vulnerable enough to receive it."

Kate stared at him, unsure if he was serious or not. Waiting for him to burst out laughing and shove a finger in her face all, "Gotcha, *veana*." But he didn't. Instead, he took her hand and led her deeper into the crowd.

"I say we give it an hour, then head to another club," he said, his eyes scanning every corner, every body, every table.

But Kate was still thinking about what he'd said. Those weren't the words of a monster, a Son of a Breeding Male, a blackmailer . . . Those were vulnerable words, words that Nicholas would probably regret uttering later. Words she wasn't going to forget anytime soon. And yet she had to because her main objective was to find a way to get away from him. He was the enemy now, the master, and she was the rat in a cage, beautiful dress, beautiful room aside. She would serve him and his cause until her chance for escape presented itself; then she would disappear.

"Do you really think Dare's going to show up?" she asked as they hovered near the dance floor. "This place is packed with eyewitnesses."

"He's an arrogant little bastard. Seems to like to do things with an audience. And you have what he wants— the *balas*, not to mention your pure blood."

"Even if that blood has been in Mondrar?" she said with a contained laugh.

"I don't think he cares."

"He'd be the only one."

He glanced down at her. "What does that mean?"

"Nothing."

"We are all lawbreakers in our way, *veana*." His black eyebrows drew together. "Perhaps the crime that you committed was . . . understandable."

She lifted her shoulders in a gentle shrug. "Maybe even forgivable."

He was silent for a moment, his eyes probing hers for answers she would never ever give him. Him or anyone. Then he asked, "Why do you even care?"

"What do you mean?"

"What you did in the past is your business. Those were your choices—your mistakes—if you even believe they were mistakes. Stop caring what anyone thinks and live your life the way you want to live it."

Kate swallowed as she stared up into his fierce, feral gaze. His nostrils were flared and the vein in his neck pulsed with tension. He spoke with the passion of someone who felt everything he was saying, who believed the words that were coming out of his mouth. It was personal, and Kate couldn't help but wonder just what the hell was in his past.

The music changed then, from heavy hip-hop to a sensual groove. On the floor, couples wrapped their arms around each other and slowed their bodies down.

"Dance?"

Kate turned to him. "What?"

"Dance with me." Without waiting for her to answer, Nicholas took her hand and led her though the crowd to an empty square of floor.

"I thought you abstained," Kate said.

"Normally, yes," he said, turning her to face him, "but those animals over by the bar are looking at you like you're a porterhouse in heels, and before I fly over there, smash them in the face, and cause a scene that gets us kicked out of here, I thought I'd occupy my hands and send a message at the same time."

"I'm flattered. I think."

He pulled her into his arms, one hand holding hers, the other around her waist. Their bodies fit perfectly, and Kate allowed herself to move with him to the music and not think about her past or his, her future—or his.

He moved well, slow and confident around a sea of popping hips and curious stares. It was as though he moved to a rhythm, to music that was in his head alone. Kate's eyes lifted to his and shivered under his black, hungry gaze. He wanted to kiss her. She could see it in his eyes, in the way his lips parted just a fraction, the way his tongue raked the tips of his fangs.

She forced her gaze away, tried to focus on the crowd, on the DJ, anything that reminded her where she was and why she was here.

Then she spotted a figure over by the restrooms, a male she recognized. He was skulking as he always did, looking for flesh to sell, drugs to sell—anything money could buy.

Anything.

The skin on her arms tightened as a thought, just the first rustles of an idea came to her mind.

Anything money could buy.

She broke away from Nicholas's embrace. "I need to go to the little vampires' room."

"I'll take you."

She looked up at him, smiled reassuringly. "It's right over there. Keep your eyes open for Dare. I'll be back in one minute."

"Not a chance, *veana*. I'm not letting you out of my sight tonight for anything. And you shouldn't want me to."

Kate hesitated. What the hell did she do? She couldn't press him on this . . . There was no good reason for her to go alone.

Shit.

Finally she gave up. As she walked toward the bathroom through an ocean of sweaty, writhing bodies, Nicholas was right behind her, no doubt scanning every nook and cranny she passed. But Kate's gaze was on Cambridge, silently begging him to look up, see her, and follow her into the ladies' room.

In another club farther south, Dillon was performing another act of goodwill. Her third for the day. The first was tracking several rogue Impures over the Net, and the second had been two solid hours in a department store—aka the bowels of hell—watching some chick try on dresses.

Fuck, she was really over helping the Romans and their females. Maybe she needed to rethink her affection for them. Maybe she needed to walk out of the club she was in right now and head back to Maine where she belonged.

That would send a message.

'Course, she'd already spotted her person of interest. Might as well finish what she came here to do.

Frame, Equinox's head of security and one of the biggest *pavens* she'd ever seen outside of the Roman brothers, was standing at the edge of the dance floor, scanning the crowd for any signs of trouble.

Dillon headed his way, marveled at how he got bigger the closer she came. Handlebar mustache, eyes the color of smog, and long light brown hair that was pulled back into a braided tail.

A human woman stood next to him, trying to get his attention by slow dancing in the smallest, tightest dress ever know to man, her large cans jacked up to her chin.

"Get lost, female," Dillon muttered.

The bottle blonde turned to look at Dillon with a pair of brown eyes that screamed attitude. "Who are you?"

Dillon leaned in and whispered in the woman's ear, "Your worst nightmare if you don't get out of here and find another dick to suck." She pulled back an inch, met the female's rage-filled glare. "A lot of quality males in this place to choose from. You've been vaccinated, right?"

The woman's mouth dropped open.

"Yep," Dillon said with a grin. "Just like that."

"You bitch," the woman said, but turned right around and walked away.

Frame's nostrils flared as he glanced over at her. "Was that really necessary?"

"I needed to get rid of her."

He raised his eyebrows. "There are other ways."

"I could've shown her my fangs." She lowered her voice. "Hell, I could've shown her yours."

"What do you want, Dillon?"

"Gray Donohue. Seen him?"

"He was here last night, stayed until dawn, as usual." Frame shrugged his massive shoulders. "'Course, I was gone by the time the sun came up, so don't know what happened after that."

"Who was he hanging with?"

"Who wasn't he hanging with? The guy's a whore."

Dillon's insides curled. "Hey. Watch it." That's family, she almost told him. Almost. "Come on, old friend. Give me something. I got a few bloodsuckers who are pretty worried."

He sighed. "A couple human females, and one Impure."

"An Impure? Did you know her?"

"No. She's been in here a few times this past week. Watches your boy a lot—until last night." Frame had spotted two idiots on the dance floor fighting over something thin and leggy. "I gotta go, D."

"Hey. What does that mean—'until last night'?"

"Finally got her cherry popped by Mr. Scars." He lifted a brow. "She was still with him when I left."

And then he was off, deep in the crowd, a tree among bushes.

Dillon turned and headed for the door. Goddamn Roman family. Now she wasn't just looking for Gray, but the Impure female who was no doubt lying beneath him, eyes closed, legs spread.

18

"Well, don't you clean up good." Cambridge gave Kate the once-over two times, his oddly thick lips curling into a grin. "I wouldn't have recognized you without those eyes of yours. Twin balls of desperation and misery, I always called them, yes?"

Just seconds before Kate had entered the bathroom, the Eyes' number-one strangest member had finally noticed her, but had taken off in the opposite direction instead of trying to slip past Nicholas.

As she'd stood inside the empty bathroom, she'd figured the meeting wasn't going to happen—she was even trying to come up with a way to get to him with Nicholas around, maybe at the bar. Then, across from the marble stalls, several squares of brick wall had popped forward and Cambridge had come crawling through as though breaking and entering into a women's bathroom registered zero on the crime meter.

And to him, it probably did.

Cambridge continued to look her over as her hip pressed into the sink. "You know, if you ever consider selling that lovely flesh, kitten, I would guarantee a sizable payday."

Kate didn't need this. "I'm a little tight for time here, Cambridge."

"Aren't we all." His eyes narrowed, as did his smile. "What do you need?"

"Information about getting lost," she said. "Permanently."

"Are we talking you or a . . . friend?" He chuckled, his strange blue eyes seeing only dollar signs as he watched her. "I'd hate to see you sent up back to Mondrar."

"Look, Cambridge, I heard something when I was on the inside, about a place, underground, where a *veana* or a *paven* could go, disappear for good." She leveled him with her gaze. "I need to know if that place is real."

His smile faded. "I may know of a place. But why should I assist you, kitten? I believe I'm mad at you. I've heard you are telling some very nasty people that I sell *balas* flesh."

"I'm sorry." She shrugged. What else could she do, say? "It was a shitty thing to do. I was caught in the middle of something—"

"I don't want your apologies," he said, cutting her off. "I want money." He rubbed his thumb and first two fingers together. "For the pinch to my rep and for safe passage to Mondalagua."

"Mondalagua," she repeated.

"The world of water. The place you seek. Your underground safe haven."

Her breath caught in her throat. "What's the price?" All she had was what her mother had left her when she'd died, just a few thousand.

"Shit." He looked behind her, snarled. "Not now."

Glancing over her shoulder, Kate saw two females walk in, head straight for the toilets.

"Go. Get out of here," she hissed, turning around.

But Cambridge was already gone, the brick wall she'd seen him enter from, now solid and seemingly untouched.

Nicholas had never been inside a ladies' room before and he certainly didn't want to start now. No doubt it was painted a color that would make his eyes bleed and had baskets of scented shit all over the counters.

But the *veana* had been gone too long. Could be that something was wrong, or maybe she was just messing with him.

She liked to do that.

Two females, human, both blond, blue dress and black dress respectively, real jumpy about the eyes, were coming out of the bathroom just as he was closing in.

They came to a cartoon-style stop in front of him and presented him with matching grins.

"Lookie here, Nan," Blue Dress said, one hand reaching for Nicholas's shoulder. "Someone we need to get to know better."

"Yes, indeed," Black Dress said, her fingers playing at the space between her nose and her upper lip as she checked him out. "Should we follow you back in there, babe? Play a little two against one?" She grinned. "There's a lock on the bathroom door."

Good to know. "Maybe some other time."

He tried to walk past them, but Blue Dress got all belligerent and started yanking at his coat. "You don't want to go in there alone, Romeo. Trust me. There's a chick in there talking to herself about escaping or something."

Nicholas stilled. Talking to herself? His skin began to vibrate.

"Come on, lover."

"Excuse me," Nicholas uttered, trying to pass.

"We're not letting you go," Blue Dress said, laughing and tugging at his arm.

A low growl rumbled in Nicholas's chest and he whirled on them. "I don't play with coked-out humans unless I'm paid. Very, very well." Nostrils flaring, he flashed his fangs all nice and deadly in the club's pale blue light.

The women's eyes grew dinner-plate wide and they backed off real slow; then, as soon as they were ten feet clear of him, took off running, arm in arm back toward the dance floor. Normally he didn't show his cards like that, but those two were so juiced up they wouldn't believe what they'd seen anyway—and neither would anyone else they decided to talk to tonight.

Without another thought, he busted through the door of the bathroom like a bull charging a cape. When he was over the threshold, he let it swing back into place and locked it nice and secure. It was a decent-sized room, two sinks and a couple of fancy marble stalls. He sniffed the air and came up with the scent of a female he recognized, many he didn't, and one putrid stink of a male.

He snorted. "Whoever was in here with you wears cologne made from a donkey's ass."

Kate, who was standing in front of the mirror, reapplying her lipstick, glanced over at him. "I suppose it's inane to point out that this is a ladies' room," she said, "and you are no lady."

He walked up to her, stood behind her so that both of their reflections were echoed in the mirror. Outside the room, the slamming of a bass-heavy dance mix could still be heard, while inside, the lights above them were agreeably dim.

Was that scent of a male someone she'd been talking to? Meeting? Couldn't be. Nicholas would've seen him go in and come out.

Kate lifted one dark blond brow. "What?"

"I can't trust you," he said softly.

"Hey, I am where I said I'd be." She seemed calm enough, but he saw her chest hitch as it rose and fell with each breath.

He leaned in and kissed the spot between her neck and her shoulder blade. Just one soft, nothing of a kiss and yet it made his entire body go up in flames. "I can't trust you," he said again, trying to control himself even as his cock grew harder under his fly, "and you certainly can't trust me."

Her eyes locked with his then, and she nodded. "At least you can admit that. I hate pretending."

His hands stole around her waist. Goddamn, she felt good, perfect against him—like no one ever had. "Don't you think I know you want out?"

Her jaw tightened, but she didn't deny it.

"To run for the freedom you've lost?" he continued, pulling her back against him so she could feel how hard he was—and that it was all about her.

"I deserve to have freedom," she said, her breath quickening.

"You do."

"But you need me."

His hands drifted up, over the silk bandage material of her dress, over her ribs. "Only for a short time," he whispered as he eased down the bodice and filled his hands with her breasts. "After that, you're free."

She sucked in air, then released on a soft moan.

"As long as you can't stop me, or find me, or . . ." she moaned as he squeezed her breasts gently, as she watched her nipples rise and jut out and beg to be pinched.

"Catch you."

Kate arched her body, pushed her breasts deeper into his hold, and Nicholas released them, let them gently bob back down against her ribs.

"Don't stop," she hissed.

He grinned, bringing his fingers to her nipples and flicking them lightly. "I haven't even started."

"Good," she said, dropping her head to his shoulder and closing her eyes.

"No, Kate," he said. "Don't look away. Watch how your sweet tits respond to being touched, and stroked, and pinched."

She turned her head back, and Nicholas watched her in the mirror as she stared heavy-lidded, mouth open at his hands on her breasts, his fingers squeezing her nipples, teasing the very ends of each bud until they were pebble hard and deep pink.

She lifted her arms over her head, draped them across his shoulders, giving him more access. And he took it. He flicked her nipples back and forth so lightly they barely moved, but so quickly and deliberately that her back arched and her breathing grew ragged.

"How wet does this make you, Kate?" he whispered into the cover of her ear.

"Feel ," she uttered, her back arching farther, her ass pressing into his straining cock.

On a growl, he grabbed hold of her waist and spun her to face him. Instantly, her arms dropped around his neck and Nicholas leaned in and kissed her hard and brazen without any thought to being gentle. As her breasts pressed against his chest, his mouth took her, his tongue sliding deep just as his cock wanted to slide into her pussy.

She tasted like the sweetest blood, the most fragrant nectar, and if he could spend a lifetime suckling at her tongue, her lips, her nipples, her clit—he would.

And he'd pay for it if he had to!

He tore his mouth from her and dipped his head. He needed to taste her, know what it felt like to have her life force between his teeth. He took her nipple into his mouth, circled the hot, hard bud, looking for nourishment. Suckling her deep, he heard her moan again above him, but this time it was louder, desperate.

He needed to feel what she felt—to know how wet she was. How warm. As he continued to feast on her nipple, pulling it, rasping it gently with the tips of his fangs, he ran his hand up her thigh, under her dress until he reached silk.

Fuck.

Soaking wet. And hot as the sun.

Hunger roared through him like a ravenous animal with prey in sight. In seconds, he was dropping to his knees and pulling her dress to her hips. He wanted shelter. He wanted his tongue inside her cunt, warm and wet and safe. He wanted to feed from her and be saved from a life of loneliness and pain and memories.

She parted her legs for him—long pale legs that shook just a little in anticipation. He eased her dress up a little higher, left it at her waist, then hooked his thumbs under the thin strips of silk underwear and pulled them down, all the way to her ankles.

Her scent assaulted him at once. The sweetest, most delectable, entirely addictive scent he'd ever encountered. It screamed at him, "Take me, drink from me and you will be reborn."

For a moment, he just sat there and stared, his breath causing her pale hair to move a fraction. Above him he heard her heavy breathing as she watched him take in every inch of her labia. Did she know how beautiful she was? How kissable her lips were? So pink and shiny and ready for him.

He put his hands on her knees and moved slowly up her thighs, enjoying the heat of her skin and the way her muscles bunched and shook beneath his palms. Up his hands raked until his thumbs dipped into her crease, spreading her wide for him.

And then he put his mouth on her and went to heaven.

Goddamn, her scent, her taste, it had ruined him forever for anything else. Savoring her, he ran his tongue over her inner lips, slowly, so slowly until she hissed and moaned and shook above him.

When he found her clit, dipped his tongue inside the little hood that housed the hot, tight bud, he drew it into his mouth.

Kate cried out and gasped for air.

Keeping her open, stretched, Nicholas continued to suckle, pulling the hard nub inside as he flicked it gently with his tongue.

"Oh God," she moaned. "Nicholas, please."

Yes, veana, he mused. *Yes, you will come hard and long and slippery against my mouth.*

He released her clit and slid his tongue inside her. "Shit," she hissed, widening her legs, her hands diving into his hair, her fingers gripping his skull. "Oh God . . ."

Her movements made him crazy, made his cock

strain to get out, get free—get inside her and fuck until they were both on the verge of insanity.

She bucked against him, his mouth and his tongue, driving him in deeper. And then insanity did hit.

Hunger.

Starvation.

Greedy lust like he'd never known.

Her blood should not be his, never be inside him, and yet . . .

He struck gently, scoring her, bracketing her lovely clit with his fangs.

She cried out. Not in pain, but in deep, unabashed pleasure. "Yes, Nicholas. Please. Deeper. God, feed from me. Don't ever stop!"

He pulled, suckled, took from her, and as her sweet blood flowed into him, as it ran down his throat and made his cock heavy and hungry, he licked her. He suckled and swirled his tongue around the throbbing clit that grew darker and thicker as she approached her climax.

Kate had never felt such pleasure, such freedom from herself and her thoughts and fears. It was like being lost in a world of delicious, happy safety and love, and she never wanted to come out, come down.

She just wanted to come.

And as Nicholas gripped her hips, his tongue moving in quick feathery strokes across her tender clit, and as he drank from her, she felt the heat inside her spread.

She was his, and her body was his to command.

Her hands had satisfied her in the past, but it was nothing to this—to Nicholas Roman—nothing to his touch, his suckle, the way he consumed her whole.

"Take it all," she cried, her fingers pressing into his scalp, pulling him closer. "My blood and my body."

Nicholas growled like a wild animal, a beast, deep in his throat, and Kate loved it, wanted to drown in that sound as she bucked and moaned, fisted his hair and surrendered herself.

As the heat spread farther and grew inside her, Nicholas quickened his strokes. Her breath caught in her throat, her mind filled only with pleasure, she cried out. Orgasm hit like a tidal wave of feeling, blinding heat and magnificent pleasure washing over her, washing her clean. She had been taken. Her first and only. And as she bucked gently against him, keeping the pace with her waning orgasm, she wished sentimentally that he would be her last and forever.

She felt him slip out of her, his fangs retracting, and the loss was palpable. She was *virgini*, untouched by anyone but herself for all these twenty-five years, and the connection she'd just experienced with this *paven* made her wish not only for his care, but for his body on hers, his thick cock easing deep into the channels of her cunt.

As she stood there, Nicholas's head resting on her belly as they both tried to catch their breath, Kate looked at herself in the mirror opposite them. She saw her fingers threaded in his black hair, her arms still taut with tension, her face flushed with the aftermath of climax, and her bare breasts moving with her chest as she breathed in and out.

And she saw a small bruise on the curve just above her right nipple, on the spot where she had a freckle—a freckle she'd had since birth. She grinned. How had that happened? she wondered. Was it when his hands had stolen around her, yanked down the top of her dress and squeezed her nipples until she cried out? Had he been so rough?

Her grin widened. She liked rough.

His rough.

But her grin began to fade as over the course of a moment or two the bruise did not. Purebloods couldn't hold a bruise for longer than a few seconds—and this had been far longer than that. In fact, his playful tugs on her nipples had been ages ago.

Nicholas still had his head resting against her belly, no doubt contemplating the ramifications of what they'd done, what they'd allowed to happen.

And now so was she.

Screw the mirror. She glanced down at her skin, at the bruise that wasn't really a bruise at all. What . . . It was more of a faded shape. Curves to it.

She squinted. It was something she'd seen before. A sign or a symbol—

It hit her like a baseball bat to the skull and she shifted her gaze from her skin to his—down to the strong, intelligent, devilish face of the *paven* who had just granted her the climax of her life.

Her skin started to bristle and her head felt heavy,

dizzy, like it wanted to blow up. There within the Breeding Male circle on his cheek was a faded shape.

The lower curve of a lip.

Her head came up, and she stared at her reflection in the mirror. Gone was the flushed, happy face of a *veana* who had just connected with someone for the first time in her life. Those brown eyes of hers were filled with shock, horror, and disbelief. But there it was, just above her right nipple.

The pouty double curve of an upper lip.

It all made sense, she thought breathlessly—the undeniable attraction they both shared, the hunger for his blood.

Nicholas Roman wasn't just some random male she found irresistible.

He was her other half.

Her true mate.

19

"I'll be out in a second."

"I'll be waiting."

Nicholas left the bathroom, intent on giving Kate the time she needed to get herself together—both mentally and physically—despite his concerns over the male's scent he had detected earlier. Granted, she was hiding something, but then again so was he, and he didn't think her secrets had anything to do with meeting someone in the bathroom.

There were a few women waiting outside the door, their expressions heavy on both interest and embarrassment.

Nicholas nodded at them. "Just a few more minutes, ladies."

They smiled at him like they knew what had happened behind the bathroom door and they wouldn't mind a repeat performance. Listening, watching, or participating.

Shit, neither would Nicholas.

After scanning the dance floor for Alexander, who

had been hidden so undercover that Nicholas had yet to connect with him, he moved into the shadows of a nearby curtain and watched the bathroom door like a hawk. Any male that went by and so much as paused by the door elicited a soft, fierce growl from his throat. The severe reaction surprised Nicholas. He had never been a possessive *paven*—it wasn't something that worked well in his profession—and he had no interest in becoming one now. It was just her. He'd seen no mark on her skin and yet he couldn't stand the thought of anyone touching her, scenting her, taking her blood . . .

His fangs dropped and he licked his lips, wanting more of what was on his tongue and rushing through his veins and belly right now. Was this how it would always be for him—hell, for them? A constant state of desire mixed with distrust? Would either of them break or bend, even for a second?

Would either of them reveal their secrets to the other?

He stared at the bathroom door, ready to see her emerge in that dress, her face flushed, her eyes still heavy with the aftershocks of orgasm as she searched the dim passageway for him. Would she be as desperate to see him as he was to see her? And when their eyes connected, maybe even their hands as they moved through the club to get outside and to the car, would she despise herself for feeling that desperation?

His questions went unanswered. He never saw

Kate, couldn't wait for her to come through that door. The scent that hit his nostrils and flared into his lungs was rank, poisoned—deadly.

Dare was here.

And he was close by.

One second ticked by as he weighed the option of remaining where he was, waiting for Alexander to emerge, waiting for Dare to get close enough to Kate so he could take the bastard out. But Dare wasn't stupid. Just as Nicholas possessed the power of scent, Dare had it too. Besides, waiting was bullshit.

Nicholas took off, his hand closing around the gun at his back. He hated following his nose like a dog, but that's what he was now thanks to morpho—an animal. Predator in search of prey.

A slow groove pounded a deep bass through the speakers as he circumvented the dance floor, which was packed, patrons barely able to move more than an inch in any direction. For one brief second he lost Dare's scent, and he was so amped up to capture and kill he wanted to grab the first thing that walked into his path and dive-bomb into their throat with his fangs. But then it returned, the sewer stench of the Impure who was feeding off something evil, and Nicholas resumed the hunt, through the crowds, past the bar, to the stage . . . There was no performance going on out front, but his instincts told him, warned him that it was all happening behind the scenes.

Pocketing his weapon, he eyed the oversized human male who stood guarding the backstage area and quickly moved to his left, where a frat party was taking place. Knocking two drunken spiky-haired boys together caused an instant brawl, and as the guard leaped down to break it up, Nicholas headed up and behind the curtain.

He barely got three feet before—

Motherfucker!

In a rush of movement, Nicholas jumped on Dare, pulling him down, needing to get a hand free to grab his weapon. But it was limbs and fists and head butting, until Nicholas brought his elbow down on the Impure's neck. Still on the ground, he reached behind him for his weapon, and in under a second had it trained on Dare's temple.

Problem was, Dare had a gun pressed against Nicholas's temple, too.

Nicholas locked eyes with the Impure, a deadly clash of wills, nostrils flaring, fangs dropped.

"This is fun," Dare whispered.

"Not as fun as hauling your rotting carcass to the Order," Nicholas returned.

"Perhaps," Dare said. "But *you* won't be the one to do it, Son of the Breeding Male."

Nicholas remained silent, but released the safety on his gun.

"In fact," Ethan continued without even a hitch of concern in his voice, "you will be the first to drop your weapon."

Nicholas pressed the muzzle deeper into the Impure's temple.

"Not ready to surrender just yet, eh?" Dare's eyes drifted to the ceiling. "Perhaps if I offered you something? Gray Donohue's life?"

Nicholas's lip curled. "Gray? What do know about Gray?"

"Or perhaps an incentive that only you could appreciate." His eyes slammed back to Nicholas. "How about cash? Or would you take a personal check?"

Aggression rushed over Nicholas like an avalanche threatening to bury him alive, and he snarled at the Impure. This was fucking out of control. Maybe he wouldn't mind getting his own head blown off if he could manage to take Dare's off first.

"But maybe I should ask," Dare continued, amusement greasing his tone now. "What is your going rate now, *Nichola*?"

Nicholas froze.

Dare grinned. "Did one of your patrons give you that name, or was it your pimp?"

The world suddenly imploded. Nicholas saw nothing but red, and sixty shades of it at once. In that moment, Dare could've put a bullet in his brain or his body and he would've done nothing but drop.

"What did you call me?" he rasped.

Dare's grin widened. "The name of a secret whore, one who's been working for a long time, one who continues to sell his cock, his mouth, his ass—"

"Shut up!" Nicholas roared, his finger shaking on the trigger.

"Do it and I'll flash," Dare warned. "And I'll be

bringing all my new information with me. Who knows who I'll run into on my way home? Your brother out there in the club tonight?"

How was this possible? Nicholas thought, his brain squeezing inside his skull. His two worlds colliding like trains running the same track.

Shoot. Shoot the motherfucker.

"What do you want?"

Dare exhaled. "What do you think I want, *paven*? I want the *balas*. I want you and yours to back off and let the uprising come to pass. Let the Impures free so they can finally have what they deserve."

"And what is that?" Nicholas growled.

"Choice."

"You deserve nothing but a long, pain-filled death, you piece of shit."

"But you'll still do as I ask, won't you?" His eyes were heavy with purpose now. "And one more thing."

"Fuck you."

Dare shook his head. "Don't think I carry enough cash. Bummer."

"I think I can arrange for a freebie just this once," Nicholas said menacingly. "I think you'd like it. Or maybe your ass is already being serviced." Nicholas cocked his head to one side. "Who is pulling the strings back there?"

But Dare wasn't taking the bait. "I want the *balas* and the *veana*."

"Not a fucking chance," Nicholas bit out.

"Bring them to Time Square tomorrow night, just

after sundown"—he leaned in closer and whispered— "or your Impure sister-in-law will never see her brother again and your brothers will have every detail of your long and very rich career as a cock-for-hire."

Dare flashed from the alcove, leaving Nicholas sitting there, alone, on his knees, air trapped inside his lungs. A cyclone of self-disgust and self-hate spinning within him.

Nicholas let his head drop forward and lifted his gun, trained the muzzle that had moments ago been on Dare, on himself. It felt good, cool on his temple. It was the easy way out. Quick, messy . . . but he wouldn't have to be the one to clean it up.

He didn't move, barely breathed, his lips feeling so dry. His secret, his shame, in the hands of the enemy.

He itched to squeeze the trigger.

Which was worse—let Lucian be morphed, let him be turned into a Breeding Male, let Gray die, give an innocent child over to a demon . . . and then there was the *veana*—or let his brothers know he was a liar and a filthy whore who had never stopped fucking anything that walked upright.

Nicholas shut his eyes, his lip curling with ire and desperation. Alexander and Lucian saw him as the honorable one, the *paven* they counted on for rational thought and a controlled manner—the *paven* who had left his hole and his profession in France for a new life and a clean future. But it was nothing but a joke.

He was nothing but a joke.

A worthless piece of gutter trash.

For a moment, he remained there, still and trembling, no thought in his head as he forced air in and out of his lungs.

Then he eased the gun from his temple and opened his eyes.

Kate.

Her blood pulsed through his veins, her life force, her passion, her ferocity—her drive for freedom, all gripping hold of every cell in his body and attempting to reorganize his will and purpose.

She waited for him in the bathroom. Or had she left, gone into the crowd looking for him?

A new fear gripped him.

Dare.

Was he looking for her? God, had he found her?

Nicholas was up and out of the alcove in under a breath, his gun back in his waistband where it belonged.

Kate ignored the knocking on the bathroom door. *Back off*, she wanted to yell through the wood. Didn't they get it? Didn't they understand how insane and complicated her life had just become, and that she needed a minute in front of the mirror to process?

Or ten.

'Course they didn't.

She couldn't stop staring at the mark just above her right nipple. Twenty minutes ago, it'd been a freckle, a tiny little nothing from birth, and now it was the mark of her true mate. Granted, this wasn't uncommon. A *veana* could develop the mark of her true mate at any time before Meta, the transformation at age fifty into an adult vampire female. But to develop the mark following a sexual encounter—her first, in fact—well, that she'd never heard of.

She reached up, touched the spot. It was softer than the rest of her skin, as though it were coated in oil.

Top lip. Bottom lip.

A kiss.

"Come the fuck on, bitch!" someone called through the door.

Yanking up her dress and grabbing her purse, Kate unlocked the door and charged through it like a feral cat. Her nerves driving her irritation, she took on the first female she saw, number one in the long line.

"Who are you calling bitch, bitch?" she challenged, chin deep in the woman's face.

The black-haired female blanched, her pale brown eyes trained on Kate's mouth. "Sorry. Holding it for ten minutes. You know."

Fangs in, Kate. Jesus. Get ahold of yourself.

She quickly curled her upper lip over her teeth, gave the woman an apologetic, toothless smile. "Sure. Sorry."

Stepping back from the terrified woman, Kate walked past the line of girls and headed for the dance floor. Thankfully, the *paven* she sought stepped right into her path only seconds later.

"I'm here," she said, her hands itching to touch him. "Just like I said I'd be."

"Good. That's good."

He looked distracted, to say the very least. "What happened?" Her eyes moved over his face, his eyes the blackest she'd ever seen them. "You look upset. Are you hurt? Did you see Dare?"

He didn't answer, just grabbed her hand. "Let's get out of here."

Kate followed him into the sea of swaying bodies. "Nicholas—hey—"

"Come, Kate, please," he called back to her, picking up the pace. "We need to go."

"Where to? Another club?"

"Back to the house."

He walked ahead of her, straight across the dance floor, his eyes scanning the crowd, his body tense as an alpha wolf. Kate was no wilting flower by any means, but things had changed. Back in that bathroom, things had changed big time—whether she wanted them to or not. Nicholas was her mate. And though she would never give up her freedom, even for love, she would protect him, care for him for as long as they were together. Her DNA demanded it be so, and though she hated to admit it, so did her heart.

She squeezed his hand and hustled forward.

He glanced back, his eyes a weary, indecipherable question she didn't have the answer to, but she gave him a soft smile and a nod of encouragement anyway.

The flash of pain-laced desire that crossed his black eyes cut her to her core, but the look was gone in an instant, and the moment they exited the club and hit the sidewalk, so were they.

The limousine and its driver were left waiting at the curb.

20

Nicholas landed just outside the back door of the house, and without ceremony took Kate's hand and led her inside. He needed time, as much as could be spared, to figure out what his next move was going to be. How he was going to silence Dare forever, find Gray, all while keeping his brothers in the dark. He wasn't about to bring them in on this; this was his problem to solve.

As he passed by what was now the kitchen, he saw Sara preparing rations on the counter. She glanced up, and before Nicholas could even get a word out, Kate jumped in with a question for Sara.

"How's the *balas*?" she asked, true concern in her tone.

"Sleeping," Sara told her. "He asked for you, and I told him you'd check in on him when you got home."

Kate smiled at her. "Thanks."

"'Course." She looked from Kate to Nicholas, then back again. "How did everything go tonight?"

Kate nodded. "Fine."

"Good to hear."

"Is Alexander back yet?" Nicholas asked with un-disguised impatience. "Lucian?"

Sara shifted her attention to him, and Nicholas saw the worry in her eyes, the tension of unanswered questions. *Not to worry, female. I will get your brother back safely.* "Alexander hasn't returned, but Lucian's in the library."

Nicholas nodded, then led Kate out of the kitchen, through the living room, and into the main hall. At the base of the staircase, she stopped.

"You don't have to walk me to the door, Nicholas."

"Maybe I want to," he said. Maybe that was all he wanted to do, follow her upstairs into her room, strip them both naked, and get in bed beside her. Pull the covers up over their heads and breathe each other's air as he buried himself deep within her.

And yet duty called.

"Are you going to tell me what happened tonight?" she said, her large brown eyes probing his.

That was the problem. She wanted to talk, and the only thing he wanted to do with his mouth was taste her cunt again.

God, he was a crude bastard.

"Nothing happened tonight," he said easily. "Futile search."

"Is that really the story you're sticking to?"

He nodded.

And she didn't fight him. "Okay."

"You know, I'm not talking about what happened between us when I say that, right?"

"Sure."

Always playing the cool card, *veana*. "Because what happened there was something. Really fucking something." He caught the sudden whisper of a smile on her perfect lips, and he leaned in to her and whispered, "I want it to happen again. Every inch of me wants it to happen again."

She held on to the banister with one hand and leaned toward him too, stopping only when their chests connected and their heads nearly collided.

She didn't say anything more, didn't confirm or deny her body's need for him. But she didn't need to. The hot scent of her arousal drifted up to him and played in the space around his nostrils, teasing the air that he pulled into his lungs. Christ, just the thought of handing her over to Dare made him want to kill. The idea was so preposterous and impossible for him to conceive of, for a second he could almost convince himself the demand hadn't happened.

But seconds last only seconds for a reason, and if Nicholas wanted to birth a plan to combat Dare's he needed to get on it fast.

He leaned in and kissed her softly on the mouth. "Good night, Kate."

She took a deep breath, exhaled, and said, "Good night, Nicholas," then turned and made her way up the stairs.

Alone.

The Supreme One stood at the water's edge in his reality, the sunlight and easy breezes warring with the mood of their creator. He was growing weary of the male before him. In fact, he wished he could end the Impure's life this very minute.

But that was not wise.

Not until his plan was complete.

"Not only do you not bring me the *balas* I seek," the Supreme One began, his lip curling, "but you flaunt your beating heart in front of an entire club of humans, chasing after the Roman brothers."

Dare stood by Pearl's chair, his hand gripping the pregnant human's shoulder as if he could protect her, or the *balas* inside her.

A fool among Impures.

"Who do you have spying on me, my lord?" Ethan asked easily, though the worry was bright in his dark eyes.

The Supreme One smiled. "Alistair observes your movement."

"Alistair."

"The male reports to me now."

Ethan lifted his chin. "Your trust for me and my actions wanes, then."

The Supreme One laughed at the male's idiocy. "I have never put my trust in you, Impure—only my blood. And if you wish to continue taking from my vein, you will listen closely. The Romans gain in strength, ability, and motivation; they will take any and every chance to kill you. Do not underestimate them—and do not play cat and rat games with them. You will lose."

And so will I.

"Do you understand me, Impure?"

Ethan nodded, but his face was a mask of irritation, of frustration—of a male who had been elevated to a station far greater than he deserved.

Yes, the Supreme One mused, he would love to end this male's life himself—and make him suffer before he did. But the Order would not morph the third Roman brother if Ethan Dare was dead. And the Supreme One needed Lucian Roman to go through morpho if he was ever going to see his plan hatched.

21

His mind spitting out thoughts, ideas and impossibilities, Nicholas stalked into the library. He found Lucian in front of his laptop, a stack of books beside him—several open and scattered around the table.

"Have you heard from Alex?"

Lucian glanced up. "He texted me about ten minutes ago. He thinks he may have something. A possible location of the recruits—he followed two of them from that club you were in."

Perfect, Nicholas thought, his insides ready to jump, ready to sink his fangs into the heart of the Impure who had caused havoc in his world, changed their lives forever. Alexander and Lucian could handle the recruits, take down the compound, while Nicholas took down Dare once and for all.

"You look like you're ready to explode, *Duro*," Lucian said. "We will end Dare."

Yes, he would, Nicholas mused, his lip curling. He nodded toward his brother's portable library. "Studying for a test?"

Lucian snorted. "Genetics."

"Ah, right. You saw Bronwyn, then."

"You mean Pain in the Ass? Yes, I saw her."

"You gave her the sample?"

Lucian nodded. "She needs a couple of days."

"You couldn't persuade her to hurry?"

"Please."

A dark grin spread over Nicholas's features. "Didn't pull out that Roman charm that I have to assume is in there somewhere, but have never actually witnessed?"

Lucian's pale eyes flicked up and he cursed. "Here's the problem, *Duro*. When I'm around that *veana*, I want to tear the fucking walls apart."

"That's because you want to mate with her."

"No," Lucian said quickly. Too quickly. "Maybe." He shook his head. "But not in a pure way."

"What the hell does that mean?"

"It's a drive, not a lust. I don't know." Lucian slammed the book shut. "I think this is all a fucking lie."

Nicholas's guts constricted. In his rational mind, he knew that Lucian wasn't talking about his own situation, about his past, and the lies he'd been shelling out for more than fifty years—and yet his younger brother's words felt directed toward him anyway.

"I think the Order's bullshitting all of us," Lucian continued. "I think even if we drop Dare's carcass at their ancient feet, they're still going to morph my ass." He shook his head, his mind working. "Maybe that's what I'm feeling when I'm around Bronwyn, the beginning of morpho—overwhelming aggression. You've felt it, so has Alexander. Does that sound right?"

"Aggression is exceptionally strong after morpho," Nicholas conceded. "But I wouldn't go there—not yet. Not for another hundred years."

Not if I succeed in wiping Dare from the earth tomorrow eve.

"Or maybe this is our father's doing," Lucian suggested, his tone dark with disgust. "His cursed blood is sending me through morpho before my time—straining to get out, escape from my cells and flow freely through my veins."

"No," Nicholas said through clenched teeth.

"Easy as that? Say it and it isn't true?"

"You're not in fucking morpho!" Nicholas said, his tone almost a snarl. "Christ. You're not going to go through morpho until it's your time. I will make certain of it."

The aggression that had surrounded Lucian so heavily a moment ago dissolved, and he really looked at Nicholas. His pale brows knit together and his tone softened as it rarely did. "You know you can't protect me from my destiny, *Duro*."

Nicholas blew him off. "I don't know what you're talking about."

"Yes, you do, and so do I. That debt you believe you still owe was repaid a hundred times over."

"Shut it, Luca," Nicholas spat, his eyes combing the room for something to pick up and throw at the wall.

"We are blood," Lucian said, standing, his books forgotten. "It was my duty and pleasure to do what I did that day. The sound of slit throats and heads rolling was the sweetest fucking music I'd ever heard, then or now."

Images flooded Nicholas's mind. His shirt ripped, his pants ripped, his face smashed into the concrete over and over until he lost consciousness.

"I still carry that bloodlust within me," Lucian said softly.

As do I, Nicholas thought.

Lucian offered him one more look of solidarity before he returned to his chair, his books. "Maybe someday I will get a chance to use it again—and on dear old Daddy, perhaps."

As a member of the Order, one was expected to counsel, lecture, set limits, and hold those guilty of crimes accountable for their actions. So it had always been for nearly seven hundred years, for as long as the Order had held power. Members had come and gone, seeking authority, then seeking everlasting quiet beneath the stone pillars in the Tomb of Nascita.

Within the gardens of the Athens *credenti*, just one mile from the Plaka, Titus Evictus Roman sat beside his fellow Order member Jaxelon, on a large flat rock, a group of the *credenti*'s elders seated on the grass around them.

Covered from head to ankle in his burgundy robes,

Titus remained quiet as Jaxelon, a *veana* who at last count was nearing her three hundredth birth year, attempted to spread calm throughout the small gathering. Though his Breeding Male brands had dissolved back into his skin, Titus was still the intense-looking *paven* he had always been: with a shock of white hair and nearly pink eyes. Every time Cruen took his blood, he'd assured Titus that at some point his features would fade into an obscure appearance, but until then Titus should remain covered if he wished to keep his anonymity within the Order. A choice the members had always respected.

"We have heard of the abductions of the *veanas* in the States," one *paven* commented, his black beard cut short and square as was the Greek vampire custom. "And the news is spreading throughout the *credenti*, making our citizens nervous."

"It will be short-lived," Jaxelon assured him, her voice as calm as a parent to a tired child.

"The perpetrator has been apprehended, then?" the *paven* asked.

"We have reason to believe it will be very soon."

"Good thing. We don't want any of the *credenti* citizens here or around the world to think this problem requires a dire solution."

"No indeed," said a black-haired *veana* beside him. "The Breeding Male must never return."

Jaxelon's gaze was steady, though Titus felt apprehension move through his body. "It will not happen,"

Jaxelon assured them. "At present, no Breeding Males exist, and our eyes are always on their descendants. I am pleased to say that none, to date, has acquired the gene."

The *paven* with the square beard raised one ink-black eyebrow. "And if one did?"

"He would be caged." Jaxelon said the words without hesitation.

Too easy, Titus thought. Words too easily said and actions too easily taken—and yet he knew the wisdom and experience behind the decision to cage, contain, watch.

An animal will kill to feed and to breed.

And a Breeding Male, as Titus knew firsthand, is at its core an unfeeling, immoral predator.

"If I remember my history correctly, one or two of the Breeding Males escaped their confinement," the *paven* remarked. "Elimination seems a wiser, more prudent choice should the Order come across a *paven* with such a genetic structure."

A collective murmur of agreement rippled through the small crowd, and Jaxelon nodded her understanding, put her hands in the air and called for calm. "We hear your concern, and will take your thoughts under advisement."

As she steered the conversation away from Breeding Males to blood distribution within the *credenti*, Titus felt his insides curl and wither beneath the protection of his robes. There would be another Breeding Male, one whose genes were dangerously close to being activated were he not careful.

Granted, there was only so much interference Titus could manage without risking his seat on the Order. But for his youngest son, for all the children he had sired, he would do what he could.

22

"Mommy!"

Kate heard the scream like it was right beside her, and it triggered a reaction in her that was tantamount to panic. Lying nude on the bed after stripping herself of the red dress and heels, she grabbed a robe from the back of the chair and threw it on. She was out of her room and flinging open the door to Ladd's just as another cry stole from his throat.

"Mommy!"

He was writhing on the bed, his sheets crawling up to his belly.

"Ladd." Kate went to him and dropped to the mattress. "Ladd," she said again, her hands on his shoulders, then face. "It's okay. Ladd, wake up."

His eyes jumped open and when he saw her, he looked momentarily devastated. She wasn't the one he wanted. But the look lasted only a brief second, and with a cry, he threw his arms around her neck and clung to her. She wasn't the one he wanted, but she was there and she was female, a worthwhile substitute and she was patting him as gently as she could manage.

"Kate?"

Ladd spoke against her chest, his small voice tired and confused.

"Yeah?"

"Is my mom really dead? Did it really happen?"

Kate's throat tightened, but she answered him. "Yes."

He was quiet for a moment. Then he said, "I don't know what to do now."

"You don't have to know. You don't have to decide anything. Everything will be okay."

"Are you going to go away again?"

Fuck. It wasn't fair—not that he shouldn't be able to ask the question, he should—but that she felt so compelled to give him the honest answer. "I don't know."

He pulled back so he could look at her. His eyes were red. "Maybe you could stay. For just a little while."

Her insides twisted, her still heart too. But she nodded, because it was something she could give him. "Sure. For a little while."

"Okay." He gave her a small smile, then scrambled away from her and lay back down.

Kate watched as he hugged his pillow to his chest and stared straight ahead, blinking his exhaustion. She may not have known how to rock the boy in her arms or comfort him in a traditional way, but she wouldn't leave his side until his breathing changed and he was asleep again.

Nicholas had heard it too. The cry of the *balas*.

He took the steps two at a time, reached the landing just in time to hear Kate's voice intermingled with the boy's. He steered right and walked down the hall to the door of Ladd's room. Dressed only in a white robe, her feet bare, Kate sat on the edge of the bed, her hand on the *balas*'s back. He was lying down and hugging his pillow. Kate's face was a mask of unyielding bleakness as she watched him blink his way back to sleep.

The boy whimpered and Kate soothed him with her voice and rubbed his back. Nicholas just watched, the dim hallway at his back leaving him in the protection of the shadows. Downstairs, on his cell, making demands and offers to those who would assist in his plan with Dare, Nicholas had wondered just who he'd become over the last several hours, who he was—what he'd turned into. But now, as he stared at the *veana* before him, he wondered who *she* was. What she'd done to land herself in Mondrar. She was tough and smart and could give a good punch, but the marks on her long, beautiful neck weren't little nothings. They signified a long-held secret, and a long-term stay in the vampire prison.

A lethal crime.

And yet she had saved the boy, had risked her freedom for him—a child she was in no way close to or related to.

He wondered if she would ever tell him the truth, or if they would go their separate ways knowing as much about each other as they did at this moment.

Kate brushed a bit of Ladd's pale hair from his temple and sighed. Nicholas felt a pull toward them, toward her, an invisible tightrope he wanted to run across. He wanted to take up the space behind her on the bed and watch the boy with her, over her shoulder.

She stood up then, covered Ladd with a blanket, and started toward him. Nicholas held his ground. If he didn't take off now, she'd see him and she'd know he'd been watching her.

They'd moved him.

Moved him into a room where the sounds of sex filled his brain and his ears. It was like porn sensory overload, and he couldn't keep up with the wants, needs, and cries of orgasm.

Gray sucked in air as the tape was ripped from his mouth and eyes. The stinging sensation took his breath and his sight away for several seconds. Then the room, his new world came into focus. White walls with black shapeless art—and no windows. On the floor, backs and knees to the carpet, asses swinging like pendulums, eyes closed and mouths open, couples were engaged in all types of sex acts.

This was Dare's new compound—what the Romans sought, and what they sought to destroy. Gray fought the sounds and demands of those in his head, those before him. Even fought the erection that strained against his fly.

"You like it. I knew you would."

Dare.

Gray fought the binds around his chest.

"I thought we could talk." Dare flashed in front of him, his dark eyes probing as he dropped into the empty chair beside Gray.

"I don't know about any *balas*," Gray spat out.

"But you do know the layout of the Roman compound. How to get in, how to bypass whatever charms keep it locked up so tightly."

"Harder."

"Faster."

"Oh God, yes!"

His brain spun; his cock pulsed.

"If you were to share that information with me," Dare continued with a grin, "I would be inclined to release you from your bondage. You could join Marina and the others."

Gray turned, saw Marina in the very center of the room. Her mouth on a female as a male took her from behind.

Dare had brought him here to fuck him up, both literally and figuratively. He wanted inside the Roman compound, wanted a *balas* who may be held there—and he was going to torture the information out of Gray any way he could.

Gray's nostrils flared. He wanted what was in front

of him, couldn't help it. And yet there was Sara . . . and some sense of loyalty to those Purebloods who'd taken him in.

"I have nothing for you," he uttered through clenched teeth.

"You sure?" Dare asked. "Be sure."

Gray said nothing, his eyes trained on Marina. She was about to come, her breathing heavy—her mind tossing off sounds and words that were real easy on the brain waves . . .

"I. Know. Nothing."

A flash of deadly venom crossed Ethan Dare's face and he was up and out of his chair. "You will change your mind or you will die," he called, walking through the writhing bodies and out of the room.

"Oh God. Yes. Yes. Yes."

As Marina slammed her hips back, she looked straight at Gray and smiled.

And when she came, so did he.

Kate paused at the door and looked at the boy one last time, asleep now, his breathing even and his face free of fear or anxiety. *Don't get involved here,* she warned herself. *Don't get attached to anybody, fond of anybody— don't go so soft you lose your one opportunity for freedom.*

"And it's coming for you soon," she whispered to herself.

"What's coming for you?"

Kate jerked around and came face-to-face with a set of hard black eyes and one cruel, delicious mouth.

"Nicholas!" She shook her head, breathing heavy. "Jesus. What are you doing here?"

"I heard the *balas* cry out."

And he'd come running, instincts that would make him a good father if that's who he turned out to be. And for Ladd's sake, she hoped that was how this was all going to go down. The boy deserved such a *paven*.

"It was just a nightmare," she told him, pushing away from the door and heading down the hall to her room. "He's okay. Back to sleep."

Nicholas. "Was it about Mirabelle?"

"Yes." *Mirabelle*. Poor Mirabelle.

Kate walked a little faster. She hated feeling jealous of that *veana*. It was vile and sad and foolish. And yet she couldn't stop herself.

When she reached her door, Nicholas moved in front of her and leaned back against the wood, blocking her way.

"What are you doing?" she asked, her tone tight. She needed to rest, needed to think.

"You're angry," he said, studying her. "Sudden anger too." His dark eyes searched her own. "Why?"

"It's nothing."

"Don't think so." He shook his head. "I can smell it."

She tried to reach for the door handle. "Let me pass."

"Why? So you can go to bed?"

"Yes."

"Alone?"

"Yes!" Kate's eyes flickered over his face, the brands

on his cheeks. Her breasts tightened as the mark above her right nipple hummed. Her tone went suddenly soft, even vulnerable. "Did you love her?"

"What?"

"Mirabelle. Did you love her?" God, she sounded like a fucking *balas*. Yet once again, the mark above her nipple quivered. She pulled the lapels of her robe closed. How open had the thing been a moment ago? Had Nicholas seen anything? Anything he recognized?

"My relationship with Mirabelle had nothing to do with love," Nicholas said succinctly.

"It was just sex?"

His lip curled upward. "Why do you ask me these questions? They mean nothing. I do not inquire about your lovers."

She laughed, bitter and choked. "You mean from my days in Mondrar? Not a lot of time or opportunity to meet someone in there. And then there was the *credenti* . . ."

"What about it?" he said, his eyes narrowing. "You met someone in the *credenti*?"

"Oh yeah! A lot of somebodies—all who got raging hard-ons for the convicted felon." She cocked her head, slapped the skin over her whip marks. "This is a real turn-on for most *pavens*."

He snarled, almost viciously and sent his fist back against the door. It flung open and smashed into the wall of her room. "Most *pavens* have shit for brains," he said, scooping her up in his arms. "And in this case, I'm excessively glad of it."

He carried her into her room, tossed her onto the bed, and mounted her. His face was a mask of ferocity as he stared down into her eyes, but Kate didn't cower. His reactions, his need, his feelings of possessiveness weren't about being an overbearing cretin. They were his natural instincts, carrying out a thousand-year-old ritual that was rooted within his genetic makeup. She was his true mate, and even without knowing it, his need to breed with her, possess her, and keep her away from all other males was impossible to control.

"I won't take from you," he said blackly. "Not yet."

Kate was about to voice her confusion when Nicholas began unbuttoning the cuff of his left shirtsleeve, then yanked it back up to his elbow.

Her body began to hum.

"Are you sure?" she asked, already licking her lips at just the thought of his blood in her mouth, coating her throat.

"You fed me earlier." His eyes were intense, hypnotic as he looked up at her. "It is your turn now."

Her blood heated in her veins, calling out its readiness to be joined with the blood of the *paven* before her.

"In fact, I can still taste you," he said, his voice rough and lust-filled. He laid down beside her and offered her his wrist. "Take all you want, all you can."

His words made her skin grow tight and hot, made the muscles around her pelvis pull inward. This *paven* was a dangerous, delicious drug, lying so close, his scent inside her nostrils, and his wrist just an inch away from her dry, trembling lips.

"Your first real feed from a vein," he whispered into the cove of her ear. "Strike hard, open your throat, and let it come."

Her mouth watered and her fangs elongated to pin-prick sharpness. If she drank from him, from his vein, would he know, would he suspect—would he feel the deep, unbreakable bond of his true mate's suckle?

It should've stopped her—the question alone should've stopped her. But even as her brain tried again to switch on, reason with her, she drove her fangs down into his flesh with the zeal of a starving child. And then there was nothing—nothing but blood—hot, rich, delectable blood funneling into her canines and rushing like a life-giving river into her mouth, over her tongue, and down her throat.

She turned, curved into his side, gripped the other side of his wrist with one hand and his thigh with the other, squeezing, kneading his muscle like a cat as she suckled. She heard him hiss and pull in a breath and knew he was getting turned on by her intensity, by her unabashed need for him.

Her hand groped up his leg, felt every rope of muscle as it flexed and strained, up until she brushed over his crotch. Her belly clenched as she felt his prick, stone-hard and pulsing beneath his fly. As she fed, gulping him down, draining him, she thought about another part of him she wanted to take into her mouth. She imagined it standing up tall and thick before her, her tongue lapping at the crown.

Her fingers twitched, and as she played with him

over the black fabric of his pants, she began to feel more and more aggressive, more and ever frustrated. She needed more than what she had already consumed. More than his blood. She broke the suction on his wrist and looked down into his beautiful face.

He leaned up and lapped at her lower lip with his tongue. "What is it, Kate?"

"I'm still hungry." She lifted his hand to her mouth once again, but this time she let her tongue travel up his wrist to his palm.

He watched her. "What can I give you? Anything I have is yours, you know that."

She grinned. "I was hoping you'd say that." She took his thumb into her mouth and suckled it deep, tasted the hint of salt.

Nicholas groaned, his eyes blazing with fire. "You want my cock, sweetest?"

She let his thumb slip from her lips, wet and heavy. "Will it feed me, *paven*?"

"Perhaps more than you can take," he said.

Smiling, Kate slid to the edge of the bed and knelt between his legs, her body feeling small between his large, powerful thighs. The confidence flowing inside her, spurring her on was all him, had come from his blood—and good thing too. It was her first taste of a *paven*, and she didn't want to do it wrong. Not with him, never with him.

"I want to taste you like you tasted me," she said, unzipping his fly. "I want your blood and your cum in the back of my throat."

He wore nothing underneath, and his cock jutted out, the head smooth and purple. For a moment, Kate just looked at him, the stretched skin, heavy veins, the intimidating length. Her mouth watered.

Nicholas reached out and gripped her knees, his eyes the blackest she'd ever seen them. "It can be difficult to take a *paven* so deep."

"Not you. I want it." Her hand closed around the base of his shaft. "I want to suckle you, lick your head until you can't control yourself and you—"

"Fuck your mouth?" he finished wickedly.

She grinned. "Yes!"

She lowered her head and guided him into her mouth, inch by delectable inch until he touched the back of her throat.

"Oh God, yes," Nicholas groaned as he watched her.

It was nothing like Kate had imagined. Instead of awkwardness and fumbling with something she didn't know how to handle, she was all instinct and desire. He was so hard, like hot steel inside her, and as she kept him deep within her mouth, she let her tongue play with the base of his shaft.

"Kate, look at me," he commanded, his tone heavy with lust.

Kate's eyes flickered up and she saw him, fierce as a jaguar, his nostrils flaring, his mouth open, fangs extended as he dragged in breath after breath. Her own body responded to his need, her nipples going as hard as the *paven* in her mouth, her cunt clenching, dripping with desire as it ached to be touched, filled.

"I know you're hungry," Nicholas said through gritted teeth, his fingers gripping her scalp. "But I can't feed you. Not just yet."

Kate wasn't schooled on how to give head, but she knew how a *paven* pumped his shaft into a *veana*, as a male animal thrust himself into a female. In and out and lots of suction. And that's what she did, using her mouth like a cunt, short thrusts, suckling and lapping at the tip as she listened to his breathing change, quicken.

And just as she was begging for a taste of him, a wash of cum hit the back of her throat, beads of pre-cum bubbled over on the tip of his head. Hot, salty, delicious. She closed her eyes and savored.

Perfect. He was perfect.

For her.

Greedy for more, Kate took him deep again, pulsed him back and forth, reveling in the control she had over this *paven*'s body, his climax.

Nicholas roared, groaned, and Kate prepared herself for the rush of cum that she had been waiting for.

But there was nothing.

Nicholas stilled, his hands, his thick fingers digging into the skin above her knees. And in one swift movement, he had her off of him and on her back.

It was like a slap in the face, and Kate lay there feeling cold and confused. What the hell was going on? He wanted it, wanted her—she could feel it, smell it, taste it. So what had happened to make him pull away?

Staring down at her, Nicholas spread her legs with

his knee, making the cotton folds of her robe part and reveal her naked pussy to his gaze. His eyes were ink black and hardened with a combination of lust and torment. Kate stilled, though her breathing remained rapid. Maybe he wanted to come inside her, feed her cunt—connect in the most complete of ways.

She waited, ready for him, ready for the hot, hard length she'd had in her mouth to find its proper place—deep within her, the walls of her closing in around him.

But he didn't move, just hovered above her, staring down at her with a furious, ravenous expression.

"What's wrong?" she whispered.

His nostrils flared. "I want to come, need to come."

He looked so tortured, his eyes, his expression. She'd never seen anyone look so racked with pain. Not even the prisoners in Mondrar.

Kate wanted to strip the robe from her skin, show him that she wanted him—show him that she wanted him to see her, all of her; touch her, fuck her—come inside her, where it was warm and safe.

But she couldn't.

Just as he held back, she did too. Everything, her life, her freedom, would be gone if he saw the mark on her breast. She wanted his body, wanted him—but she didn't want him to claim her, not forever. She couldn't be a prisoner again. Not even for love.

Her eyes lifted to his and she felt his hand on her leg.

"What are you doing?" she asked. "What are we doing?"

"I want to feel . . ." His eyes closed for a moment as

his hand drifted up her leg. "I want to know what my cock would feel."

"This is bullshit, Nicholas. Please." Kate stared up at him, every inch of skin he touched flaring with heat. "Come inside me!"

She sucked in air as Nicholas thrust two fingers inside her. *Oh God. Oh shit.* Long, thick fingers, working her so deep. Back and forth he pulsed, tapping against a spot so hidden and pleasurable that she forgot about begging, questioning, and even the pain that still hovered in his gaze.

She writhed under him, her hips lifting, jerking as her cunt wept against his palm. He slipped a third finger inside her and she cried out, her pelvis thrusting, rotating. It was so primal, her response to him. It was like her body surrendered to his touch anytime, anywhere.

She kept her eyes closed. God, she didn't want to see him, see his pain as she gave in to so much pleasure. She didn't know why he didn't want to be inside her— maybe he didn't want to be held captive either—but for now, she was going to pretend it didn't hurt her.

His thumb flicked her clit, light feathering, a perfect rhythm that sent shards of sensation running through her body.

"Knees up, sweetest," he said. "I want to get deeper inside your pussy, feel the hot juice flow out of you when you come."

Just the command held Kate's breath hostage inside her lungs, but she did as he instructed, bending her knees, spreading her feet wide apart so he could get closer, deeper. She was so wet, could hear the sound of his knuckles buried within her, the suction as he drew out, then thrust a fourth finger inside to join the others. He pumped her, a steady blistering rhythm as he continued to flick her clit.

Her hands fisted around the rug at her back and she slammed her hips up and held them there.

"Oh yes, there it is," he whispered. "Your hot, tight cunt is milking me now, Kate, suckling my fingers . . . and your clit is so swollen, so red like a berry I'd kill to eat. Sweet Christ, you're beautiful."

Her body convulsed, her legs shook. "Nicholas, please. Don't stop!"

She came hard, fierce, the walls around her cunt contracting with such force she could barely control the volume of her cries. And Nicholas kept thrusting, continuing to feather her clit, gentle and easy, working with the wetness of her opening until her jerks and delicious spasms ebbed and she lowered her hips, let her head fall to the side.

She just laid there for a moment, breathing in and out. It felt like many minutes before her body cooled and she opened her eyes once again, but when she did she took in the sight of Nicholas above her. His eyes were filled with misery, with failure, and she wondered what would be said between them now. He had drank from her, touched her, made her come, and yet had refused his own pleasure.

Without a word, he lifted her up and placed her

on the bed, even covered her with the blanket. When he was done, he stood at the foot of the bed like a servant.

She exhaled, shook her head. "Nicholas . . . Jesus. I— Should I say thank you?"

"No," he said, his neck stiff, his back too as he stared down at her. "But I should."

"Why? For what?" She shrugged, wanting to goad him into a reaction, something more than impassivity. "You didn't get anything out of it."

His nostrils flared. "Not true."

She crossed her arms over her chest, well aware of the mark, his mark beneath the soft cotton. "Are you going to tell me why you wouldn't come inside me? Why you wouldn't orgasm?"

"You are a *virgini*," he said simply, suddenly dispassionate.

Her soul dropped, squeezed inside her skin. "How did you know?"

"Your scent. It hums inside my nostrils, in my loins. You remain untouched, and you deserve more than this, more than . . ."

He didn't finish, but he didn't need to.

God, she hated this side of him. So cool, detached. She'd rather have him cursing at her with pain in his eyes—at least his passion would be visible; she'd know he cared.

"Are you sure it's not the same problem as the *pavens* in my *credenti*?" she asked. "It's one thing to play with a Mondrar cunt, it's another to give your desire, your seed, *yourself* to one."

His lip curled and his fangs dropped. "That's far more insulting to you than it is to me, Kate."

"I'm just looking for honesty."

He sniffed, a barely recognizable chuckle. "No, sweet one, I don't think you are."

"What the hell does that mean?"

"You lie to me, as I lie to you." He walked over and kissed her on the cheek. "We are both comfortable in that fact, it seems."

Stunned at his words, at the truth that registered within them, Kate watched him walk out the door. She hated what he'd said to her, yet she knew he was right. He was her true mate, his body craved her to the point of pain—and yet she wouldn't tell him the truth.

A fire erupted within her, beneath the smooth skin of her mark. She ripped off the blanket and the white cotton robe, tossed them on the floor, and once again lay there naked atop the mattress.

23

Nicholas entered his bedroom and headed straight for the bathroom, tearing off his clothes as he went. Cranking on the water in the shower, he drilled it all the way from hot to blistering and stepped inside. He had only minutes before he was due in the tunnels, the first step of his plan ready to be executed, but right now his cock needed relief. It was still painfully hard, the head swollen and purple, and pissed it hadn't met the sweet, tight wetness of the *veana* it craved.

Blame me, motherfucker. Blame the whore you're attached to.

He grabbed his prick roughly and started pumping himself. He'd been wrong. So wrong . . . He could've fucked Kate for hours, his dick hard and thick without any currency needed.

So what was the problem? Why didn't he bury himself inside her like he wanted to? Ball-deep like he wanted to. It had nothing to do with her being a *virgini*—he didn't care about that, only in the sense of going easy and gentle until she begged him not to.

It wasn't her.

It was him.

He squeezed his shaft, using the water as lubricant because nothing was coming out of the head. He felt nothing, no desire, no desire for pleasure, and yet he kept beating himself off, determined to break down the rod of pain he'd created.

He tried to picture Kate on her knees, his cock in her mouth, her eyes on him, but it was no use. His sack didn't hum with the feelings of precum. He was dry as a blood whore at dawn.

Releasing his prick, he leaned against the wall of the shower and let the water pummel his back and ass. For years he'd told himself that he could never be with someone simply out of desire or care, or love, because the whore in him wouldn't allow it. But that was a lie he'd obviously needed to tell himself to continue breathing, functioning. Truth was, he didn't deserve anyone. He was a whore for life—a *sacro witte.*

Dirty animal.

Truth was, Kate Everborne was pure and good and, though he hadn't seen his mark on her skin, may very well be his true mate. But his dirty used-up cock didn't belong anywhere near her.

In Mondrar, Kate had survived by keeping her mind from the ugly and from the things she couldn't change. She kept her eyes down, her nose clean, and didn't rely on the buddy system that some inmates found essential.

But there were the occasional times when things got so bad, when she'd felt so desperate to vent her fear or her frustration over something that she'd reached out to a bunkmate or the criminal in the cell next to hers.

It was how she'd met Cambridge.

And though the redheaded Eye wasn't Dear Abby, he, at the very least, understood life on the inside of those dank stone walls. He could relate to her loneliness, her suffering, and her fear.

And sometimes, Kate thought as she walked through the dark and silent living room of the Romans' house, that was enough to get you through another day.

Hearing the soft muffled sound of voices in the distance, Kate let herself be drawn toward it. It was one of those nights and she was hoping to find her fellow inmate, who unlike her was only too happy to live in captivity.

She found the female in a smallish room off the library, snuggled up on the couch, watching TV. "Hey."

Sara glanced over her shoulder and though she looked surprised to see Kate, she smiled. "Hey there."

"Busy?"

She shook her head, motioned for Kate to sit down next to her. "Just trying not to worry about my brother."

"He hasn't called?"

"Hasn't called, hasn't checked in. No doubt he's barricaded himself in a room with some female somewhere . . ." She shook her head. "Instead of my fangs popping out of my mouth every time I think about it, I decided to chill out and watch a movie."

"Sounds like a good self-preservation move. And I'm sure Gray will turn up." Kate dropped down on the couch. "Where's your mate tonight?"

"Still out. Until Ethan Dare is caught . . ." She shrugged. "You know the drill. I'm sure it's the same with Nicholas."

"I don't know actually," Kate said, releasing a breath she'd been holding since she'd left her room a few minutes ago. "I don't know what Nicholas's plans are, what he wants, what's going through his mind at all."

For a moment, Sara didn't say anything, just cocked her head to the side and did this sort of half smile. Then she thrust a metal bowl toward Kate and asked, "Do you like popcorn?"

Kate smiled. "I don't know, do I?"

"I think you might."

"Okay." She delved into the bowl and took a few of the pale kernels, popped them in her mouth. Living in the *credenti*, she was used to grains and seeds and so the sensation of the popped corn wasn't unusual to her tongue. She took her time chewing them, really tasting them.

"What do you think?" Sara asked, watching her with curious blue eyes.

"Different, not what I expected." She smiled. "But pretty good."

"I'm glad you tried it, because sometimes things that are different and unexpected, and very tasty, can throw you off if you don't give them the proper chance." She lifted one brown eyebrow. "Know what I mean, girlfriend?"

Kate laughed. *Smooth, Doc.* Still smiling, she shrugged. "Thing is, what if you gave the popcorn a chance, but it won't open up to you—won't be honest with you?"

"Are you being honest with him?" Sara asked, serious now, the popcorn subtext abandoned.

Kate didn't answer.

Sara sighed. "It's terrifying to lay yourself bare before someone you don't trust yet. Believe me."

Kate pulled her knees up to her chest. "I don't know if I'll ever be able to fully trust him."

"Do you want to?"

"That's like asking me if I want to trust anyone—ever. If it's even possible for me after being where I've been, you know?"

Sara didn't know actually, and didn't even attempt to ask. Instead, she said, "Then this really isn't about anyone but you, is it? Maybe you'd better ask yourself what you do want—"

"Freedom," Kate said without hesitation. "It's all I've ever wanted."

Sara nodded. "Okay. And what is freedom to you? Life without the Order? The *balas* upstairs? Love?"

"Love." Kate laughed.

Sara's brows knit together. "What?"

"I don't know. I guess I just can't even imagine it."

"What? Loving someone?"

Kate shook her head. "No. Someone loving me."

"Oh, my new friend." Sara just looked at her for a moment; then she tossed a bit of her blanket over Kate's legs and gestured to the large TV screen. "Have you ever seen this movie?"

"I've seen only one movie. I snuck out of the *credenti* once, on a Saturday afternoon."

"Oh wow. Of course."

"But I really liked it."

Sara smiled. "What was it about?"

"A boy and all of his toys. The toys came to life and they had all these silly adventures."

"Well, this one is completely different, and possibly a bit more relatable." Sara pointed to a pretty redhead on the screen who was lying in a bubble bath, her eyes closed, singing to herself. "This woman thinks she's not worthy of love—that what she was in her past defines who she is now, what she wants to be." A man came into the bathroom, proud-looking and handsome with lightly graying hair, and Sara said, "Him too, in fact. Last thing he wants to do is change his life."

"But what?" Kate asked with a thread of sarcasm. "He does, for her, and they live happily ever after?"

"I don't know," Sara said honestly. "You never know, do you? But their journey to true love is paved with insecurity, desire, misunderstanding, loyalty, and finally revealing themselves to each other—their true selves. After the credits roll, it's all up to them."

Kate nodded, smiled. "Should I be paying you for this, Doc?"

Sara laughed and placed the bowl between them.

"Just have some more popcorn while we watch the movie, *veana*. Gets better and better the more you try it."

Nicholas moved through the tunnels, his eyes sliding over the Impure guards stationed at several random junctures. Normally, as he walked the dark, frigid passageways lit every ten feet or so with torches he didn't even notice the Impure males he and his brothers had hired to live and work below the Manhattan streets. The males had left their *credentis* long ago after being blood castrated by the Order so they wouldn't pass on their weak half-breed genes, and had always remained to themselves, making contact with the Romans only when they came to collect their payment once per month.

Nicholas wondered about them now, wondered what they thought of themselves. They were incapable of becoming aroused, incapable of giving themselves to anyone. Were they ashamed of what had happened to them? Did they want to remain hidden in the tunnels, or did they yearn for companionship and love?

The tunnel widened in front of him and Nicholas made a sharp right down another length of passage, this one thinner and colder as he got closer to the exterior, where snow tended to collect.

Is that what Dare was after? he wondered. Was the uprising the brain child of Impures who were unsatisfied with the hidden and miserable lives they were leading? Or was it just Ethan Dare wreaking havoc, creating a reason to take what he wanted, kill whomever he wanted?

Nicholas left the guards behind and went to the very edge of the tunnels, where someone was waiting for him, his trash can stink in full bloom.

"Well, this is an honor." Whistler's beady eyes moved warily over Nicholas. "Being allowed within the Roman tunnels."

"I need something from you, Whistler."

"Really?"

"And I intend to pay you well for it."

Nicholas could do nothing about his feelings surrounding Kate, but his war with Ethan Dare still raged, and even in his misery he would protect his family.

Whistler's grin was as disturbing as his worn-down fangs. The Eye needed to lay off the *gravo*; every hit of that shit broke down enamel until it destroyed both the house and its hardware. "I am anxious to hear your offer."

"This is no offer, as you will not have the option of saying no."

"You are more hostile than usual, Son of the Breeding Male."

"Am I?" Nicholas eyeballed him. "Perhaps it has something to do with you opening your fetid piehole to Dare about my personal business."

Whistler blanched. "It was a mistake. And you and I did not have an agreement—"

"Cease!" Nicholas hissed, "before I take these ribbed

fangs you find so fascinating and drag them across your skinny neck."

The head member of the Eyes shuddered, but he found the will to nod. "What do I need to do?"

"Keep your mouth shut." Nicholas tossed a stack of clothes at him. "And put these on."

Dawn was breaking just as Alexander dipped into the subway, then hauled ass down the secret passage that led to the tunnels. After catching sight of two of Dare's recruits in the club he was watching he'd remained hidden instead of taking them on or attempting to strong-arm them for information. He'd thought if he could just wait them out, maybe they would lead him right to Dare.

And it had looked pretty good there for a while. He'd followed them for hours, into several clubs, then to what had seemed like the journey home. But somewhere on the Hudson's East Side they'd disappeared. It had been like a fucking magic act. There one moment, snow dropping on nothing but the grand mansions of Millionaires' Row the next.

Alexander took the secret staircase down into the beginnings of the Roman tunnels, so ready to see his *veana*, take her to bed for a few hours—more if she would allow him—then get to mapping out the Hudson area for tonight's recon. He was willing to bet that one of those river homes was Dare's new compound.

But a sound stopped him, froze him midflight.

Voices, a pair of them—and as he used the power of morpho to tune in to what was being said, he realized it was Nicholas standing there in the entrance to the tunnels. But Alexander couldn't make out whom his brother was talking to.

He palmed his Glock, but remained where he was, listening. It wouldn't do to get too close, have Nicholas scent out his presence if he was involved in something clandestine. Wasn't Alexander's style to mess with anything romantic the *paven* had going.

But the voices were distinctly male and what Alexander heard next was anything but romantic. It was Nicholas and that fucking piece of shit Eye from his past, and they were talking Dare and a sting op that was going down in Times Square at first dark.

Times Square? Was Nicholas serious? At first dark in one of the busiest spots in the city? Sounded insane, and completely ineffectual. Alexander was about to tackle all six steps in one leap and give his brother his opinion himself when he heard something that made his unbeating heart stutter.

"My brothers hear about this and I will use your blood to repave every street in lower Manhattan."

Fangs descending, Alexander pocketed his Glock and reversed course up the steps. What the hell was Nicholas trying to prove? He stood in the shadows near a pylon waiting for Whistler to scuttle past like the cockroach he was, and go up into the subway.

He would give his brother time to get back too.

Maybe rethink his fool plan, and Lucian and Alexander's part in it as he walked the frigid passageways.

From the shadow of the massive pylon, Alexander growled with irritation. The hours in bed with his mate would have to be skimmed down now. To one . . .

Maybe two.

24

"We're going to die."
  "I want to die."

Lying on his back, Gray's eyes were trained upward.
Again, he had been moved. This time to a hole in the
floor of the mansion Dare and his recruits had taken
over from some Hollywood actress who seemed to like
all things "fang." The pit he was in looked as though it
had been an indoor pool at some point. But now it was
dry and stank of bleach and mildew.

Above him, Ethan Dare circled the pit that held him
and the other seven captives, who were shooting off
pitiful little whines and thoughts every other second—
that is when they weren't praying for their masters to
come and get them.

"Do you think they give a shit about you?" Ethan
called down, his voice echoing off the stained white
walls. "Do you think that the Purebloods who held
you captive even know you're gone?"

"Yes."

"Yes."

Gray's head ached, the continual sound and manic voices were like a jackhammer in his brain now. But he forced himself to remain calm, remain lucid as he was moved around like an animal in a trap. He needed to find out where they were. He needed to listen to Dare and his recruits for any clue. Because if he got free, he could lead the Romans right to Dare's front door.

"Perhaps they do care," Ethan continued, chuckling to himself. "But only because their beds are not being made and their asses are not being wiped." He stopped then, glared down at them. "Is this all you are? A slave? Is it all you want to be?"

"I want to go home."

"Please. Please."

"Perhaps he's right, but . . . oh God."

"I offer you more," Dare shouted, his eyes traversing the oval space. "I offer you a new life, freedom. I offer—"

"You don't offer," Gray yelled back, his head pounding so hard he was pretty sure he was going to vomit. "You're just like their masters, Dare! You give them no choice."

"Oh God. Cease. Cease before he kills us all."

Ethan's gaze slid over to Gray.

"If I didn't have to use you . . . If that balas *didn't dictate my feeding schedule, I would run you through and toss your bleeding carcass out the front door and into the Hudson."*

Gray's limbs went light and hummed.

Hudson River . . .

"You will drink," Ethan said, continuing to walk the perimeter of the pit. "And you will join us in this fight."

"Fight?"

"No! No!"

"Feast, my brothers," Dare called, waving his arm over the empty pool.

In seconds, males and females jumped in, crash landing on the concrete and heading straight for their victims—all holding terrified looking *veanas* in their grasp.

"Purebloods."

Gray spotted Marina heading straight for him, dragging one helpless *veana*, while two males closed in around him.

"He looks scared."

"He looks hungry."

"He is mine."

"Fuck you," Gray said to Marina as she sidled up next to him.

But the female just smiled, grabbed the wrist of the *veana* in her arms, and tore open a vein.

"Time to feed, pet."

As the *veana* screamed, as every *veana* inside the pit screamed, Gray fought his bindings like an animal fighting his steel trap.

But it was no use.

In seconds, his head was forced back by the males, and the *veana*'s wrist was yanked over his mouth, and as her blood slithered down his throat, Gray stared into her tearstained eyes and wished to God he could answer the prayers she spoke reverently inside her head.

"Well?" Kate said as the credits rolled on the huge television screen above them. "What did you think?"

In the light of day, the Romans' house went dark, and it had become increasingly difficult for Kate to come up with new and fun ways to entertain the *balas*. But today she'd really hit it out of the park.

"I loved it!" Ladd exclaimed, his small body tucked into one of the corners of the couch in the small den off the living area.

"And the popcorn?" she asked.

He nodded and said dramatically, "A lot better than seeds."

Kate laughed softly. She hadn't meant for it to happen, but the kid was really growing on her. She supposed it was inevitable, but even in their strange, tragic circumstances, they had fallen into a very copacetic rhythm. Bedtime, playtime, meals.

As young as he was, Ladd needed blood only once a week, but he did require sustenance several times a day. His system was used to the diet of the *credenti*, and Kate had made sure he had everything he needed.

"Who was your favorite, Kate?" Ladd asked, his dark eyes bright and curious.

"Hmm, I think I like the cowboy best. What about you?"

"It's so hard to choose."

Kate laughed at the expression of exaggerated pain on his face. "Don't hurt yourself, kid."

He grinned. "All right. I will say Sid is my favorite."

"The mean one?" Kate asked incredulously.

His grin widened. "What? Maybe he's just misunderstood." He drew the word out, then shrugged. "That's what my teacher at school says about me."

Kate burst out laughing, even reached out and tickled the bottom of his feet. "You're nuts, you know that?"

He dissolved into laughter. "Yeah, I know."

"What's going on in here?" Nicholas walked in, eyed the two of them on the couch, and said in a stern voice, "Having a good time in this house in strictly forbidden, *balas.*"

Ladd's smile died and his eyes went silver dollar–wide as he stared up at the Pureblood *paven* whom he knew could be his father.

"He's kidding," Kate whispered to the boy, then turned to Nicholas. "Aren't you, big scary vampire?"

"No," Nicholas said, then flashed Ladd a quick, hard grin. "So what kind of illegal fun were you two having when I walked in?"

Kate rolled her eyes. "We were discussing our favorite characters in the first *Toy Story* movie."

"It's Sid, hands down," Nicholas said without hesitation—or being asked.

"No," Kate cried. "Not you, too."

Ladd started laughing again, and Kate couldn't help but follow.

Nicholas looked from one to the other. "What?"

"Nothing," Kate said, shaking her head. "Last night, Sara introduced me to movies and popcorn, and I'm passing on her genius to the boy here."

"Do you eat popcorn, Nicholas?" Ladd asked, jumping up, off the couch.

"Never had it."

"Me neither. Not until today." He grabbed the bowl with his small hands and thrust it toward the *paven*. "Try it. It's kind of like the rations at home."

Nicholas sneered at the contents of the bowl. "I am a Pureblood *paven*, *balas*, not a *credenti* rat who consumes—"

"Hey." Kate shot him a fierce look.

He grumbled. "Fine." He grabbed a handful of popcorn and shoved it in his mouth.

"So?" Ladd pressed, too excited to wait for Nicholas to swallow. "Is it good?"

"I will stick with blood."

Ladd nodded. "Me too."

Nicholas eyed the child, his intensity and ferocity easing a fraction. "However," he began, walking over to the television, "this movie you are watching—"

"It's over," Ladd said quickly.

Nicholas glanced over his shoulder. "It has a second part."

The boy gasped. "It does?"

"I'm sure Lucian left it in here." He thumbed through a large collection of DVDs before pulling one. "Ah-ha. Success."

"That's Lucian's movie?" Kate asked, her eyebrow drifting up.

"Yes."

She nodded. "Okay. Not at all weird."

Nicholas slipped the disk in the player and grabbed the remote.

As he came toward the couch, Kate looked up at him. "Aren't you supposed to be on the hunt?"

His face was unreadable, his eyes too, but his words said everything his expression did not. "When the sun is down, I go. Until then, I think we deserve to spend this time together." His eyes moved over Ladd, then her. "All three of us. Yes?"

Ladd nodded, then smiled. "I want to sit by you, Kate."

"As would I," Nicholas said, then before he dropped down beside her, raised a brow. "If that would be all right."

"Sit, *paven*," she said good-naturedly. "But no hogging the popcorn."

"Nothing to fear from me," Nicholas said, then added dryly, "But I'd watch the boy's hand, if I were you."

As Ladd giggled sweetly, Kate relaxed back in the center of the couch. She refused to give way to the feelings—the trappings of sentimentality and romance. It wasn't a family sitting together watching the second *Toy Story* movie, or a picture-perfect moment to revel in—the *veana*, the *paven*, and the *balas*. To be real, Ladd still thought about his mother's death every other second and Nicholas remained closed, his eyes heavy with a pain he wouldn't share and a burden he refused to unload. And Kate, well, she was caught somewhere between wanting to run from her past to a future she couldn't see, and fantasizing about an unpredictable now.

And then the boy tucked his small feet under her leg and Nicholas put his arm around her shoulders.

25

It was close to five o'clock when Nicholas descended into the tunnels and headed for the weapons hold. He'd left Kate and Ladd in the hall on their way to the kitchen for the boy's evening meal, but not without requesting that the two stay in their rooms after dark. It was a nearly impossible thing to suggest, especially without giving a reason, but that couldn't be helped. He didn't want them tooling around the house when his brothers returned from their recon tonight and starting asking questions—like why the "bait" wasn't out with her date.

Shit, the lies were really starting to pile up, he thought, rounding the corner, spotting Alexander, Lucian, and Dillon. What the hell was the bodyguard still doing here?

"Perfect timing, Nicky," Alexander said on a growl, grabbing two Glocks from the holder on the wall and settling them into the holster at his sides with a bit too much force. "Dillon was just telling us she might know where Gray is."

Nicholas walked up to the small group, his guts

constricting like a tire iron was around them. If the bodyguard knew that Gray was with Dare, Nicholas was good and fucked.

"Not where he is," Dillon corrected, leaning against the weapons cage, "but who he's with."

"Well?" Nicholas said, his tone heavy with irritation.

"Yeah, out with it, D," Lucian said, grabbing a box of bullets off the shelf. "One person in this tunnel's interested."

Alexander glared at his brother.

Lucian shrugged. "Hell, just speaking the truth."

"The bouncer at Equinox," Dillon began, "that's the club Gray's been hanging out in, saw him with an Impure female. Some chick named Marina."

"They leave together?" Alexander asked.

"The Pureblood thinks so. I tried to find out something from the Eyes, but nobody's talking." Dillon fingered a shiny black bowie knife. "I'm going back to the club tonight, to ask around about her and Gray."

Lucian snorted. "All we need's an address; then Alexander can go pick him up and bring him home for his nap and diaper change."

Alexander turned on the near-albino and backed him up against the dank wall. "Seriously, I'm going to knock you the hell out."

Lucian grinned. "Hell no you're not—it's nearing dusk. Time to go hunting." He flashed his fangs. "Hudson River, baby. I can't wait to see which McMansion Dare's hiding out in."

Pulling away from his younger brother, Alexander

turned to Nicholas. "That's where I tailed his recruits to last night. And where I lost them."

Nicholas didn't have time to feel relieved. He had a job to do, real delicate work. "Hand me two Bersa Thunders and a Diamondblade," he said to Lucian, his gaze steering clear of Alexander's. "While D's at Equinox and you two are checking things out near the river, I'll be doing the club bait thing. Second time's the charm, right?"

"Actually, that's three," Lucian said, grabbing the guns and the knife Nicholas asked for, while Alexander kept the conversation rolling with Nicholas. "We're stronger as a crew, Nicky."

"I agree," Nicholas said, his gaze on his weaponry. "And if you get Dare cornered, IM me. I'll be there in a flash. Literally."

"Is that really what you want?" Alexander asked him, forcing Nicholas's eyes up, on him.

"What does that mean?"

"Just asking you to think about the plan, your plan. Is it the right one? Is it good strategy?"

"Jesus, Alex," Lucian said, "what's with the third fucking degree? You sound like your true mate."

"Go back to handling those tiny bullets of yours, Luca," Alexander returned sharply, his gaze never leaving Nicholas's. "You sure you know what you're doing?"

It was impossible for Alexander to have known what was going down in a few hours in Times Square, but there was no denying he suspected something.

"No worries, *Duro*," Nicholas said easily. "I have a

feeling that tonight is the night I'll be bringing Ethan Dare's body back to the Order. Whatever's left of it."

Ethan walked through the sand toward the water, toward the two *pavens* staring out at the waves. How sweet, he mused. The Supreme One had a friend over to his reality—a dark lord playdate. Both dressed in white linen with straw hats that made them look, from the back at any rate, like retirees from Boca. The pair seemed deep in conversation.

Seated at a round table near a wedge of sea grass, Ethan's baby mama Pearl was absorbed in a platter of fried food and a tabloid, completely careless about the goings-on in front of her. Ethan rolled his eyes at the tragic sight. Granted he cared about the girl, but he needed a partner, and that was no Head Female of the Impure revolution sitting there with a chicken wing between her teeth. She was only a human, a vampire wannabe—an *Imiti*—and after she gave birth Ethan was going to have to return her sweet ass to the world she'd come from.

He neared the Supreme One and his guest. The news that he was on his way to get the *balas* would be sure to please, and perhaps win him a much-needed feed. Granted, Ethan would have to fabricate how he'd managed to get Nicholas Roman to agree to the drop, but he was a very skilled liar.

Nicholas Roman's face flashed before him. The face of an utterly destroyed *paven*. It was a welcome sight to an Impure, and yet there was a small part of Ethan that felt for the Son of the Breeding Male—a deeply concealed part of him that understood the ugly and destructive trappings of a past, of a *balashood* you couldn't control or change.

Unfortunately for Nicholas Roman, Ethan never allowed even the smallest hint of empathy to guide his actions.

The *paven* beside the Supreme One glanced back at Ethan as he approached. At first, Ethan thought the male was a member of the Order, but this *paven* was like no vampire male he'd ever seen. The male was terrifying to look at, eyes like twin diamonds, with no soul or life behind them, and where his hands were supposed to be, the claws of a beast resided.

"We will discuss this at another time, Erion," the Supreme One said softly against the sound of the waves.

The beast bowed and uttered a gruff, "Yes, Cruen," before flashing in a small tornado of seawater.

Ethan froze, his boots anchored in the pale sand. The Supreme One never allowed that name to be uttered in his reality. There wasn't a moment when Ethan even thought about who the *paven* who'd become his partner, his meal ticket, truly was—it was far safer that way. To Ethan, he was the master, the lord, the Supreme One.

But to the rest of the vampire world, he was Cruen, one of the ancient ten.

One of the Eternal Order.

Ethan proceeded forward with far more caution than when he'd entered the reality moments ago.

26

The sun had just kissed the horizon when Nicholas exited the tunnels and headed for the subway. He was going tourist, all the way. Drawing any kind of attention to himself was not the intent of this meet and drop. Not yet anyway. Besides, he had Whistler with him. The ugly-ass Eye was dressed as a female in a heavy coat, hat, scarf, gloves, and a towel hidden around his middle that carried the delectable Pureblood scent of Kate Everborne.

They headed down Broadway into the 24-7 hustle of the city's epicenter, the streets thick with human cattle and blaring billboards. Nicholas kept his eyes peeled for Dare, who could be anyone from a scalper hocking theater tickets to one of the crazy fans crowding around that nearly naked cowboy and his guitar.

"Your Ethan Dare is clever," Whistler said, pushing a stroller that looked like a bundled-up child sat inside—Ladd's scent all over it. "A very pointed spot, don't you think?"

"I don't know what you're talking about," Nicholas

said, his gaze sliding over to a group of males outside the Virgin store.

"Ah, yes, you and your brothers came to Manhattan after the Depression." Whistler glanced around. "This place, it's all neon and tourists now, but back in the nineteenth century it was packed with thieves and prostitutes. Longacre Square it was called then—a very profitable time for the Eyes."

Nicholas didn't give a shit what the Impure's reason was for choosing this spot. All he wanted was to get Dare in his sights and Gray back home to his sister.

The gun hummed at his back, ready to be fisted and fired. It was going to take some fancy maneuvering to get Gray and bring Dare down within a crowd—all before the gifted Impure realized Nicholas hadn't brought along the boy and the *veana*.

"Got any change?"

Nicholas whirled on the voice, his hand reaching for the soft flesh of a neck before he even saw who it was.

The panhandler looked up at him with terrified eyes.

Nicholas patted him on the shoulder. "Sorry. Nothing today, brother." Then moved on.

They were nearing the barricades when a car slowed down beside them. Over the din, a male voice shouted out, "The *veana* and the boy come with me."

Nicholas's hand was already fisted around the gun at his back. Under the bright neon lights, he stared into the interior of the town car as hundreds of tourists milled passed. There was a driver, who was probably a recruit, but no Dare.

Nicholas shook his head at the Impure. *Not going to happen*.

"Bring them now, whore," the male called out.

"You're blocking traffic, dickhead," some human male said, tapping the car door as he walked by.

With a crack, Ethan Dare flashed into the backseat of the town car. The window slowly descended. Dare grinned out at Nicholas. "Is there a problem, Son of the Breeding Male? This was our agreement."

Nicholas felt Whistler stiffen at his side. The Eye better be head and eyes down. "Where's Gray?" Nicholas called out.

Dare leaned back, just enough so Nicholas could see the blond male beside him. Gray was gagged and seemingly immobile, but his eyes were solid and strong and trained on Nicholas.

"You want them," Nicholas shouted, "you come get them."

He grabbed Whistler's arm and steered him into the very center of Times Square, the triangle. There he waited.

It took Dare a moment, but he finally got out of the car and walked through the masses of people, nice and slow until he was about ten feet away. There he stopped, his eyes even with Nicholas like they were two gunslingers about to go at it.

But both of them knew there could be no shoot-'em-ups there—not unless they were close enough to do it without being seen. And at ten feet the risk was too great.

"Time's wasting in Times Square," Dare called, his eyes lit up like the billboards around him.

"What about the male?" Nicholas said, his gaze shifting to Gray. "There's no trade without him."

"He will be released the moment I have the *balas* and *veana*."

What a crock of shit, Nicholas thought. Dare wasn't going to release anything—least of all Gray.

Nicholas stilled, stared, narrowed his eyes on the male inside the car. Gray had nodded his head—he was sure of it. The Impure had nodded his head. What the hell did that mean? Was he drugged, sick? Had Dare—

Gray shook his head. A small movement, but Nicholas saw it.

Holy shit! Could the male hear inside Nicholas's head?

Gray's nod came quicker this time.

It was a rare Impure—

"It's now or never, Roman," Dare called, snatching back Nicholas's attention.

"Come and get them," Nicholas returned with a grin, his brain running a mile a minute as he attempted to hatch an escape plan for Gray. "Don't worry, I won't bite."

"But I might."

Dare took two steps closer, all confidence and intrigue, then stopped. His gaze had caught on something to Nicholas's right. Suddenly, he growled, his eyes flashing. "You stupid *witte*!"

Nicholas didn't even have to turn his head. He scented them, coming closer, completing the triangle within the triangle. Dare at one point, Nicholas at another, Alexander and Lucian at the third.

"If you can get out now, Gray, do it!" Nicholas silently urged the Impure.

As crowds moved around them, not hearing or caring what was going down between them, the four vampires stood only ten feet apart, each waiting for someone to make a move.

"Get out of here, go home," Nicholas called over the madness as all around them the energy of the Square bubbled and brewed.

Alexander, whose expression exposed both his confusion and his ire, spotted the stroller and called out, "What the hell are you doing?"

"What I was enlisted to do," Nicholas said. "Now, get out of here."

"This would be the time to hand over the *balas* and *veana*," Dare called over a group of four female tourists who were weighed down with shopping bags.

"Yes, give Whistler over to him, Nicky," Lucian said loudly. "Might as well make him happy; it's the last night of his life."

"Whistler." The sound came out of Dare's throat like air rushing from a balloon. He narrowed his gaze on the supposed female beside Nicholas. Rage glittered in his dark eyes as he realized he'd been duped. "Nice to see you, Whistler," he said. "Helping out an old friend tonight, are you? Or is this a barter for services rendered?"

"Shut your mouth, Impure!" Nicholas shouted.

"Or was it a freebie?" Dare continued. "He looks good on his knees, doesn't he?"

Lucian growled. "I'm starting to not care where we are."

Nicholas felt as though his entire existence was about to be extinguished. "Leave now," he nearly screamed at his brothers.

"No," Dare called, his expression a mask of pleasured hate. "Please stay. Hear all about how your brother spends his time."

"Shut it, you fucking bastard," Nicholas yelled.

Dare laughed. "The illustrious Nicholas Roman is a whore. Did you know that?"

Alexander grinned. "Old news. Way old."

"No," Dare said harshly. "Not just in the past. Now. Nearly once a month for as long as you've been in New York."

"You are a sack of shit, Dare," Lucian called out. "A lying sack of rotting shit."

"Ask him. Ask Whistler. He can tell you everything you need to know." He grinned as the Eye removed the hood that covered his head. "Hell, he might even be able to get you in touch with the couple who hired his talented cock last week."

Nicholas felt his brothers' eyes on him. They wanted the go-ahead to close in, take Dare down, flash him away and cut him into pieces behind the alley of their house—and shit, under all this raging neon the tourists wouldn't notice a thing. But Nicholas had died inside, self-hate and pity keeping him unresponsive, his eyes still trained on Dare.

He flashed from the triangle and landed directly be-

side the town car. Gun cocked and ready, he shot the
driver in the head, yanked Gray from the car, and flashed
out of his living nightmare and out of Times Square.

Nice, France
1909

*Nicholas had no blood left in his body. It had run from his
veins and from the cuts on his head, nose, shoulders, and
knees into the sewer grates outside his flat. He lay against
the hard ground and told himself that if he survived this
he was done with the life of a blood seller, a cock seller. At
twenty-five, he could start over, claim a new life—find a passion other than gravo.*

*Above him stood the angel in white, the one who had
come to his aid, taken down the males who had cornered and
beat him.*

"Who are you?" Nicholas uttered hoarsely.

"My name is Lucian," said the angel. "I am your brother."

*Nicholas could barely breathe, much less understand.
"My mother's balas—"*

"No, no. A Son of the Breeding Male."

*"No," Nicholas said, lifting his head. "My father was a
putan, just as my mother was—just as I am."*

"We need to go now. I'm going to lift you."

*Nicholas felt arms underneath his knees and back, but he
was so tired, so limp. "How did you find me?"*

*"My mother. She knew each of the veanas who laid with
our father."*

"Where are you taking me?"

"Away. There is another like us, in America."

As the paven *walked the darkened streets of what was once Nicholas's home, he kept his eyes moving.*

"I owe you my life, Brother," Nicholas rasped as he slowly dropped into unconsciousness, never hearing the paven's *final words.*

"You owe me nothing, Duro."

Stay in her room for the night?

Kate zipped the fly of her new jeans and threw on a sweater. He had to be kidding. While he was out with his brothers hunting Ethan Dare, she was just supposed to what? Hang out in her room and stare at the skyline?

Not going to happen.

She had things to do too, and the first was getting in contact with Cambridge.

She left her room and went down the hall. Despite her own choice with regards to remaining indoors, she was all for keeping Ladd inside and safe. She did a quick check on him, and after she found him sleeping, she went downstairs to look for Evans. She knew she took a risk in telling the servant that she was going out for a while, but he needed to listen for Ladd, and hell, the *balas*'s welfare always seemed to come before her own these days. No point in changing that now.

She was on her way to the kitchen when the sound of a loud bang outside the back door of the building stopped her. She was about to turn around and head back to the stairs when two tall, fierce-looking *paven* crashed through the door. They were carrying something in their arms, cursing and arguing with each other all the way down the hall.

"How the hell did Dare get his hands on him?"

"Shit, Alex, all he had to do was walk into a bar and take him. Gray's a newly hatched Impure with minimal fighting skills—and a stupid brain to boot."

"Shut up, Luca, I mean it."

"The truth's not pain-free, Brother. We saw that tonight."

They stopped talking when they noticed Kate, who was staring at the male passed out in Alexander's arms. "What happened to him?"

Alexander sneered. "He was dropped off at our back door."

"Dropped off? What? By who?"

"What do you care?" Lucian practically barked at her.

Before Kate could say a word, Evans rushed in with one of the Impure guards. "Sir, shall I call for the doctor?"

"He's not hurt," Alexander said without feeling. "Just put him in his room." His eyes went bloodred. "And don't say a thing to my mate, understand? I will be the one to tell her of this."

Evans nodded sagely; then he and an Impure guard eased Gray from Alexander's grasp and took him away.

Kate stood there in her coat and gloves and tried not to draw too much attention to herself, but it wasn't easy. What did she do now? Move forward or back?

"It's not a good night for a walk, *veana*," Alexander said, his eyes on her winter gear.

Though her insides trembled with nervous energy, Kate kept her chin up and her eyes cool. "I'll see for myself."

"Don't think Nicholas wants you to go anywhere."

"What do we care what Nicholas wants?" Lucian bit out, his almond eyes flaring with hostility.

Alexander shot him a glare. "You need to chill the fuck out."

"Where is Nicholas?" Kate asked, knowing it wasn't the brightest idea to get in the middle of these two, but after the thing with Gray, she was getting concerned.

Eyes narrowed, Lucian sidled up to her, got right in her air space. "None of your fucking business."

"Back off, Luca," Alexander warned.

"Sounds like a plan," Kate uttered tightly.

Lucian didn't move. "Scared of me, are you, little *credenti* rat?"

"Shut it, Lucian—" Alexander began.

"Of the Pureblood Son of a Breeding Male who has *Toy Story* on DVD?" Kate returned hotly, unthinkingly. "I don't know. Should I be?"

For a moment, Kate wondered if she'd gone too far. Lucian really was a terrifying creature. He towered above her, truly aggressive in manner, his nostrils flaring, eyes narrowed into deathly little slits. But then a slow smile began to tug at his full mouth, and he backed off, shrugged. "Gotta love that Sid."

Kate released a breath. Jesus . . .

"Go run off your anger in the tunnels, Luca," Alexander said. "Meet me in the library in an hour."

Lucian slid his gaze back to Alexander and gave him a sardonic smile. "Sure, why not. Running my vampire ass off in the freezing fucking tunnels should wipe out everything that happened tonight, right?"

He strode from the room, and when he was out of earshot, Alexander turned his attention on Kate. "You really don't want to get into it with him. He has a difficult time controlling his anger. You were very lucky."

She shrugged. "Or very funny."

For a moment, Alexander said nothing. Then he snorted. "I see why my brother is taken with you."

"What's going on, Alexander? Where is he?"

"Don't know."

"Are you going to go look for him?"

He seemed to weigh his words. "It will be discussed."

Kate watched the Pureblood's body language, his expression. Something had happened. Something bad enough that the eldest Roman brother couldn't even look her in the eye when he'd denied it. "Is he in trouble?"

Alexander laughed. But it wasn't a happy sound. It was bitter and disappointed. "He had a bullshit sting set up with Dare. Had a deal to give you and Ladd over to the Impure in exchange for Gray, and for keeping what he knew about Nicky from me and Lucian."

Kate's skin began to heat up, her mark—his mark— going from warm to red hot in under a second. "What does he know about Nicholas?"

Alexander's upper lip twitched, displaying an impressive set of fangs.

"Tell me," Kate urged. "Please."

"Tell her," Sara said, walking into the hall, her coat on over her lab scrubs. She must've come in the back door without them noticing.

Alexander reached for her at once, curling her into his side as though their bodies belonged together. He had something to tell her, something he knew would hurt her. But not yet, not now. He gestured in Kate's direction. "She is nothing to this family, my love."

"She is everything to him," Sara said, her blue eyes resting on Kate's concerned brown ones. "She is the one."

It was as if the moment stole Kate's breath from her lungs. Nothing going in, nothing being released. How? The female knew. Had Kate been that transparent the other night?

"The one what?" Alexander said brusquely.

Sara looked up at her mate and smiled. "The *veana* who found a *paven* resting against the door to her apartment at dawn."

Alexander's expression changed instantly from rigid to calm, from worried to hopeful. "You're certain?"

Sara nodded.

"If you use this against him in any way but for care," Alexander said, turning back to Kate, "I will kill you myself."

Kate swallowed, her breath returning, her lungs filling. "Understood. Now, please, tell me."

As Alexander stood in the hallway, arm around the waist of his true mate, he told Kate the history of her own mate. It was difficult to hear, and yet oddly satisfying because now she understood why he was who he was.

She didn't say a word until Alexander was done; then she grabbed her scarf off the kitchen counter and said, "I'm going to look for him."

"This is a massive city," Alexander said tightly. "There's no way you'll ever find him."

"Yes, I will." She didn't know what made her do it, and no doubt she was going to regret it as soon as she left the house. But Alexander had told her when he didn't have to, and Sara had befriended her, believed in her when she'd needed it most. Kate figured she owed them something.

With her eyes on Alexander, she lifted up her sweater and inched down the right cup of her cotton bra.

27

He needed to fuck.

Hard, deep, and preferably from behind.

The promise of currency did that to him.

Nicholas ran his tongue over one distended canine as he entered the club. Ribbed for pleasure. A mutation gifted by his father, the dual sensations of heat and vibration when sunk between a customer's thighs had always granted him extra funds when he'd worked the streets as a *balas*.

Now it was his calling card.

Metro wasn't the hottest club in town or the hippest, but it had plenty of dark corners, bathrooms that were rarely used for their proper purpose, and a lackluster room upstairs for minor celebrities and their catalog model companions. Nicholas had been there a few times in the past year, and he knew the lay of the land—and the land knew him.

He had decided to lay off the tricks until Dare's capture, but after what had just gone down in Times Square, what was the point? He could manage both. In fact, a good green fuck might be just the thing to center him, get his focus back—get him amped up to kill.

Because, if it was the last thing he ever did, Dare was going to lose his life, his ability to breathe—his everything.

Just as Nicholas had.

His nostrils flared at the scent of a female with an appetite to match his own. With one glance at the bartender, Nicholas knew this was his trick and treat. Dark hair and eyes to match, she hovered near the bar, her drink nearly gone. She was new to him—but the moment his gaze locked on hers, he knew she had either heard about him or seen him in action.

When he walked over to her, stood over her, she looked up at him and moistened her red lips. She was a nervous creature, human and somewhere in her late twenties—but Nicholas could see the raw excitement in her eyes, scent the wetness already glistening between her legs.

He loved it—loved that he felt nothing but revulsion for her. That was how his cock did its best work.

"What do you need tonight, *mon truc*?" he asked, the French slang for "trick" sliding off his tongue as though he were right back in the dilapidated flat in Nice.

"You," she returned breathlessly.

Nicholas grinned. The word was simple enough, but the sound, the tone, belied her need. Nicholas knew that sound . . . Desperate, hungry. Ready to pay to play. And she would—for his rates were steep. Granted, he didn't need the money anymore, didn't need to make sure his ailing and aging mother was taken care of or that she had her day's supply of *gravo*—but the sickness inside of him demanded he always receive payment for his services.

"I need you inside me," she whispered. Then she grinned. "I need you to be rough, yes? I need you to slap my ass, my face, my tits." Her grin widened, her eyes belying just a hint of embarrassment. "I need you to call me a dirty little whore."

Ah. God, yes. There it was.

Perfection.

And maybe if he screwed her blind, she would return the favor.

"I think you need this first," she said, opening her way-too-precious flower-shaped purse. His eyes moved over the ten one-hundred-dollar bills sitting inside.

Come on, now. You know you want it. You know you like it. His cock stirred. *That's right. Do what you're supposed to do, motherfucker—all you're good for.*

Her dark eyes glistened with anticipation. "If this works out well, I'm going to bring my husband next time." She grinned. "He needs his ass spanked, too."

"I am here to serve," Nicholas said smoothly. Any and all. It mattered not.

He was about to take the female's hand when the scent of home and concern and life-giving blood suddenly hit him like a baseball bat to the nostrils.

Shit, no.

Not here.

Not now.

Goddamn her. He fought the urge to turn around, spy her at the door to the club. She had no business coming here. He didn't want her here, didn't want her bringing that part of his existence anywhere near him right now.

But the scent grew stronger, deeper, until it was so intense it forced him to look or be suffocated.

Fuck me.

She was already inside the club, dressed in jeans and a sweater, her coat over her arm—the complete opposite of the female behind him. To anyone in Metro that night, Kate Everborne was as nonsexual as it got. But to Nicholas, she was the most beautiful, most desirable creature that had ever walked the earth. And he had walked it longer than most.

Kate's large brown eyes spotted him then, and she offered him a small smile—a sad smile. Not exactly pity, but close.

His guts twisted, and he wanted to stab something— the bar, himself . . .

She knew.

And his brothers were going to pay.

"I'm waiting here," came the irritated voice of the female who had been—this close—to hiring his cock for an hour.

Nicholas turned and flattened her with a dark glare. "You will wait."

Her eyes widened, both frightened and turned on by his blunt command. He didn't even wait for her nod, knew she would remain affixed to the barstool all night if that's what it took to get pounded both in body and in soul.

Kate stood near the exit sign, red light bathing her like ethereal blood, and Nicholas wondered if he recalled their last time beneath a sign that glowed red.

His eyes moved over her, every inch as he approached. "What are you doing here, Kate?"

"Looking for you."

He despised how much he loved hearing that. "How did you find me?"

"Our blood is bonded, Nicholas. It will always lead me to you, whether you want me or not."

She had no idea how badly he wanted her. "You aren't supposed to be out."

She looked past him, to the female at the bar. "Looks like we're all doing things we shouldn't tonight."

"Go home, *veana*."

"Come home, Nicholas."

He shook his head. "Not tonight."

"Why? So you can screw that skank at the bar? Seriously? She's wearing a wedding ring, for Christ's sake."

"Not my problem."

"What does she want you to do to her? Fur handcuffs and a pole to get up that tight ass of hers?"

"I have a pole."

"I know," she countered. "I had it in my mouth last night."

Nicholas's cock went north—instantly. "Shit, Kate. What are you doing to me?"

"Trying to wake you up, jackass. This isn't your life—doesn't have to be your life."

"You know nothing about my life."

"Not true. I know enough. And as a fellow sufferer of the past, I know it's damn hard to crawl out of the gutter, even if you want to. It's cold and it smells like shit, but it's familiar and sadly comforting, right?"

"You need to leave."

Her expression went tight, resolute. "I have money. Is that what it'll take? To get you away from her, from here." She grabbed a stack of twenties from her back pocket and shoved them against his chest. "It's all I've got, but it's yours."

"I'm not leaving."

Her eyes blazed into him. "Then fuck *me*. Take *me*."

"Stop it."

She grabbed his shirt, fisted the material. "If it's all about money for sex, then what does it matter whose hole you're in?"

Nicholas grabbed her arm and yanked her back into the dark hallway that led to nothing, nowhere—just like them. "You sound ugly."

"This is ugly." She pushed him away. "All of it."

He spun her around to face the wall, unbuttoned her jeans, yanked down the zipper. "This what you want?"

"For a start," she returned harshly, her cheek pressed

against the cool black wall. "Tell me what you have to offer me besides rough hands."

He hissed, his fangs dropping. "Nine and a half inches, *veana*," he said, yanking her jeans down to her ankles, then unzipping his fly, letting his prick loose. "It would fill your hand nicely, as it did your mouth."

"Would it fill my cunt?"

His cock wept for her because his eyes could not.

He kicked her legs as far apart as the denim would allow. He thought about the twenties, all over the floor of the bar. He thought about her face, her eyes.

"I paid you," she said sharply over her shoulder. "I paid for a fuck and I want it."

It was a gut reaction, one built out of decades of work for hire. He yanked her hips back and entered her in one hard thrust.

She cried out, her nails digging into the dirty club walls.

Nicholas froze inside her, in her hot, wet, insanely tight virgin cunt. It was Kate. Kate, who cared for the *balas*, who had risked her life, her freedom. Kate, who was trying to save him right now, even as he tried to take her back down into the gutter with him.

He hated himself, despised every inch of his skin, the steeled prick inside her. His hands gripped her hips, dug in as he fought his need to thrust. "You are something else," he uttered. "You deserve something else—something clean."

"That's bullshit," she said on a moan, breathing

heavy as her body stretched to accommodate him. "And you know it."

"It shouldn't be here. Not here."

"Yes." She started to move, rocking her hips back and forth slowly. "Yes, it should. Here. Now. Anywhere. Doesn't matter as long as you're in me."

"Kate." The blinding pain of pleasure nearly ended him.

"Fuck me! Now!"

His mind shut down and he pounded into her, gripping her hips as she held up the wall. People could've walked by, seen them—hell, watched them— and he wouldn't have noticed or cared. This was his home. Right here. Her cunt, her body, her voice, her unfathomable, unrequited care for him. It's where he belonged.

He heard her breath hitch, her quick rhythmic moans. She was so tight, impossibly, deliciously tight, and he entered her with quick, short thrusts. He knew he must be hurting her, and yet her body, the way it moved beneath his, the constant rain of her desire against his shaft, screamed otherwise.

"Oh God," she uttered. "I can't hold . . ." Her chest jerked, her hips too, and her arms shook.

Suddenly, the walls of her cunt contracted, fisted him so tightly his fangs dropped and he growled. He was going to come inside her—defile her with the flood of his despicable life.

He started to ease back.

"Don't you dare," she uttered hoarsely. "I paid for a full fuck. Your cock in me, your cum in me."

Shit. Never in his life did he want to come inside someone so desperately—mark her, brand her.

He pounded into her, wild and untamed. And she met him, thrust for thrust. She cried out, her muscles clenching, bathing him in her juices until he couldn't contain it any longer. He slid all the way in, deep as her body allowed, then thrust his hips upward. He came hard, growling like a rutting animal, and Kate held still and tight around him.

In the dark hallway of a club she didn't even know the name of, Kate breathed her way back to sanity. Though she didn't really want to get there anytime soon. The feeling of Nicholas inside her was harmony and bliss, perfection and peace. And regardless of the way they'd gotten there, she now understood the chemical connection of a true mate. After that initial thrust, after her body had registered him, his size, it was as though they'd been making love forever. No pain, no soreness—just extraordinary pleasure. Their bodies were literally made for each other.

Nicholas slipped out of her and gently turned her to face him, drew her pants up. It was relatively dark in the back, in the shadows of the club, but a streak of red light from the exit sign lit their faces weakly.

Their mouths were so close, nearly touching, and Kate felt his breath mingle with hers, felt the apology that was close to coming. She didn't want it—didn't need it.

She tilted her head to the side, stretching her neck. "Do you still want to know about these?"

His gaze slid over the slash marks. "What I want is to run my knife across the throat of every *Similis* guard who did this to you."

"It wasn't the guards. It was the Order." She took a breath. "Once a year, I would wake up to the most intense pain, another mark being seared into my skin as I lay there helpless on my mattress." She reached out and touched his brands with the pad of her thumb. "Similar process to these, I'd imagine."

He growled, low and feral.

"Ten marks for ten years," she said, keeping a close eye on his expression. "Ten years for murder."

He looked at her for a moment, then leaned in and kissed the marks on her neck. Ten kisses, soft and wet and sweet.

Kate closed her eyes and inhaled. God, if this could only work. Them. Her and him. If she could just give up her perception of what freedom needed to be, and he could come to believe he was more than a cock for hire, maybe they could have something.

"As you know, gifts can be given when a Pureblood needs them most. That could be at birth or death or anywhere in between," she said softly, leaning against him, her chin on his shoulder, her eyes on the wall. "My father gained his after he mated my mother. And it was a good one. He could change the emotions of anyone around him—anyone but the Order, of course." She sighed. "He always said he loved my mother more than anything in the world and he just wanted that same love in return. Supposedly when his gift had first surfaced he'd tried to change my mother's emotions into a deeper love for him. You know, amp them up. And I guess for a time that worked. But soon he grew insecure. He thought my mother was unhappy with him and her life—he thought she was hot for the Impure who worked our fields. He thought they'd slept together."

"They had not," Nicholas said gently.

"No. My mother was a fricking saint. But it didn't matter." She sniffed, shook her head. "He got rid of the Impure and soon after, whenever my mother would piss him off, which seemed like all the time to me, he'd use his gift on her—really fucked with her mind, took away every bit of happiness she had inside her and forced her into days of nothing but despair."

Kate felt Nicholas's hands on her back, his fingers brushing her, petting her softly.

She looked straight ahead, seeing nothing. "It was the most god-awful thing to watch. I almost wish he'd used his fist instead. He may have blackened her eyes, but at least he wouldn't have robbed her of every shred of hope."

Nicholas's hands were on her shoulders now, easing her back so he could see her and she could see him.

"My mother tried to kill herself once," she said. "But she failed, and my father made her pay for trying to leave him. He lost his mind one night, sending images into her head so fast she couldn't even process them much less react to them. It was total emotional overload. One moment she was on the floor, her hands over her head, the next she was in the kitchen grabbing a knife. She stabbed him until he stopped, until the pain in her head stopped."

There were no tears as she spoke—Kate could never manage tears, even seeing the whole thing again in her mind. But in that moment, with Nicholas's gaze so intent on hers, she wished she could produce something to ease the tension within her.

"She'd been through too much," Kate said, shrugging like a child. "She would've never been able to live through Mondrar, so—"

"You said it was you," Nicholas finished, his black eyes raw with understanding.

"Yeah."

"Oh God, Kate. You must regret that every day of your life."

"Never," she said passionately. "Not once."

"And your mother? Where is she now?"

"She went onto the afterworld a few years ago. But she lived in peace after that horrible day."

Nicholas's hands came up, touched her face, her nose, her eyes. "Kate, listen—"

"You don't have to tell me anything, promise me anything," she said quickly. "That's not why I told you."

He brushed his thumb across her lip. "Why did you?"

"I just wanted you to know that I understand." She

lifted a brow. "I want you to know that I feel dirty too. Used up. Unworthy of anything good. After what I've been through, seen . . . But it's not the truth of what I am."

He smiled and pulled away from her. "You've done nothing wrong, only saved someone else from more hell."

"So have you."

"At one time that was true, but . . ."

As she watched him right his shirt and zip his fly, she realized that she wasn't going to convince him of anything. His worth as a *paven* wouldn't come out of her assurances or attempts at mutual understanding. He was comfortable in his beliefs.

"Come." He took her hand and led her out of the shadows and into the electric lights of the club.

"Where are we going?"

"I'm going to take you home."

She lifted her chin. "What about, Miz Bar Back over there?"

He didn't even glance in the woman's direction. "I'm out of service."

"For tonight?"

He smiled that half smile of his, that impossible-to-read smile, and said, "Let's go, my dear," then ushered her out of the club and into the night.

28

Ethan stood before his master, ready to take his medicine. Or rather, to not. He was getting no blood meal today.

"The *balas* remains with the Romans," Cruen hissed, his pale blue eyes changing color to match the stormy sea behind him. Wearing white robes and standing knee-deep in water, he was trying way too hard to channel Jesus. "You disappoint me once again."

"Displeasing you is never my intent, my lord," Ethan said tightly. "I live to serve."

"Yourself," Cruen said, his lip curled into a sneer. "Let's not play games anymore. I grow weary."

"Whatever you wish, my lord," Ethan said, his eyes searching the beach for Pearl, finding her several yards down, on a raft, floating in the water.

Things were growing uneasy in this little world with this uncontained, ancient powerhouse. He needed to get his human, his *balas* off this plane soon before there was trouble, an implosion of some kind.

"You placate me for blood," Cruen continued, "just

as I use you and your idiotic crusade for the Impures to get the sons of the Breeding Male morphed."

The sounds around Ethan ceased—the tide, the breeze—everything went silent. He turned to face his master, the one who had championed his cause so long ago, fed him, made him strong, gave him powers beyond all other Impures, beyond Purebloods. And it had been nothing more than a way to morph the Romans.

Cruen was grinning at him, red fangs descended. "And soon Lucian Roman too will be morphed and I won't need you anymore."

It was a lie. All of it.

Staring at the ancient one, Ethan understood now, saw everything clear as glass. Cruen had no Impure blood, no shame, no hope for the Impure Uprising to succeed.

And as he'd said, soon no need for Ethan himself.

Kate remained close to Nicholas as they entered the house. She felt as though they were something of a couple now—a disjointed, unsure, mishmash of a couple, but something bound together. There was a protection in their closeness, as though whatever and whomever they encountered as they walked through the living areas, up the stairs, down the hall, wouldn't be able to intrude or harm them in any way.

Maybe it wasn't the prudent thing to allow herself such a romantic fantasy when things were so up in the air and new, but Kate had rarely, if ever, let herself be drawn into the safe and peaceful feelings of a *paven's* care. Was it really such a big deal to let it continue for a few more minutes, until she got to her door and said good night?

But Nicholas didn't stop at her door. With his arm around her waist, he continued on to Ladd's room, where he opened the door.

The light from the hall spilled in and illuminated the bed and the *balas* in it. As always, Ladd hugged his pillow to his belly as he breathed even and peaceful.

"He's a fine boy," Nicholas said softly.

"He is."

"Funny . . ."

She laughed softly. "Very."

"And decent to look at, yes?"

"Very handsome. Just like his father."

Nicholas looked over at her, his eyes soft with affection. "I must do right by him, Kate."

"You will."

"He needs to know he is worth something. He needs to feel as though he belongs to someone." He turned back to the boy and said with fierce passion, "Everyone should feel that—everyone should know that they belong to someone, don't you think? Even if it's only for a little while."

Nicholas may have been talking about the boy, and maybe even himself, though she knew he'd never admit it. But regardless of whom the words were intended for, they cut straight into Kate's chest and squeezed her unbeating heart.

It was time. Had probably been time back at the

club, but that chance was over now. No matter what happened between them, what their future looked like after tonight, and even if it was only for a little while—he needed to know that he too belonged to someone.

Kate slipped out of his embrace and took his hand. "Let the boy sleep. I want to show you something."

Nicholas closed the door gently, then followed her to her bedroom. Inside the large, yet cozy space, Kate led her *paven* to the armchair beside the unlit fireplace. The blinds were open, revealing the half-moon light and the city that was like a vampire herself, sleepless and untamed. She sat him down, but didn't back up. She needed him to have a front-row seat—to see everything, every line.

For one moment, she gazed at him, at his long, lean legs stretched out past her, his wide chest and shoulders taking up residence, as though the chair were an extension of himself.

"I've kept this hidden," she began, her skin humming with nervous energy. After revealing herself to both Alexander and Sara earlier in the night, Kate had begged them to keep her secret until she could reveal it to Nicholas herself. "I've kept it hidden until I knew I could trust you with it."

Nicholas didn't say anything, just watched with a heavy brow, lips that were set and eyes so black they mimicked the night outside. With deft fingers, Kate pulled her sweater over her head and tossed it on the bed. Then she unclipped her bra and let it fall too.

She could barely breathe, she was so nervous. His reaction, she realized, meant far more than she'd ever imagined it would. Probably too much. And as she stood there naked from the waist up, her nipples hardening in the cool air, her eyes lifting to meet his, she found herself actually praying that he wouldn't reject her.

A low growl sounded in Nicholas's throat, and as Kate locked onto his face she saw that his eyes, glittering like black sand in the sun, were sweeping hungrily over her flesh, his nostrils flaring as he took in her belly, her breasts, her nipples. Then suddenly, his expression changed. His eyes narrowed as he fought to register what he was looking at. It felt like hours . . . hours of being inspected like a—

He reached out suddenly, took her hand, and pulled her onto his lap. Kate gasped at the abruptness of the move, then braced herself both physically and emotionally for what was coming next. Would he be angry? Hungry? Would he want to get the hell out of her room and never come back?

But Nicholas didn't say anything. Not at first. Transfixed, he put a hand on her belly and slowly worked his way upward until his palm covered her right breast. He stared at the mark, his mark, through his splayed fingers.

"How long have you known?" he whispered, his voice hoarse and heavy with wonder.

The club, the bathroom mirror and her reflection in it surfaced in her mind. "That night in the club bathroom. It appeared just after we were together."

His lids flipped up, his eyes locked on her, jaguar black and hungry. "After you came?"

She nodded, her breath tight inside her chest. There was no denying it, this *paven* made her body weak, made her skin itch to be touched. Made her feel an affection that she was sure was the blossoming begins of love.

Without another word, Nicholas was up and on his feet, carrying her in his arms as he walked across the room and into the bathroom.

"What are you doing?" she asked, all of sudden slightly panicked.

"Drawing you a bath." Nicholas set her down on the thick bath mat, then turned and cranked on the water in the tub. Steam began to rise, thick and predatory.

She didn't understand. "Why?"

He didn't answer, just started unbuttoning her jeans.

Was he angry? She couldn't tell—couldn't tell what he was feeling.

He pulled down both her underwear and her jeans and tossed them aside, then went to lift her into the tub.

"Stop," she said. "Nicholas, seriously. Stop for a second and look at me."

He glanced up. "What?"

She stood in front of him completely nude, her eyes searching his for answers, for the reason why he was trying so hard to get her in the bath, get her clean. And then her insides began to twist. "Oh my God."

"Kate—"

"It won't come off, Nicholas, if that's what this is about."

His brows drew together in a frown. "What?"

She shook her head. "No matter how hard you scrub, it won't come off."

Nicholas looked perplexed; then his gaze dropped to her right breast. "Oh, my beautiful Kate."

His arms went around her and he leaned in and kissed her. A slow, gentle kiss that made her dizzy and properly breathless. Then he dropped his head and kissed her mark too, lapped at it with his tongue until Kate's eyes closed and she moaned with the delectable sensation of it.

"This is mine," he growled, running the tips of his fangs across the imprint, the brand, the curve of an upper lip—the kiss. "You are mine." He lapped at it with his tongue. "I thought . . . God, I wondered if it could be true. If such a perfect creature could be mine."

His words, his claim on her should've made her want to push him away and run. She did not want to be owned, claimed. But this was different. Something else entirely. Something biological, in her code, DNA, that got her all hot and wet for his fierce, animallike declaration. And then there was the small fact that she was falling in love.

He took a step back and removed his shirt. She watched—stared eagerly, in fact—at the visual gift before her. It was a first, her first time seeing him bare, and he was impossibly beautiful, like a statue in his perfection. His skin was smooth, hairless, and the color of light caramel, and from tapered waist up to wide powerful shoulders, he was one ripple of muscle after another.

Kate felt her fangs drop, felt saliva form in her mouth. She wanted a taste, a suckle at each of his nipples. Lord, at the very least she wanted to feel him . . . She leaned in to him, let the tips of her breasts brush against his skin. He hissed at her and she sucked in air through her teeth.

"Bath first, Kate," he said, lifting her from where she stood, the muscles in his arms flexing impressively as he placed her in the water. "After my rough manner earlier tonight, I thought a soothing bath was in order. Relax your muscles a little before I take you again." As she lay back in the water, her body stretched out before him, he dropped to his haunches and placed his hand over her mark again. "Because make no mistake, my beautiful *veana*, tonight I will take you. Again." He brushed his thumb over her nipple. "And again"— another featherlight brush—"and again."

Heat surged within Kate, and she wanted to tell him to forget the bath and take her right now. Better yet, get in the water with her. But before she had a chance, he was standing up and heading for the door.

"Where are you going?" she asked, sounding forlorn even to her own ears.

Oh Lord. Pathetic, needy chick, party of one.

"A surprise." Grinning, he left her, closing the bathroom door and leaving her in darkness, except for the strip of light where tile met the hardwood.

For a moment, she felt strange, almost claustrophobic—like she was in prison again, and the idea of sitting up and waiting for him to return sounded like a stellar plan. But soon the heat of the water mixed with the cozy darkness began to calm her, cast a spell on her mind and body, and she relaxed. Her breathing slowed, her mind brought forth the image of Nicholas without his shirt and his pants and suddenly her hands were diving below the surface of the water and resting on her core.

Her eyes closed and she played, her fingers running through her hair to get to her clit. Even in the water, she felt her slick juices. Nicholas. He did that to her, would always do that to her . . .

She didn't notice when he came back into the room, didn't notice he had knelt beside the tub until she felt his hand over hers.

"Yes, Kate, just like that," he whispered.

She smiled as he followed her movements, adding just a hint of pressure to the ridge of her clit as they stroked her together.

"Sore, my dear?"

She shook her head. "Not even a little."

"What about here?" He guided her fingers lower, inserted all four of them gently into her cunt.

She moaned. "Oh, Nicky, please . . ."

He laughed softly. "I like when you beg. And I like when you call me Nicky."

She smiled in the dark. "Please, Nicky, spread my legs and put your thick, hard—"

His brutal growl cut off her words, and she felt arms under her, lifting her out of the water. Once she was tucked against his chest, he yanked open the bathroom door so hard it nearly flew off its hinges. They were through it and in the bedroom in under five seconds.

Through drowsy eyes, Kate stared at what was happening in the bedroom. A fire was lit in the hearth and several white towels were stacked up nearby. The bed was turned down and there was music coming from somewhere she couldn't see—a soft groove that was nowhere near romantic, but more like Nicholas—driving and a bit plaintive.

His surprise.

He carried her over to the fire and stood her up on the rug before it. Then he knelt down, grabbed a towel, and began to dry her skin. Her feet to her ankles, the sensitive backs of her knees to her thighs, to the curls that still glistened with both bathwater and excitement. His gaze lingered on her core a moment, and after exhaling heavily, he leaned in and drew his tongue all the way from the entrance of her cunt up to her swollen clit.

Kate moaned softly and reached for his shoulders to steady herself.

"You taste so sweet," he whispered against her, the heat from his breath teasing her sensitive skin.

"And so wet," she whispered.

"So wet when I should be drying you off."

She laughed softly, then sucked in air as he circled her clit with his tongue. His strokes were featherlight and quick, and within seconds she was breathing heavy, her hands moving in his hair, gripping his scalp.

Nicholas slipped his hands around her, filled his palms with her ass as she continued to ride his mouth, easing her hips toward the rapid movement of his tongue.

With the buildup in the bathtub and the quick slashes of Nicholas's rough, hot tongue, Kate couldn't hold on. She shuddered against his mouth, moaning loudly as she continued to thrust, as she gave herself over to the sweet torment of climax.

Nicholas drew back and stood, his face a mask of impatience as he picked her up and dropped her on the bed. Kate was soaking wet, and still clenching from her orgasm, but in that moment there was nothing she wanted more than him inside her. She watched with greedy eyes as he stripped down to nothing but glorious skin and hard, thick cock. She opened her arms to him, and he lowered himself on top of her, took her mouth hungrily. His kiss took away her breath, every thought, and she moaned into his mouth, then whimpered as he slid his tongue deep inside.

Every inch of Kate was alive, electric; this is where she belonged—this is the *paven* she belonged to. She wrapped her legs around his waist and rubbed her wet cunt against him, circling, begging for his shaft.

"Tell me you want me, Kate."

"I want you," she said breathlessly. "I want you so much."

"Tell me where? Where do you want me?" Nicholas

placed both of his hands on her inner thighs, near her opening, and spread her wide. "Right here, sweetness. Where it's so wet, so warm."

"Yes, Nicky, please!"

It was all she had to say. He pushed back just enough to grab the head of his cock and direct it straight toward the entrance to her body. With one crashing blow, he was inside her.

Kate gasped for air, deliciously impaled.

"Is that what you want, Kate?"

"Mmmmm," was all she could say as he slipped his hands under her and lifted her hips.

Nicholas began to move inside her, long heavy strokes, warming up her body, filling her all the way, until she could barely breathe he was so deep.

She moaned as he drew all the way out, then cried as he thrust back in. God, she loved the weight of him, how she anticipated every thrust, how her mind went blank when he slammed back into her—how his balls slapped against her backside like a hand.

And then his hand left her hip and tunneled between their bellies, his index finger finding the hard nub his tongue had lapped at earlier.

"Come for me again," he said, staring down at her as they moved together, their breathing labored. "I want to see you, watch your face, your eyes as you shudder."

As he drove into her faster and faster, his fingers dancing on her clit, she felt the walls of the room closing in—or maybe she was expanding. Maybe she was going to explode . . .

How could she tell him? How could she make him understand how she felt at that moment? So safe, so happy—so filled with pleasure. So . . . in love. She gasped, her legs shaking, the walls of her cunt clenching, her fangs elongating, and when Nicholas dropped his head to her shoulder, gave her the full expanse of his neck, she struck.

The moment blood hit her tongue she came.

Fast and hard, and stars behind her eyelids.

A groan escaped Nicholas's throat as she shuddered and quaked around him, as she greedily drank from him and clawed at his skin, as she fastened her legs around his waist and held on for the ride.

"My Kate," he uttered with a deep groan. "My sweet Kate."

He took her with one last earth-shattering thrust, and as she suckled his neck, as her cunt suckled his cock, Nicholas spilled hot seed into her body.

29

Gray knew he was coming.

Alexander—not his true mate.

It wasn't that Gray could feel the Pureblood's presence near his room or hear heavy footfalls moving toward the door. No, it was as it would always be. He heard the thought. The single and only thought.

"Little shit better be conscious."

Gray smiled. He had packed his duffel and was standing beside the twin mattress in his sparsely furnished room—the room that had once attracted him because of its resemblance to the hospital rooms he'd lived in most of his life.

It didn't take long.

One hard rap on the wood and Alexander Roman walked in. He looked as he always did—impenetrable and fierce. But Gray knew where his ferocity stemmed from—the love he had for his true mate, Gray's sister.

"It's like the old days," Gray said, tossing one last piece of clothing in his bag. "Coming to save the lost half vamp from himself."

Alexander shut the door and leaned against it, arms crossed over his chest. "Was never looking to be your life raft—then or now, Brother."

"I'm not your brother." Gray said the words with no malice, just the strength of truth.

"Why? Because I'm not blood."

"No, because you're *Pure* blood."

"My mate is like you," Alexander pressed. "Blood matters not to me."

"No, but I think it matters very much to me."

With a sigh, Alexander shook his head. "This is Dare."

"Dare fucked with his mind."

As the words played in his head, Gray stopped fiddling with his duffel and stood to face the *paven*. Perhaps it was the pure blood he'd been forced to drink or maybe the intense overload at Times Square had shut off the panic button in his brain, but the sounds of voices were muted now, even placed in separate tracks inside his mind so he could register them all individually. It wasn't normalcy by any means, but it was a relief to feel almost calm for once.

Gray eyed Alexander. "You need to know that Dare is holed up somewhere on the Hudson River, and he will do anything to get the *balas* you keep here. He is morally unreachable, his vision and goals skewed. I want nothing to do with that." He held up a hand. "But it is time for me to see my own goals clearly—search out my kind, learn, even fight for the cause, if I think it's a just one."

A slow, tense hum moved through Alexander. "What cause is that?"

"Equality." Gray leaned down and grabbed the duffel, tossed it over his shoulder.

"This is bullshit."

Alexander pushed away from the door. "If you leave, walk away from the protection of this house and its *pavens*, and join some fools on a quest, know this—the Order will hunt you."

Gray's eyes flashed gunmetal. "You too, right? If the ten call on you."

In that moment, Alexander's thoughts were of Sara. Only of Sara. How this was going to cause her such pain. Gray smiled. He was glad his sister had such a *paven*.

"We want nothing to do with a war between the Purebloods and the Impures," Alexander said, his tone as tight as his expression. "And if it does come to pass, we will not choose sides."

Gray raised a brow. "You may have to."

As he walked past Alexander, the Pureblood called after him, his voice deadly, "Say goodbye to your sister before you leave or I swear to God I *will* hunt you down. Family or not. Pureblood or not."

"Whether you love your sister or not."

Gray opened the door and walked through it. "I love my sister, Alex, make no mistake about that."

He was halfway down the hall when he heard the *paven* growl, "What in hell?"

And he was down the stairs and halfway to the door when he ran into Dillon.

She was dressed for travel, packed up like him.

"There he is." She gave him a big artificial smile. "You know, I looked all over for you. Taken by Dare, huh?"

He nodded. She was angry with him, but he wasn't sure why. Wasn't sure if he cared.

She sniffed. "And I thought you were in the bed of some female, as usual."

"You pissed at me, D?"

"Nah. I'd have to care about you to have those kinds of feelings."

Gray studied her, tried to read what was going on behind those cat eyes. But nothing doing. She was as closed as ever. "You leaving?"

"I think I'm done here," she said. "Need to get back to my life, my work." She eyed his duffel. "You?"

"Yep. Me too. Life, work."

For a moment, she was quiet, her eyes on him. Then she gave him a quick wave and headed for the door. "Goodbye, Gray."

"I'll be seeing you, *veana*," he said, watching her walk outside and hover a moment on the step before she flashed away.

Nicholas had never felt so warm. He'd never thought about it before, but he was a cold-blooded animal. Or so he felt at times. But with her . . . things were different.

It was night, but he had no idea what part of the night it was. Outside the window, the lights of the city still twinkled against the black sky.

Beside him, Kate snuggled into the curve of his arm, her cheek on his chest. "Have you ever slept with someone?" she whispered, her breath grazing his nipple. "In the same bed, all night?"

"No," he said. "You?"

"No."

"Good, because I'd have to cut his dick off and serve it to him raw."

She laughed, pressed her body closer to his side. "Morphed *pavens* are nuts."

"True mated *pavens* cannot be helped," he clarified, feeling his cock jump as she pressed her wet core against his hip. It had been a half hour and yet she was still wet—from his seed, his mouth . . . "And who says you're sleeping tonight, *veana*?"

He pulled her on top of him, groaned at the sweet weight of her, the softness of her belly against his shaft, the press of her nipples against his chest, the beauty of her eyes and face and expression as she looked down at him.

"Slave driver," she chided, her mouth kicking up at the corners.

"Come here," he whispered, feeling suddenly soft and sentimental about her, like he wanted to protect her from even the slightest thing—a willful breeze or a *paven* who could stay inside her for days if she'd allow him.

He threaded his hand in her hair, cupped her scalp and gently brought her lips down to his. He kissed her passionately, tasting her tongue, suckling her lower lip, and she followed him. They were a perfect match, designed to fit and complement each other. And yet their need for each other seemed to be so much deeper than just the body. Nicholas felt an urge to consume her, take her goodness into himself and resurrect into a being who was worthy of her care. Even her love.

Kate sat up, straddled his waist. With her large heavenly eyes she watched him as she fisted his cock in her warm hand, smiled sensually as she stroked the swollen head against her core until it shined with her juices. Lifting her hips up slightly, she guided him inside her body, then sat down with a sigh.

A deep growl escaped Nicholas and he gripped her hips, ready to rock her back and forth, lift and lower. But Kate had other ideas. Placing her feet on either side of his head, she stretched back slightly, her hands bracketing his thighs.

Nicholas stared at the sight before him. Her cunt and his shaft, joined, wet, pulsing together in a rhythm that made his breath seize in his lungs.

As she began to move, pumping her hips forward, finding her pace, he reached out and stroked her from his buried shaft to her swollen clit. She released a soft moan and let her head drop back as her hips continued to take him in and let him out.

Nicholas could barely hold himself together. She was like a goddess writhing above him and he wanted to make her climax over and over until all she saw were stars, and all she wanted were his arms around her.

Panting, she rode him hard and he followed her rhythm, flicking her clit in quick little movements. Moisture dripped from her core like honey, and his mouth watered.

Suddenly, the mated male inside him unleashed, and he snarled, flipped her to her back in one easy movement and bit into the mark near her right nipple.

Kate gasped, cried out, and opened her legs as wide as they would go. "Oh yes. Fuck me, Nicky."

As he rode her hard, he filled his mouth, his throat, and his belly with her blood, never stopping, never slowing, not even when she bucked and shook and shattered beneath him.

An hour later, Nicholas stood beside the bed and gazed down at his true mate. She slept on her side, looking young and sweet and so achingly desirable all he wanted to do was get back into bed and put his arm around her waist, pull her close to his chest. He had never wanted anyone like he wanted her. She was like *gravo*, only better, richer, and more satisfying in every way.

But no matter how much he craved her again, he had something to settle downstairs. They were waiting for him. He could feel it.

He dressed quickly and left the room. He would be back, he mused, heading for the stairs, and this time he would have her in the bathtub. Or the shower. Or both. God, the thought of water raining down over her breasts, her nipples, his mark . . .

He was grinning as he entered the library, but the moment he saw Lucian, his mood soured.

Standing near the wall where a map of the Hudson River had been tacked up, the near-albino looked positively fiendish. He turned and glared at Nicholas. "Ah, has the whore left the bed of his latest trick?"

Bloodshed and carnage raged through Nicholas in that moment. Whatever was standing there mocking him wasn't his brother. It was his enemy. Without thought or question, he ran at the *paven* and tackled him, sent him to the ground. With a grunt, he smashed his fist into Lucian's gut, then jacked his knee up into the *paven*'s chin. He heard the rattle of teeth and snarled—until Lucian flipped him over and cracked his jaw with a hard right. For a good five seconds, Nicholas saw stars, but after he shook his head clear, he jumped on the bastard again.

The two rolled around like pigs in the mud, cursing and punching each other in any and every available spot until Alexander kicked them off each other. "Get the hell up, you idiots."

Cursing, they broke apart, and Nicholas stumbled backward. He stood there panting, his eyes narrowed on his younger brother. "Just say it."

"What? That you're a fucking liar?" Lucian wiped blood off his mouth. "Fine! You're a fucking piece-of-shit liar!"

Nicholas was so amped up he wanted to run at the albino again. "Keep going. You know you want to."

"Oh, I want to."

"Then, get it out, Luca," he snarled. "Come on—say it, asshole. SAY IT! Tell me I fucking disgust you."

Lucian jabbed a finger at Nicholas. "Yeah, you do!"

"Tell me I've disappointed you."

"Fucking right."

"Tell me you wish you'd never saved my ass that day in the alley behind my house!"

Lucian opened his mouth to strike back again, but when he realized what his brother had said he froze, went ghost pale.

Swallowing his own blood, the aggression dying off as his brother's face grew more pained, Nicholas shook his head. "Tell me that maybe I deserved what I got that day."

"Stop it," Lucian ground out.

"Tell me seven wasn't enough—that I should've been beaten until I bled out."

"Shut up! Christ."

"Enough, Nicky." It was Alexander. He'd allowed the yelling, the bar fight, and the accusations to fly. But only so far. "Don't you think that's enough, *Duro*?"

Nicholas realized he was barely breathing, that air was trapped inside his chest, that his face was wet with something too, and his fangs were dropped so far down they were nearly to his chin.

"Shit." He took a breath. "I'm sorry. I'm really sorry. I swear to God I never meant for this to happen."

Lucian stared at him. "Which part? The lying to

us, or having Dare shout it out to us in fucking Times Square?"

"Both."

"Did Kate find you?" Alexander asked, trying to ease the tension in the room.

Nicholas nodded.

"I told her, you know." Alexander shrugged. "Maybe I shouldn't have, but she cares about you, and maybe you need that or something."

Yes, he'd needed it. He needed her.

"So?" Lucian put in, his rage defused, but not totally gone. "It's done, then? You have her, so this fucking for money thing is over?"

Nicholas wanted to give them both the answer they were looking for. Hell, he wanted to say it for himself and mean it—believe it. But he couldn't lie to them again. Whatever he decided to do from that moment forward, it was with full disclosure to his brothers. "Listen, I shouldn't have lied to you, but what I do in my personal time is mine to choose."

"That sounds like a no to me," Lucian said, then turned and headed for the door. "I'm going to work out in the tunnels. Smash some heads down there. Hey, if you're interested in joining me, Nicky, I'd love to re-introduce you to my fist. Maybe I can reconnect some wires or something."

When he was gone, Alexander didn't waste any time beating the injured horse. "You have a mate now," he said. "And you seem to care for her."

"Of course I care for her." Shit, he may even love her. He wasn't exactly sure what that felt like, but whatever he was feeling had to be something close.

"Are you willing to give her up?" Alexander asked. "Are you willing to let her walk away, out, into the arms of another *paven*?"

The rage that boiled within Nicholas at that moment could've set the house on fire. It was possible, to walk away from one's true mate. The pain would be excruciating, and the blood of another would never truly satisfy, but it could be done.

"All for something you don't need," Alexander continued, "for something that gives you no love, no honor."

Nicholas's nostrils flared. "How about for something you love, you need—something you fight to keep safe."

"What does that mean?" Alexander asked, wary.

"The deal I made with the Order after I went to get Kate. It's not just Dare's body they want anymore. I must bring Kate back to the Order or they will morph Lucian anyway."

Alexander looked horrified, as if he were trying to imagine the same scenario with his Sara. "Your mate's life or your brother's."

"Yes," Nicholas said, realizing that the wetness he'd felt on his face earlier were tears. His first. "The one who saved my life then or the one who offers me a new one now."

*   *   *

Kate stood outside the door to the library, her lips dry, her throat too as she listened. She had come downstairs to find him. She'd come downstairs thinking she could talk him into snuggling—or something equally cute and nauseating—on the couch in the den, maybe watching something sexy and funny while she force-fed him popcorn until he growled at her.

God, she was so stupid!

He was talking about her in there like she was a choice he had to make. Like he had control of her body and her life, and her goddamn future. And she'd let him think that.

She stood there and shook her head. Romanticizing the nights they'd had together, letting her mind and her unbeating heart believe they were anything more than mutual satisfaction, wasn't her best move.

What happened to self-protecting? Enjoying herself to a point, then moving on? What happened to the promise she'd made to herself? The long days and even longer nights in her cell, unable to sleep, listening to the weeping and the anger—she'd gotten through it all by promising herself that someday she would be free.

She heard movement in the library and forced herself to turn around and head back to the stairway. He couldn't see her like this—all sad and disillusioned. He couldn't know she'd heard him.

She started up the stairs. She wasn't getting in the middle of blood—not even as a true mate. Nicholas had an impossible decision in front of him and she wasn't going to force him to make it. After that insane meet-up with the Order, he'd said that if she got "lost" he wouldn't come looking for her. She hoped he'd stand by his word.

"You work too long, my daughter. It is time you rested."

Bronwyn looked up from her desk, from her computer screen and smiled. "I'm almost done, Father."

"See that you are," the old *paven* said, his green eyes warm with worry as he stood in the doorway of her office. "Then come down. Your mother and I would like to discuss something with you."

"Is it about my future happiness, Papa?" she joked, knowing that finding her a mate, even if he was not true, weighed heavily on them.

"Hurry up now," he said. "I've brought Edel to help you."

I don't need help, she wanted to say. But what was the point? They didn't hear her cry for independence, and allowed her to work inside the house only because the Order had sanctioned it. They were not modern vampires, and she would never expect them to be.

Edel walked in then, and her father closed the door.

"What are you working on?" the older *veana* asked.

Turning back to the screen, Bronwyn closed the window. "Something personal."

"Involving a certain clan of brothers, perhaps?"

"Perhaps."

Edel's sigh could've been heard all the way to Beacon Hill. She didn't like the Romans, especially Lucian, and wanted Bronwyn to steer clear of the whole gang.

"Please don't get involved with them again," Edel said, her eyes heavy with worry. "It's already taken a toll on you."

She appreciated her friend's concern for her, but the *veana* didn't understand what was happening inside Bronwyn, where her recent bouts of weakness and lack of appetite were coming from. It certainly had nothing to do with the Romans. Meta was soon to be upon her, just as the need to find her true mate would overwhelm her good sense.

Bronwyn gave the *veana* a soft smile. "You can retire now, Edel."

"But your father—"

"Is not the boss," she finished firmly, yet good-naturedly. "But please don't tell him I said so. His feelings would be hurt."

The older *veana* smiled. She knew a losing battle when she was playing one. "All right, Bron. I will see you tomorrow."

After Edel was out the door, Bronwyn reached for her cell phone. As she dialed the Manhattan number, her eyes slid to the computer screen again. What stared back at her was remarkable, and yet she hesitated believing it. One more time perhaps?

She disconnected the call and placed her phone back on the desk.

She would run the test once more to be certain.

30

Nicholas removed his clothes and slipped into bed beside her, breathing deep as he felt the warmth of her skin curl around him, sheltering him, easing him from the rage and uncertainty of all that happened downstairs. His hand went immediately around her waist, and he slowly pulled her back against him. An almost imperceptible growl escaped his throat. Her round bottom fit so tightly against his groin, the curve of her back was pressed softly against his chest, and her hair, scented with a night of blissful sex, teased his face and the brands on his cheeks.

He was caught between wanting to make love to her again, and just holding her, telling himself that she belonged to him.

"Kate," he whispered near her ear, "are you awake?"

"Yes," she returned, her voice soft, yet devoid of all the pleasure he'd heard in it earlier.

Concern flooded him. "Are you all right? What is it?"

"Nothing. I . . . I just want to sleep."

He didn't believe her. "Kate—"

"No." She grabbed his arm, the arm that was around her waist, and pulled it closer beneath her breasts. "No talking. Please. Just hold me."

Encouraging *veanas* to bare their feelings aloud wasn't Nicholas's way, but this was Kate. His Kate. And not knowing what was going on in her mind, what pained her heart at that moment, made him crazy. He would fix it, always, whatever it was that hurt her. And yet she wasn't asking that of him. She wanted his arms around her and his breath against her neck.

And so he closed his eyes and tried to regulate his breathing. For tonight, he would be still and at ease because tomorrow would bring with it a mountain of uncertainty, and the fate and freedom of two vampires he cared for more than anything in the world.

It had snowed overnight, and the morning light in Washington Square Park was lovely. Kate made her way toward the Garibaldi Monument, passing trees frosted with white, joggers puffing out steam, people crossing the park to get to work, and babies being pushed by tired moms and nannies.

Nicholas and his brothers were in the tunnels, had been since dawn—since he had left her bed. They were training for the night's battle, and had taken Ladd with them. In any other circumstance, Kate might have objected to a boy so young learning fighting techniques and combat strategy, but he was a descendant of the Breeding Male. The battlefield was in his blood. Besides, Nicholas was the only family he had left, and seeing them bonded was far more important to her than protecting the *balas*'s tender age and sensibilities.

After all, tonight she would be gone, and unable to protect him any longer.

As she approached the monument, she spotted Cambridge, his red hair a beacon in all the white, circling the bronze statue like a rat with an inner-ear problem. When he noticed her, he stopped, his eyes flickering in every direction.

"I don't like working against the Romans," he said, coming toward her.

"You're not working against anyone," she said tightly. "You're working *for* me. Besides, you don't care who you work for as long as you get paid."

He didn't dispute that. "That *paven* of yours know where you are and why?"

"He's not my *paven*." The words felt wrong exiting her lips.

"Didn't look like that to me."

"Well, then, maybe you need your eyeballs removed and given a good cleaning. I think I remember a fellow in Mondrar who did that kind of work." Her brows lifted. "Ebox, wasn't it?"

Cambridge recoiled. "Do not speak to me of that vile thing. I couldn't see or hear for a week after he attacked me."

"Then let's get this done," she said, her tone rigid. She wanted it over. She wanted to be on her way, wanted to start forgetting this city and everyone in it as soon as possible.

"You must understand," Cambridge began, "Mondalagua is underground, beneath the water. Can you live in the dark again?"

She looked up at the monument of Giuseppe Garibaldi, a freedom fighter of sorts and said, "I can live anywhere I'm free."

"Five o'clock tonight at Pier 90," Cambridge said quickly. "You have five grand?"

Her gut clenched. "All I have is three."

"Fine. Bring the three thousand and you'll be taken . . . home."

Home. The word stabbed at her insides. For one glorious night, she'd thought that maybe she had a home, with Nicholas and Ladd.

She nodded at Cambridge. "I'll be there."

When Ethan Dare landed in Cruen's reality, he could feel the change, the shift in the Supreme One's mood and purpose immediately. Gone were the homelike beach setting, the paintings, the bed and chairs, even the plant life. The only things that remained were sand and water.

Cruen was nowhere to be seen and Ethan glanced around looking for Pearl, nervous energy kicking around inside his gut. He should've taken her with him the last time he was there. Oh God, his child . . .

His eyes caught on movement a mile down the beach, near the water's edge. Squinting, he walked toward it. The sand was blisteringly hot, as was the sun, a perfect storm for being cooked alive. As he started to make out the lines of a pregnant female, he closed his eyes and flashed, taking form directly in front of her.

Pearl gasped when she saw him. "He's gone," she choked out, sweating profusely, her hair plastered to her face and neck. "And there's something here, something watching me."

"Don't worry. I'm taking you."

She shook her head. "When the Supreme One returns and finds me gone . . ."

"He won't find you," Ethan assured her.

"Ethan!" she cried, her eyes fixed on something behind him.

Ethan whirled around, saw a massive figure charging toward them on all fours. As he got closer, Ethan recognized him as the Beast he'd seen with Cruen a few days ago. Long black hair, white diamond eyes, death and destruction in his expression.

Erion.

Wrapping his body around Pearl, Ethan flashed.

When he landed outside his newest compound, his mind spun with what he'd just seen. Cruen was gone, and he'd left that monster behind to clean up his mess.

Ethan's veins were growing hungry again, the power beginning to deplete. Cruen would never feed him again, but he might come calling. And if he did, Ethan needed to have a plan in place.

He needed a bargaining chip.

31

A boy, whether vampire or not, can be confined for only so long before he becomes a battering ram—running up and down the hall, smashing into the doors, pleading with his "jailer" for release—desperate for a little air and a lot of sky.

Four Impure guards stationed ten feet on either side of her, Kate sat on the steps in front of the SoHo house, watching Ladd weave in and out of the three trees near the curb, bending down every so often to inspect a bug or a scrap of paper towel or a cigarette butt.

It was a beautiful day, sunny and warm in the middle of February, and she hadn't the heart to force him back inside after the five minutes she'd promised him.

After all, today was her last day with him. She wanted to give him something nice to remember her by.

"What is it?" she called, as Ladd dropped down on his haunches again.

"Piece of wire, I think."

"Don't touch it," she warned, hearing sirens in the distance. "Could be sharp."

"What's that sound?" Ladd asked, looking over his shoulder.

"Police siren."

"Ooh, I want to see."

"You stay where you are," Kate instructed.

It was getting closer, the wail nearly upon them. Then out of nowhere, like something from a movie, a cab came screeching around the corner followed by several police cars, lights flashing. With another squeal of tires, the yellow cab raced down the street and crashed into two parked cars just a few feet away from the house.

"Ladd, get up here," Kate called, as one cop after another jumped from their cars and surrounded the vehicle, guns drawn.

"Ladd," she called again, running down the few feet to the tree where he had been investigating the wire, the guards right behind her. "Come on. Inside."

But he wasn't there, wasn't by the tree.

Oh, God. Oh, God. Kate screamed at the top of her lungs, her gaze flashing everywhere at once.

But it was no use.

The boy was gone.

The search went on all afternoon. Those who could handle the sun were out trolling the neighborhood, checking bus stations, arcades, movie theaters, anywhere a child might wander off to. While inside, Nicholas and Alexander connected with the Eyes and the Internet to see if there were any reports of a found child.

For obvious reasons, they couldn't go to the police, but Kate knew in her gut this was no random act of kidnapping or Ladd just taking off. As she entered the house, the sun still high in the sky, she knew there was a decision to be made.

Nicholas pulled her into his arms and gave her a reassuring kiss on the cheek. "We'll find him."

"Not like this, we won't." She hated that he was being so understanding, so damn nice to her. She didn't deserve it. Forget the guards. Ladd was her responsibility, and she'd just allowed someone to take him—right out from under her nose. "We know who has him," she said darkly. "Those bastards wanted him from the start."

A low snarl sounded from Nicholas. "If it is the Order, then I will go. At first dark. They will not deny me my *balas*."

Kate nearly laughed. The Order was not a sentimental lot. They didn't give a shit about keeping a child with his parent—especially if that parent was a descendant of the Breeding Male.

She pulled away from Nicholas and left the room, went upstairs. He would have an easy decision now. His flesh-and-blood of a brother, or the *veana* who had allowed his son to be taken.

If only the boat could come for her sooner.

She sat down on the bed, put her head in her hands. Ladd. Goddammit! He'd just lost a mother, and now this. He must be scared out of his mind. He must hate her . . .

Licking her dry lips, Kate slid her gaze over to her bag, which sat empty in the center of her bed. The plan had been to wait until it got dark, until Nicholas and his brothers left for the hunt.

Fuck!

Her freedom waited at the docks, an unknown, uncharted destination that had filled her with at least a modicum of hope. And here she was again. Two directions in which to run. Yet this time, there was no question in her mind where she belonged.

She dressed quickly, and left the room in the very clothes she'd originally entered it in. In the hall, she paused and looked at Ladd's door, then headed past it to the room she knew from Sara's true mate love story boasted a fire escape.

Nicholas felt as though he were being stabbed over and over. Not by the cool metal of a blade, but by the knowledge that he could do nothing save sit on his hands until the light changed. While the *balas* who could be his son was held by the treacherous ten.

"You look like a dog who needs to piss," Lucian grumbled, standing in front of the recon map in the library, growing irritated with Nicholas's incessant pacing near the door.

"I feel useless!" Nicholas slammed his fist against the door, leaving a mark like an animal paw print in the wood. "I need to find him, get to him."

"I'll go before the Order," Lucian offered. "Christ. I'll demand the boy be returned."

"No." Nicholas pointed a finger at him. "You're not giving them any more reasons to morph your ass than they have already. I am trying to reach Dillon, but even if she does agree to go, I think it may only anger the Order." He sniffed darkly. "They want me to come before them and beg. I know it."

Alexander burst through the door at that moment, nearly colliding with Nicholas. "Any news on the *balas*?"

"No," Lucian said, returning to his map. "But Sugar Ray here believes the kid's being held by the Order."

"I'm leaving for the mountain at first dark," Nicholas said. "If Ladd is my offspring—"

Alexander cut in quickly, "There is no more 'if,' *Duro*."

Both Nicholas and Lucian stopped and gave their eldest brother their full attention.

Alexander nodded. "The test is complete."

"You spoke with Bronwyn," Lucian said, an edge to his tone that was always present whenever the *veana* was mentioned.

"She called a moment ago," Alexander explained. "I spoke with her very briefly because Evans came in and I thought he had news—"

"Is he mine, *Duro*?" Nicholas interrupted.

"Yes."

The room went silent for a moment, and within it Nicholas took quick inventory of his emotions. No highs, no lows, just a feeling of confirmation, as though he and his insides had known all along that Ladd was a part of the Roman family.

Evans rushed into the room then. He looked anxious as his gaze flickered in Nicholas's direction, but his eyes refused to focus. "Sir . . ."

Sudden fear replaced every shred of contentment within Nicholas. "What's wrong? Is it the *balas*?"

The Impure shook his head, muttered something about "females" and "fire escapes."

Nicholas was on top of him, coiling over him like a cobra ready to strike. "Speak, dammit!"

Shaking, Evans looked up at him. "Your *veana* is gone."

It was as though his world had imploded, and the cry that he released from his burning lungs made the windows throughout the entire house tremble and threaten to shatter.

32

Unlike New York, Vermont hadn't embraced the early call of spring yet, and as night fell around Kate in wicked blues and haunting lavenders, she felt the familiar chill of a familiar land invade her bones.

Getting inside the *credenti* had been difficult as her blood was no longer welcome at the gates. She'd had to go through a narrow slit in the hedgerow, one she'd heard about from a student several months ago. The branches and vines had cut her up something fierce, but it mattered not. Her wounds would heal quickly, just as she hoped her actions now would heal the boy's.

There was no one about, no sounds but the wind. Picking up her pace, Kate hurried toward the school, then stopped once she hit the steps. Fresh white snow now covered the spot where Mirabelle's body had lain.

Where her blood had run.

She closed her eyes.

I'm here.

She waited, her lungs having trouble taking in the freezing air. Five minutes went by, then ten.

"I'm here!" she shouted. "Take me, dammit!"

Why didn't they hear her? Sense her?

Frustrated, she left the school grounds and went walking toward the graveyard. Would she be here? Kate wondered, stepping over drifts and tree roots. She hoped so. For Ladd's sake. Someday he would want to come back, see her . . .

Snow blanketed every inch of the cemetery, uniform headstones popping up out of the white covering like stone dominoes. Kate walked up one side and down another, looking for a new burial, a simply carved stone.

There. She spotted it, far back and to the right, a newly dug grave, snow only an inch or two instead of a foot.

Mirabelle Letts.

It was carved by hand and quite lovely.

Her throat felt tight, and she remembered that day, that moment, wishing again she could've done something to stop it. She reached out to brush the dusting of snow from the top of the stone, but before her fingers made contact, she was flashed.

"Welcome back, Prisoner 626."

Out of the tundra and into the desert, the ancient ten were seated, per usual, at their long table—ready for judgment. The first to speak had been a *paven* with light blue eyes and a pointed black beard, and without fear this time around, Kate walked toward him.

"My name is Kate Everborne, and I want to see the *balas*."

He attempted to look confused. "What *balas* is that?"

"Mirabelle Letts's child, Ladd."

"He is not here. You took him from us, remember?"

"Let him go, and you can have me."

There was a smattering of laughter up and down the table.

"What a bargain that is, 626," the blue-eyed *paven* remarked. "An escaped prisoner who stole—then lost—a *balas*." He leaned over the table and smiled, his brick-red fangs stretched down past his lower lip. "Here is *my* deal: Do not fight the guards as they return you to Mondrar and I will think about sparing your life."

"You're lying," she said, though the few small taps of panic that had been inside of her a moment ago turned into blips of acid rain.

"There is no reason for us to lie, 626," said a white-haired *veana*, her voice lacking the amusement of the *paven* beside her. "We have no one but you, and I ask that you go quietly."

Oh God. He wasn't there.

Ladd wasn't there.

She had just given herself up, her freedom, every-thing for nothing at all. And Ladd was still missing . . .

Her head squeezed with pain and her belly con-tracted. She would be sick.

Guards were flashed to the empty spaces on either

side of her, and as they sank their meaty hands into her arms, the *paven* laughed. "Take her."

Screaming for Ladd, for Nicholas, for justice, Kate kicked at the *pavens* holding her, smashed her head into one's shoulder, even ripped a hole in the back of another with her fangs. But it was no use. She was flashed away before she even had a chance to see the blood flow.

Cambridge skulked around the exterior of the building, trying to decide the best way in. He'd followed Kate to this wrecked warehouse space after their meeting in the park earlier. At the time, he hadn't really given a shit as to why she was lying low in such a dump, especially when she knew the Roman brothers—who were pretty much on par with the Rockefellers in the city—but maybe he should have. Maybe he should've checked her and her situation out a little more carefully before agreeing to hook her up with a few very important vampires because the bitch hadn't shown up for her ride to Mondalagua.

Rounding the side of the building, he saw a window open just enough to slither through. Cambridge had shelled out a few hundred just to get her the meet, figuring he'd recoup the loss when she showed up with the three grand. Now he was skint and she was going to hear about it, pay him back double—or else.

Using a thick hedge as a step up, Cambridge lifted himself toward the window, but he barely touched the apron when a knife was pressed to his throat.

"What are the Eyes doing here?" came the deep growling query of a morphed *paven*.

Cambridge stepped down very slowly. "Nothing."

"Looking for a *balas* or here to return the one you stole?"

"What?"

The *paven* came close to his ear. "Where's the boy, you piece of shit?"

"You have me confused with someone else, *paven*. I don't know what—" Cambridge couldn't say another word because he was being twisted around and slammed back into the side of the building, the steel blade once again pressed against his windpipe.

"Shit," he uttered on a weak gasp, then froze as he realized who was in his face, fangs extended and face contorted with rage.

Nicholas Roman snarled at him, his eyes so black, so narrowed, they seemed almost dead—like a shark's.

"I'm going to ask you one more time," he said with a terrifying calm, "then you will be dead. Where is the boy?"

Cambridge felt the knife cut into his skin, just a hair, but it scared the shit out of him and he rattled off the truth. "I don't know about the *balas*. I came to find Kate."

The *paven*'s face changed so abruptly it was almost as though he had been wearing a mask—from deadly to demonic in under five seconds. "Why would you be looking for Kate?"

Cambridge swallowed against the knife, tasting his own blood. "I need to talk to her."

"What about?"

Cambridge said nothing.

Nicholas inched the blade deeper.

Fuck me. He gritted his teeth. "She booked passage tonight on a ship going to Mondalagua, to the underground *credenti*, but she never showed up."

The Roman brother's brows slammed together. "Why was she going to Mondalagua?"

"She said she wanted freedom."

Cambridge saw a quick flash of pain cross the *paven*'s vicious mug, and wondered if he could use that to his advantage.

But he didn't have to. Nicholas cursed and released him, let him fall to the hard ground.

"Get out of here," he muttered. "I need to find her, bring her back home."

"She said she wanted a new life," Cambridge said, holding his throat. "Was willing to pay for a new life."

"If she's gone to where I think she's gone, she's just ended her life," Nicholas said in a fierce whisper before flashing out of the side yard.

33

Lucian had a hard-on for violence tonight.

Bred out of an eye-popping, ball-busting few days, he wanted nothing more than to bring down the one piece of shit who had started the whole fucking mess in the first place.

Nicholas had gone in search of his *veana* and the *balas*, and Lucian would go with Alexander to find the mess maker himself. This was not just a hunt and kill mission anymore however; this had upgraded to full-on torture and disembowelment.

He eyed his tomahawk propped up against the wall. That could hack into some serious bone.

Grinning, he grabbed his clothes from the back of the chair. He was pulling on a pair of black jeans and zipping up his fly when there was a knock on his bedroom door. Alexander was way early, but maybe he wanted to get a jump on things.

He pulled back the heavy wood and was more than a little surprised by what he saw. Or whom he saw. "Don't have time for a social call right now, princess."

Bronwyn Kettler didn't grin or roll her eyes, or shoot him a sarcastic response as she normally did. She took a breath and said, "I gave Alexander the news about Ladd."

"He told me," Lucian said, eyeing her. She didn't look so good. In fact, she looked a little pale, tired. "I am sorry for the *balas*, our DNA in his tiny body. It is a fate I would not wish on any vampire, Impure or Pureblooded."

"I need to talk to you." She closed her eyes for a moment and gripped the doorjamb. "Can I come in?"

He was on her in an instant, taking her against him as he helped her inside. Jesus, she weighed nothing. "What's wrong with you?"

She settled in her seat and again took a breath. This time, when her eyes opened, she smiled. Well, forced a smile was more like it. "I'm fine. Just been working a lot."

Lucian didn't buy it. "Are you ill?"

"No."

But the moment she said the word, something unseen hit her in the belly. She doubled over and sucked in air.

Lucian knelt in front of her. "You need a doctor. Why did you leave your *credenti* when you felt like this?"

She didn't respond, just moaned softly.

Goddammit. He tipped her chin up. Her eyes were closed, her face bone-white. "Have you fed today?"

Her eyelids fluttered.

"Bronwyn!"

Nothing. God, he hated this. What the hell had she done to herself? He cupped her face. "When was your last feed?"

"A month," she uttered.

"What?" he roared. She didn't mean it—couldn't. A *veana* could go without blood for a week, maybe two, but after that her body would go into shock, deep, painful starvation. "Are you fasting? Is this coming from the Order?"

"No. Just me." She gripped her belly and flinched. "I've tried to take rations. Can't get the blood down."

"You are ill." He lifted her in his arms and carried her to the bed. "I'm going to call Leza."

But when he tried to release her, she gripped him, her head tucking into his neck. At first, Lucian didn't know what she was doing; then her scent slammed into him, desperate and starving, and he realized she was sniffing him.

Fucking sniffing him.

Without thinking, he bit into his wrist, waited for the blood to climb to the surface of his skin, then slipped his arm between their bodies, right up under her chin.

He heard a savage growl and she broke free of him. Her eyes glittered at the sight of his bright red blood. She lowered her head, and Lucian watched as her tongue drifted out, swiped at the blood on his wrist.

"Oh God," she uttered, her chest going up and down so quickly it looked as though there were an invisible string attached to it.

Lucian's skin went tight and the bulge in his pants screamed to be released. But he barely had time to register the thought. Bronwyn's hands shot out, gripped his wrist, and pulled it up to her waiting mouth.

The moment her fangs plunged into him, Lucian felt as though a bolt of electricity had hit his entire body. Shocking, painful, and intensely erotic. No wonder he'd avoided feeding a female—he'd have screwed every single one of them whether they'd wanted him to or not.

His own fangs dropped and he fought the urge to rip away Bronwyn's purity cloths and bite into her pale neck, taste her—finally taste her. But she needed *him*, *his* blood to regain her strength—not the other way around.

She drank, fed, suckled until Lucian felt almost light-headed. And when she released him, dropped back on the bed with her eyes closed and the color returning to her cheeks, he felt something move through him. It was snakelike in its progress, slow and calculating, and for the first time in his long life Lucian felt a twinge of fear.

Then he was pulled, yanked from his room and dropped at the mouth of a cave.

Lucian had never seen the Order, but he was pretty sure that the *paven* who stood in front of him with a wine-colored robe and a hood that covered his entire face, was a member.

"Who the hell are you?" he demanded, his gaze shifting from the Order to his surroundings. He'd been to this place before. It was the same cave he and Alexander had flashed to when they were waiting for Nicholas to return from the Order. The Hollow of the Shadows. "What do you want from me?"

The *paven* reached up and pulled back his hood. Lucian braced himself to see some nasty sci-fi special effects instead of a face, but the horror that hit him had nothing to do with gore.

It was like looking into a mirror. The *paven* was ancient, but his hair, his facial structure, and his grim mouth were the very image of Lucian.

"The Breeding Male," Lucian uttered.

The *paven* nodded. "Your father."

34

Mondrar was no home.

And Kate was no criminal.

But there she sat, once again, in the freezing five-by-five cell, no walls, just bars on every side so that her fellow inmates could observe her. It was proper humiliation in the most disgusting, despicable, and most demoralizing of settings. Typical Order.

By now, Nicholas had to know she was gone. What did he think? she wondered. Did he believe she'd run away? Did he believe she felt nothing for him, had never felt anything for him but the built-in sexual lust of a true mate?

Or did he think her freedom had meant more to her than him . . . or Ladd.

And maybe he'd be right. Maybe not . . .

Didn't matter now, she told herself, forcing a hardness into her soul that she knew she would need if she was going to survive in this place again. Nicholas would find out soon enough, and at the very least, her capture would mean that Lucian would be safe.

The *veana* in the cell next to hers banged on the bars with the head of her bed. "Who are you, pretty bitch?"

Kate sat down on the edge of her metal bed and put her head in her hands. "Prisoner 626."

She was out of fight.

As night overtook the mountain, and the moon's glow became the only source of light, Lucian stood near the cave's mouth and stared at the *paven* before him—the Breeding Male.

His father.

Lucian wasn't at all sure how to feel about this choice piece of news. In one respect, he wanted to wrap his hands around the *paven*'s neck and squeeze very slowly until his eyeballs popped. Hell, did a Breeding Male who had taken countless *veana* against their will, left them alone and terrified and filled with hatred for the *balas* they carried deserve anything less?

Lucian thought no.

And yet he had questions. So many questions. Was it possible to ask them and get the answers before he lost his mind and attacked?

"It is good to see you, my son," the *paven* began, his voice a low, dark mystery.

Growling, Lucian moved nearer. "Don't call me that."

"Very well." He inclined his head. "Lucian."

"What is your name?"

"Order 10."

"Your real name."

"Titus Evictus."

"Am I a Breeding Male, Titus?"

The *paven* nodded, and around him the wind picked up, scattering leaves on the hard ground. "The moment you gave your blood to the *veana*, the change began."

Lucian stared at the *paven*, no rush of cataclysmic shock barreling through him. For years, maybe forever, he had felt a self-imposed don't-even-go-there-dickhead sign when it came to feeding females of any species. And yet, faced with Bronwyn's hunger, he hadn't been able to control himself—hell, he hadn't even paused to consider it.

"So it's done," Lucian said tightly. "I fed the *veana* and now I will become a rutting animal with no feeling, no care, and no conscience."

Titus shook his head. "The change has only begun, it hasn't taken hold. Not yet."

"Are you saying there's a way to stop it?"

"If your brother fails at killing Dare, the Order will morph you early regardless, and you will become a Breeding Male. If not, there is a way to prolong the change until the time of your true morph one hundred and seventy-five years from now."

"How?"

"You cannot breed with the one who holds your blood," Titus explained, his eyes heavy with significance. "If you mate with this *veana*, the gene *will* take hold and you will be changed quickly. It is not a road you would appreciate. For the rest of your existence, you will feel the undeniable pull to breed with every female around you. And you will take them whether they accept you or not."

In other words, if he didn't steer clear of Bronwyn Kettler he would become a piece-of-shit raping monster way ahead of schedule. Really fucking fabulous. Lucian eyed the *paven*. "You still feel this, even now?"

"No," Titus said, the blatant look of relief unmasked. "It is why I gave up my existence for the Order. All urges, controlled or not, have been stripped from me."

"By who?" Hell, he might need that information someday.

But Titus only shook his head. "That matters not. What matters is that I am only a justice now."

Lucian snorted. Whatever else his "pops" was spewing today, the innocent, justice-for-all Order rap wasn't getting past Lucian's bullshit detector. He knew better.

Inhaling slowly, eyes closing, Titus grew silent for a moment. Then, like a switch being turned on, he flipped open his lids and announced, "I must go."

Lucian raised a pale eyebrow at the *paven*. "Tell me something first, *Dad*. Is this justice? What you're doing for me now?"

Titus didn't answer. Instead he replaced his hood on his head and flashed from the cave.

Inside the Hudson River compound, Ethan stood beside the long dining table and watched the *balas* as he flicked seeds and fruit around his plate. An hour ago, he'd taken blood from several of the Pureblood *veanas*, and although it hadn't offered the Supreme One's sudden onslaught of power, it had given him a welcome rush of clarity and strength.

Two vital skills he would need for the battle ahead.

"Eat, boy," Ethan muttered as the child continued to pick at his plate. He wasn't about to have the child die before he could be used.

"I want to go home," the boy whined.

Ethan chuckled. "Do you even know where that is anymore?"

Ladd's lip trembled. "My family will come for me."

"Are you speaking of the Romans? Because if you are, then I hope so. I would love to make them all bleed, just as I made your mother bleed."

A loud gasp escaped Ladd's throat and for a moment he looked sick to his stomach. But the look quickly faded, and changed into something strong and resolute. "I am a descendant of the Breeding Male," he said, inching up his chin. "The most powerful of all vampires."

"For now," Ethan replied, then spotted his female and the son nearly grown inside her belly, and left the *balas* with his recruits.

Lucian snapped back into consciousness. He was in his rooms. Bronwyn sat before him on the bed, concern in her eyes and on her expression.

"Where did you go?" she asked.

"What do you mean?" He tried to appear casual, but he really didn't know what the hell had just happened to him—where he'd gone or how.

"You just looked like you were lost in thought there for a second."

A second? Lucian's gut clenched. This wasn't right. It wasn't how things worked, had ever worked. The Order couldn't pull a *paven* from a protected home. Their power didn't stretch that far. He would've had to have been outside, and even then his body would've been taken—not just his mind.

Firecrackers were being lit up inside of him. *Kabam. Pow.* Daddy dearest and all that shit.

Maybe it was Titus. Something in their blood connection . . .

He eyed Bronwyn.

She didn't need to know about any of it. He shrugged roguishly. "Maybe I passed out. You nearly drained me dry, princess."

She smiled, sat up a little straighter against his pillows. She looked beautiful in his bed. She looked like she belonged there—belonged to him.

She needed to go.

His life and the lives of many depended upon his never seeing her again.

"No one could drain you dry, Lucian Roman," she said. "You may be a pain in the ass, but you're invincible."

And she needed to stop looking at him like that— like he was a fucking hero when all he wanted to do was tie those purity cloths at her wrists to the bedposts and screw her until she was as weak as when she'd first come into his room.

"Lucian." She went serious for a moment. "I want to thank you for what you did."

"It was just a little blood, princess. Let's not make it into a big thing."

"You didn't have to, is all I'm saying."

He stood. "I have an Impure to hunt, and you should probably return to your *credenti*."

For a moment, she didn't move; then, like a cat, she crawled off the bed and stood beside him. "Listen, I never got to tell you, never got to finish what I was saying before. The reason I came here in the first place . . ."

"What are you talking about?"

". . . and Alexander hung up on me before I could explain further."

"Is this about the *balas*?"

She looked up, nodded. "His DNA."

"What are you talking about?" he said impatiently. "Is he Nicholas's relation or not?"

"Yes. They share blood." Her tongue swiped at her upper lip as though there was still a trace of him left on her to enjoy. "But the *balas* is not his son."

35

"Where is she?"

Nicholas stood before the Order, his black eyes narrowed as his boots sank into the sand. After he'd left Cambridge and flashed to the mountain near the caves, it had been only seconds before the ancient ten pulled him in.

"She has been returned to us," Cruen said in a calm voice. "Now, if you have Dare hidden somewhere behind your back, we could consider our dealings with the Romans settled."

Nicholas snarled. "Where is the *balas*?"

"As we told the *veana*, we have no *balas*."

"You lie. You are all a bunch of motherfucking liars!" Nicholas ignored the rumble of outrage by the other Order members and focused on the one who seemed to rule them all. "I want to see Kate. Now."

Cruen's pale blue eyes narrowed. "Prisoner 626 will remain in Mondrar. After her escape and abduction of the *balas*, she now has a life sentence to fulfill."

Nicholas fairly leaped on the table, his fangs popping out of his gums like switchblades, his voice as deadly as a scorpion's sting. "I will do nothing to apprehend Dare until I see her."

Flashing his brick-red fangs in return, Cruen said, "And we will morph Lucian Roman unless we get Dare. So where does that leave us, Son of the Breeding Male?"

"With your drained body at my feet," Nicholas spat out, ignoring the whispers of the other members. He was barely able to contain himself. A part of him was missing, and he would have it back, even if he had to slit the throats of every vampire at the table to get it. "Kate Everborne is my true mate," he declared. "And as such, I have a right to see—"

"It is you who are the liar now," Cruen cut in, not even a shred of calm left in his tone.

"She bares my mark, completes my mark."

"That is impossible. It is Mirabelle Letts who—" Cruen cut himself off, his eyes flickering toward the Order members to his left.

Warning sounds went off inside Nicholas, and he leaned against the wood table, getting closer to the ancient *paven*, a mere breath away. "What did you say?" he whispered fiercely. "What do you know of Mirabelle?"

Cruen slammed his eyes shut, and started performing some kind of heavy breathing act through his nostrils as his mouth began to work a silent chant.

In seconds, there was a crack in the air, a hum, and Kate appeared behind the table, two guards bracketing her. She looked startled, as though this was the last place in the world she expected to be. Her gaze shifted around the Order's reality—sand to table to members, as she tried to get her bearings.

Nicholas nearly lost his mind. She was chained, shackled, and garbed in nothing but a strip of cloth. And as she finally found his gaze, he saw that her eyes had lost their fire, their hope.

Mine.

Tossing his head back, Nicholas roared, then headed straight for her, his brands going hot and heavy against his jaws.

"Stop!" Cruen screamed. "Or she is dead!"

Nicholas froze, nearly on top of the table, his nostrils flaring, his chest spasming. Desperation and need and fury and impatience whirled like a cyclone inside him. She belonged to him, and in that moment, nothing else mattered—not his brother, not his past, nor his present or future.

She was everything.

"Kate," he moaned.

She shook her head, her eyes beseeching him. "Find Ladd. Please. Dare must have him. He's got to be scared and—"

"Cease," Cruen commanded, glaring at her. "This *paven* has claimed you are his true mate. I know this to be impossible. But to satisfy the remaining nine, we shall strip you down and prove it."

"No!" Nicholas yelled so loudly every member of the Order jumped.

"Try it and lose an ear," Kate warned one of the guards who made a move to touch her. "Muzzling me is about the only way you're going to get me naked."

Cruen nodded. "So be it."

"You fucking touch her and I will find Dare and *help* him!" Nicholas threatened. "I will help that piece of shit Impure destroy the race and the Order. I swear it! Now . . ." He turned to Kate and nodded. "Show them, sweetest one, show them my mark so we may end this."

Kate's eyes turned from angry to blisteringly sad as she looked at him. Nicholas felt an overwhelming urge to comfort her, but all he could do in that moment was beg. "Please, Kate."

Dropping her head, she pulled the ratty fabric down over her right breast, almost to the nipple until the mark could be seen.

The seconds ticked by as the Order stared, first at her mark, then at Nicholas's facial brands—the ones they themselves had been responsible for implementing.

"It is true," one member remarked. "She completes his kiss. Kate Everborne is Nicholas Roman's true mate."

"But she has broken the law," said another. "Ran from her probationary period, with a *balas* of the *credenti*."

"Yes, but we need Purebloods to mate," said the white-haired *veana* beside Cruen. "Now more than ever. She has paid for her original crime. We could forgive her mistake with the *balas*."

"We could."

"We are the Order."

Cruen stood, slammed his fist on the table three times until silence was obtained. "Enough of this. She is not worthy of a Roman. She is Mondrar *witte*, a murderess of her own blood."

"It is I who am not worthy of her," Nicholas shouted over the din, his gaze locked on Kate's. "I offer my life for hers."

Kate's eyes went wide. "No," she uttered, shaking her head. "Nicholas, no."

It was in that moment that Nicholas understood love. Truly understood it. His life meant nothing without his other half, without the *veana* before him, and he would do anything, including destroying himself, to see her have the one thing she had always wanted.

Freedom.

"I will accept punishment in her place," he said, his tone harsh and resolute. "I demand it."

"Nicholas, please." He heard Kate beseech him, but he didn't turn from the Order.

"We do not want you in Mondrar, Son of the Breeding Male," said the white-haired *veana*. "We want you hunting Dare."

The *paven* beside her nodded. "Indeed."

There was a moment of silence; then the white haired *veana* spoke again. "Bring us Dare tonight before the change from eve to morn, and you will have your mate, Nicholas Roman."

Seething and realizing that he'd lost control of his position, Cruen attempted to reason with his members. "This is unjust, my brothers and sisters. It will set a precedent with the inmates—"

"It will be done, Cruen," the *veana* said. "Dare must be eliminated."

His face tense with hatred for the Roman brother before him, Cruen could barely spit out the words. "Fine. But if he fails, the *veana* dies and the third brother is morphed."

As each member of the Order nodded, Nicholas turned to see Kate flash out of the reality.

Nicholas sat down across from Whistler at the empty chess table in Washington Square Park, his brothers bracketing him. It was closing in on seven p.m.—five hours to find, kill, and drop Ethan Dare. No time to waste.

"Here." Nicholas shoved the bag toward the Eye. "Quarter of a million, in cash."

"The Romans have deep pockets tonight," Whistler said, his eyes gleaming with satisfaction as he checked the contents.

"This isn't Roman money," Nicholas said tightly, feeling both sets of eyes on him. He wasn't looking for approval from his brothers, or the I'm-so-proud-of-yous. The raid he'd made on the safe he had hidden below the floorboards in his room wasn't about anything except getting clean, coming to his mate free and clear, his past remaining there forever. "I'm going to say this only once, Whistler," Nicholas said. "The whore is dead and buried. Understand?"

Whistler's eyes shifted to Lucian, then Alexander, then back to Nicholas. "Got it."

"Now. That kind of cash is going to get us location *and* entry points."

A slow smile broke on Whistler's ugly mug. "The compound's on the Hudson, owned by an actress, some goth vampire wannabe type."

"Does Dare have the whole operation there?" Nicholas asked. "Recruits, *veanas*, females?"

The Eye attempted to look confused. Wasn't a good look on him, might get him strung up if he wasn't careful. "Don't know about any operation."

"You can stick coy right up your ass, Whistler," Nicholas hissed, "or I'll do it for you."

The Eye blanched. "I hear there are recruits and the ones who lie beneath them."

Nicholas said, "I need you to find out where Dare keeps the *balas*, then text us."

Whistler nodded. "Are we done?"

"Go," Nicholas said, flicking him away like a gnat.

As the Eye jumped up and scurried off with his trick-or-treat bag of cold hard cash, Nicholas rose too.

"Let's go," he said, grabbing hold of Lucian.

Alexander nodded. "Suit up and pick weapons."

They flashed from the park without one thought as to who might be watching them.

*   *   *

Inside the reality he'd abandoned days ago, Cruen stood at the water's edge, looking out at the miles and miles of calm sea.

"You need to get to my Impure," he said to the Beast at his side. "He must not be killed, not until I have the pleasure of doing it myself."

Erion inclined his head, said with a deadly baritone, "Yes, my lord."

Cruen looked up at the shape-shifter, who was in his vampire form at the moment. "I must see Lucian Roman morphed, Erion."

The male's diamond eyes glittered in the sun. "It will be done, Father."

Enclosed in a shelter of trees, the Hudson River mansion of Hollywood's girl next door rose up like a mini White House. Pretty fucking stunning, Nicholas thought as he quickly surveyed the area, looking for recruits patrolling in the night.

"I think we need to move," Lucian whispered, checking his weapons stash to see if it all had made the journey safely. Two Glocks and that goddamn tomahawk. "I belong in this place."

Two Glocks of his own at his chest, Nicholas tossed his brother a quick grin. "Could be available real soon, Luca."

"Let's roll," Alexander said, nodding at one lone recruit on the north side of the lawn. "I'll take him and meet you near the pool entrance."

Nicholas nodded, and he and Lucian hightailed it across the lawn, their eyes peeled for more recruits.

"Twenty feet," Lucian whispered, knocking his chin in the direction of another Impure near the driveway.

Nicholas took off silently, flashing directly behind the male. He struck with one brutal slash across the throat, then tossed the male into the nearby fountain. Mere seconds later, he caught up with Lucian and Alexander, who were waiting near the side of the house.

Nicholas could hear the now familiar sounds of a heavy bass line and hard-core sex. Just another night of making Impures, he mused. He moved with his back along the wall until he came to the floor-to-ceiling windows Whistler had told them about. With a quick glance into the massive living room, he saw no armed recruits near any of the exits. They'd paid enough for the element of surprise, and the Eyes weren't about to have their money reclaimed for selling information to a second party.

Nicholas motioned for Alexander and Lucian, let them know all was well and ready. The plan was get to Dare and the boy. Thanks to Whistler's text, Nicholas knew exactly where to go.

Alexander counted to three; then all of them lifted their Glocks and shot through the glass. They rushed through the shattered holes and burst inside the den. The surprised recruits scrambled from their female companions and reached for their weapons.

Nicholas spun into action and slit the throats of three Impure males who were locked in the throes of climax. Two other Impures leaped at him, smashed him up against a chair. He retaliated with a quick set of blows to one and a bullet to the temple of another.

With a swift glance at Alexander and Lucian, who were engaged in bloody hand-to-hand combat with at least six recruits, a couple of them bare-ass naked, Nicholas deemed them under control and stole out of the room.

Whipping out his BlackBerry, he followed the signal that Whistler had sent him, moving down the hall with the speed and grace of a morphed *paven*. Halfway up the stairs, a recruit leaped out behind Nicholas, plunging a knife into his calf, ripping into muscle. Pain slashed at him, and he whirled around. Quick and deadly, he grabbed the recruit by the neck, crushed his windpipe with one squeeze, and tossed him.

Bastard.

Got a nice red trail to follow now.

Bleeding, his wound only an irritant to his body's drive to kill, Nicholas continued up the stairs, his eyes on the signal his BlackBerry was flashing—down one hallway, then another. It was too damn quiet in this place. He didn't trust it. When he got to the door where Ladd was supposed to be, he fisted both Glocks, then smashed in the wood with his foot.

No more games.

He scented Dare, heard the bastard's heartbeat.

This was it. The end.

He released a furious snarl, scoping out the room and its contents: an armed recruit, Dare, Ladd, and a pregnant female who was cowering in the corner. The recruit jerked up his guns and started shooting. Reacting instantly, Nicholas launched himself at Dare, while firing off three rounds straight into the recruit's chest. The male hit the ground dead at the same time Nicholas landed on the Impure he sought.

Refusing to let the bastard flash without him, Nicholas dropped one Glock near a shaking Ladd and gripped Dare by the chest, cold-cocked him to the side of the head.

Lying flat on his back, Dare looked as though he were trying to get out, flash. But nothing was happening.

"Has the plug on your power cord been pulled, Dare?" Nicholas snarled. "Out of pure blood?"

"No," Ethan said, grabbing Nicholas's gun and training it on the child. "He's right here."

Perhaps Nicholas should've been worried, terrified even. But he wasn't. "You'll never touch a hair on his head."

"Wanna bet?"

Lightning fast, Nicholas yanked the blade from his thigh and thrashed it across Dare's neck, all the way to the bone.

Shock froze the Impure in place, and the gun dropped from his hand. He lay there, staring and panting, as if he couldn't believe this was it, how he was going out, his end.

Ladd ran for Nicholas, as the female in the corner screamed and blood gurgled and seeped from Dare's neck. Nicholas pushed the boy behind him.

"Please," Dare uttered, his eyes flickering in death.

Nicholas sneered. "What is it you beg me for, Impure? A quick death?"

"I . . . didn't hurt . . . your son," Dare rasped. "Please . . . don't hurt . . . mine."

The Impure stared up at Nicholas, fear bright in his dying eyes. But it wasn't for himself.

As Lucian and Alexander burst into the room, Nicholas nodded at the Impure, then grabbed his Glock and shot Ethan Dare in the heart.

36

Cruen hovered above his chair at the Order, hearing the clock inside his head tick away. Only seconds remained until his dream would be realized. Nicholas Roman would fail and Lucian Roman would be morphed—Lucian Roman would become the next Breeding Male.

The one waiting for him, the one who sat in a cage of her own, guarded by the Beasts, her desires threatening to drive her mad, would need Lucian's quick attention.

And Cruen would see to it.

After all, the Breeding Male program had been his original creation. He had mourned the loss for too many decades now. He would have his resurrection. The Breeding Male and the Breeding Female—he would create a perfect Pureblood race, one he controlled completely, one that might someday rule even the human population. It would be his greatest triumph. He didn't regret the lies he'd told Dare or the few Impures who had been created in the name of progress, nor did he regret the *veanas* who had been taken from their *credentis*. All would be stabilized soon enough.

Five seconds.

Four.

The grin that spread on his face was catlike.

Three.

Two.

CRACK. POP.

Standing before the Order, their eyes blazing with the sheen of war and death and triumph, were the Romans—all three. A white-haired *balas* was huddled against Lucian Roman's chest, while Alexander and Nicholas held the body of Ethan Dare.

Cruen's hands curled into fists. It wasn't possible. Not possible. Where was Erion?

"I want my mate released," Nicholas ordered as he and Alexander laid the ravaged, blood-drained body on the table.

Shaking with blind rage, Cruen stood up, shook his head. "Never. Never!" he shouted, his mind unable to contain its rage. He pointed a trembling finger at Lucian. "Lucian Roman will be morphed. He must!"

Nicholas stared at the ancient *paven*, who was slowly becoming unglued before his eyes. He wanted to grin, wanted to laugh, but he remained silent and calm before the Order. They would handle the matter; he was sure of it.

"Cruen, please," the white-haired *veana* hissed, placing her hand on his arm.

"Do not touch me," he growled, yanking his wrist away.

"You are not yourself, brother."

"I am the law!" Cruen screamed. "I am justice, order—I will do what must be done."

"Stop him," cried the Order member at the end of the table, his hood still drawn up over his face. "He is going to morph the *paven*."

Closing his eyes, Cruen raised his arms and began to chant.

"He cannot," the white-haired *veana* said, true concern in her eyes and in her tone. "Not without the power of half the Order."

But Cruen was far gone now, chanting words no one understood but him. Tipping his head back, he cried out, then flashed from the desert reality, leaving only his empty chair and the vibration of his exit reverberating through them all like a mini earthquake.

There was a moment of collective silence; then the white-haired *veana* spoke.

"Kate Everborne will be released and forgiven," she said. "Lucian Roman will not be morphed, and the Roman Brothers will go in peace and freedom."

The *paven* beside her nodded. "The Order appreciates what you have done."

Several members of the Order nodded.

"We may be harsh dictators," said the *veana*, "but we keep our word. If we did not, our breed would not trust us to govern." She smiled tightly. "With that said, we fear a bigger enemy is now on the loose. Perhaps

Dare was only a small fragment of a greater problem. The strings . . . Perhaps Cruen has been the true puppet master."

"Here we go again," muttered Lucian, who was standing behind Nicholas, his hatred for the ten and all they represented palpable.

The *veana* eyed each brother. "We respectfully reserve the right to call upon you if there becomes a need."

"You can call," Nicholas said tightly. "We may not answer. Now, release my mate."

Simultaneously, the Order closed their eyes. After a moment of pure silence, there was a crack, a flash and Kate stood before them. Confusion and fear resonated in her large expressive eyes. She looked at Nicholas, then over at Ladd, then at Nicholas again.

"Nicholas?"

He grinned at her. "You are free."

There was not even a breath of hesitation. She ran at him and threw her arms around his neck.

Nicholas buried his face in her hair. "You are free, my sweetest one," he whispered again. "We both are."

37

All Nicholas wanted to do was haul ass upstairs and get to his mate. But his brothers had insisted they talk with him first. His body humming with an irrepressible need that he knew would always be with him, he stood just inside the doorway to the library in the SoHo house, his arms crossed over his chest.

"Let's get on with it, *Duros*," he said impatiently. "I have a *veana* waiting upstairs for me." In our room, in the bathtub. Christ, just the thought of it made his cock pulse. She'd whispered it in his ear, all low and sweet before she'd taken the boy upstairs to put him to bed.

Scowling, he looked from Alexander to Lucian. "Out with it before I disown the pair of you."

Standing beside the fireplace, Alexander spoke first. "It's about the *balas*."

"My son?"

"Yes, and well you and all of us really . . . Aw, shit," Alexander muttered, shaking his head. "This is hard, and impossible to accept."

"Just rip the fucking Band-Aid off already," Lucian said, dropping into a chair.

Nicholas growled. "Okay, someone had better tell me what the fuck is going on with my son or—"

"He's not your son, Nicky."

Nicholas whirled on Lucian, his head pulsing with an all-new and terrifying pain. "What did you say?"

"Bronwyn came by today. She hadn't told Alexander the whole deal—"

"Bullshit. She did tell Alex and he told us—"

"No," Lucian said too harshly. He looked uncomfortable as shit. "Alex hung up on her before she could explain the full result of the DNA test. Before she—"

"She told him Ladd is of my blood," Nicholas said, slamming his fist back into the door.

"And he is of your blood," Lucian said, his own nostrils flaring. "But he's not your son."

Nicholas stilled, grinding his molars as he tried like hell to keep himself under control. "What are you saying?" he said through gritted teeth.

"Your DNA and Ladd's DNA had so many matching markers she thought you were the father," Lucian said, "but when she looked closer, tested further, she found that there was one marker off."

"Then she made a mistake," Nicholas said on a bitter chuckle. "One marker is nothing. That's impossible."

"She thought so too," Alexander put in, his merlot eyes as tortured as the days he used to cage himself, living in his past pain, while protecting others from his insatiable hunger. "She did another test, and another." His gaze flickered to Lucian, then hit Nicholas full force. "The last marker identifies conclusively that another Roman *paven* fathered Ladd."

It was as if the room lost all its air. "What? What the hell are you—"

"You were not born alone, Nicky," Alexander said. "Your mother gave birth to a *gemino*. He is Ladd's father."

Drowning in words that were ancient and impossible, Nicholas shook his head. It was a lie. Had to be. He would know if there was another . . . He would fucking know!

"I don't—" He could hardly get the words out. "It's not possible—"

Lucian came forward, grasped Nicholas's shoulder. "You have a twin, Nicky."

With the *balas* sleeping soundly, Kate had returned to the room next door, undressed, and slipped into a hot bath.

As the water flowed over her feet and ankles, soothed her weary skin, and washed away the hours she'd spent in a prison she'd sworn she'd never return to, she wondered what would present itself next. Freedom had only been a hope, a goal to keep her breathing on the days living had seemed impossible. But now it was there for the taking. All she had to do was reach out and grab it.

And yet . . .

The mark on her right breast hummed for its mate, just as her body hummed for his touch.

Nicholas.

He was here.

When she heard the bedroom door open and close, heard determined footfalls move across the room, saw the door to the bathroom open, she smiled. She couldn't help herself. Seeing him was like seeing the sun after months of rain.

He came to stand beside the bathtub, tall and dark and beautiful. But when she studied him further, she saw confusion and pain in his black eyes.

She sat up. "What's wrong? Is it the Order?"

He shook his head. "It is me."

"What?"

His eyes caught hers and held. "There is another part of me out there somewhere, Kate."

She released the breath she was holding. "Yes, and he is well and is fast asleep in his room."

A soft smile touched Nicholas's hard lips. "Yes. It's true."

"Nicky?"

He shook his head. "No. Later, sweetest one. Right now, I need you. I need to be inside your body, your soul"—he locked eyes with her—"inside your unbeating heart, where it's warm and safe."

His words made her ache, yet worried her too. But she nodded and said, "Come."

He stripped down, and Kate watched as every glorious inch of his heavily muscled perfection was revealed to her hungry gaze.

He stepped into the tub and sat opposite her.

"You are free now," he said softly, though his eyes drifted downward to the mark above her nipple. "Free to do what you want when you want, and with whom—even free from the strings of mating, if that is what you wish."

"Is that what you wish?" she asked, then held her breath.

His lips curved into a grin. "My wish, dear one, is for you to crawl up onto my lap and take my cock inside you. My wish is for you to ride me until you come, drink from me until you are filled, and love me as I love you, for all eternity. That is my wish."

It was too good, too wonderful—too sweet to be real. And yet it was. Kate didn't have to think, to mull—she didn't even have to say a word. She leaped at him, not caring about the water splashing over the sides of the tub. She needed to get to him, feel his skin, connect their bodies. Tears sprang to her eyes, but she swiped them away. She didn't do tears. She did honesty and care, and the magnificent *paven* before her.

"Yes. I am free," she said, straddling him, just until she felt the head of his shaft meet the entrance to her body. "To choose my life, my destination, and my true love." Then with a sigh, she sat, taking his cock deep into her, all the way to her womb. They wouldn't have a perfect fairy-tale existence together—it wasn't their way, not with pasts still yet to fully overcome. But with a love this great, Kate knew they would find their happily ever after, in the arms and the smiles and the loving care of each other. "I love you, Nicholas Roman," she said passionately. "And I bind my body to yours, my life to yours, my mark to yours, if you'll have me."

Nicholas growled, wrapped his arms around her. "I will have you every day, every moment," he murmured, taking her mouth as her hips rocked and swayed, as the brands on their skin filled in and became whole, one, a true kiss. As it was meant to be. "I love you, Kate. More than I ever thought possible."

"Never stop telling me," she whispered in between nips and laps at his tongue, "and never stop kissing me."

"Never," he declared, gripping her as tightly as her tender cunt gripped his sex. "For you wear my eternal kiss above your heart," he murmured against her mouth, "and carry my eternal love beneath."

VERACOU CEREMONY

Lucian Roman stood at the very edge of the dance floor, his arms folded across his chest in a show of repulsion. Granted, he was moderately happy for his brothers, but the fact that they felt it necessary to invite the whole fucking *credenti* community to their mating made his ass twitch.

The schoolroom in the Manhattan *credenti* had been magically transformed into a medieval ballroom, courtesy of the Order. A mating gift, they'd called it.

Lucian just called it bullshit.

Impures were not welcome at the Veracou, much less allowed to take part in it, but when Alexander had gone to the Order, feral and protective, demanding that not only would his true mate be beside him at the ceremony, but any and all of her family, they'd caved immediately and given their consent.

Clearly, the Eternal Order were trying to make nice after all that happened with Cruen, and even perhaps buttering them up in case they needed to call on the Romans in the future.

Lucian eyeballed the heavily robed Order member sitting alone near the musicians. Perhaps it was Daddy who had something to do with this, he mused. Bringing everyone together as though nothing had happened. Lucian didn't like it, the Order and the Romans coexisting. It was unnatural.

His eyes shifted to the happy couple who had just completed their mating ceremony. Nicholas and Kate, dressed in their formal robes, sat at a long table, drinking each other's blood out of gold cups. Ladd sat beside them. Their *balas*. For now. Soon, Nicholas and his mate, along with both Alexander and Lucian, would be on the hunt for Nicholas's twin—their brother in blood—a mystery to discover.

On the dance floor, acting like two animals in heat, Alexander and Sara were curled into each other, swaying to the music.

Lucian snorted. Nothing more off-putting than a bunch of vampires playing medieval wedding music, he thought. Dillon must've thought so too, as her scowl from across the room was nearly as irritated as Lucian's.

"All alone, Luca?"

Lucian turned. Sara and Gray's mother—and the female who had once traveled with Lucian and his brothers back during their escape—gave him a wry grin. "Not anymore, Cellie."

"Oh, I'm only here for a moment," Celestine informed him. She had just arrived from her home in Minnesota the day before, but whenever she was around it made Lucian and his brothers feel like young *pavens* again. "There is an Impure over there who is anxious to dance with me."

"He is a lucky male."

She leaned in and gave him a kiss on the cheek. "Oh, my dear Luca. You can be a true *gentlepaven* when you want to be."

Lucian heard the hitch in her voice, and wondered if she was thinking of her son. "Have you heard from Gray?"

"No."

"We'll get him back, Cellie, don't worry."

"I'm afraid he doesn't want to come back. He searches for something none of us can offer him." She gave him one last smile, then walked away toward her male admirer.

As the song ended with an eye-rolling flourish, Lucian watched the crowds fan out toward the tables. Typical fare was being served—grains and fruits, seed cake, and all the blood one could drink. But as the Purebloods and Impures took their seats, a commotion from near the main table erupted, and two figures were pushed forward. A smiling *paven* and *veana* walked onto the dance floor and addressed the crowd.

"We wished to wait," the *paven* said, though his smile was wide with pride. "As this is the mating day of another."

Lucian sighed. How much longer did he need to stay? Hell, he'd witnessed the mating rites, and he wasn't looking for a blood meal.

"Announce your happy news, Kettler."

The call from the crowd instantly grabbed Lucian's attention and he scanned the guests for a familiar face. Bronwyn *Kettler*. God, was she here?

"Two weeks ago," the *paven* was saying, "my daughter Bronwyn went through her Meta."

Blood began to pound in Lucian's skull like a gas pump. What the hell was happening? Two weeks. That was when she'd come to him, weak, unable to take rations—when he'd fed her. She had been going through Meta.

Lucian's lip curled.

She had lied to him.

"Her mark has called forth her true mate," the *paven* continued, his eyes sparkling like diamonds. "And it is with happiest heart that I announce their engagement."

As he stared at the couple, Lucian could barely get air into his lungs.

"When is the mating service, Samuel?" someone called out.

"Wednesday next." The *paven* gestured to the crowd, and Bronwyn stepped forward, a male at her side.

Turn around.

Lucian stilled. Not his voice. Titus was in his head. He slashed his gaze to the hooded *paven* near the instruments.

Walk out.

Lucian couldn't help himself. His eyes tore into Bronwyn and the *paven*. Smiling down at her, the Pureblood grabbed her hand with its small animal-shaped brand near the base of her thumb and brought it to his mouth.

A feral sound erupted in Lucian's throat. His fangs dropped, his body went hot and heavy, and when the *paven* put his lips to Bronwyn's pale wrist, he sprang— through the crowd and toward the unsuspecting bridegroom.

Don't miss the next dark and thrilling
novel in the Mark of the Vampire series,

ETERNAL CAPTIVE

Coming from Signet Eclipse
in February 2012.

Her fangs had been inside him only once, and yet they had left an unseen mark on his skin, his blood, even his breath. In consuming his blood, she had consumed his very soul, and now—every day, every moment he existed—she moved inside him, her unending hunger deafening as she searched and slithered through his veins, circled his muscles, squeezed until his brain threatened to explode.

Lucian Roman sat perched, as he had for the past seven nights, on the snow-crested roof of Bronwyn Kettler's brownstone. Still and menacing as a gargoyle, he ignored the vibration of his cell phone in the pocket of his coat and stared without purpose into the heavy snowfall, which dropped bride white over the silent Boston *credenti* landscape. An hour ago, the streets had been alive with Impures, running about, adorning the doors of their masters' dwellings as well as the gates, fences and lamposts leading up to the Gathering Hall. The tasteful bunting and subdued winter flowers were a testament to how the Boston community viewed the binding ceremony of its true mates: with serious and reverent celebration.

Now the streets were empty and silence reigned, as did the snow, and Lucian sneered in appreciation as the decorations for tomorrow's Veracou were quickly being buried in heavy white frosting. Would a blizzard annul the binding ceremony between Bronwyn and the *paven* who claimed her mark? Lucian thought not. But he would remain, affixed to the roof, to watch. To wait. To see the binding done and over. Or—if his blood had its wish—to see Bronwyn run from her true mate, reject her body's choice.

As another wave of longing, of desire-ladened torment pulsed in his bones and brain, Lucian's fangs slowly descended and the blade in his fist trembled.

There were only two ways to stop this madness.

Fuck her or kill her.

And yet he could do neither and remain free. The former would turn him into a Breeding Male one hundred seventy-five years before his time: a rutting animal with no conscience, no control—only a hunger to claim. The latter would send him to Mondrar, the vampire prison, for all eternity.

Again, he felt the vibration of his cell phone, and again, he ignored it. He knew Alexander would never give up looking for him, and in fact he had seen his brother walking the streets below once already this week. But the eldest Roman had never looked up, and down below had found only snow and the censure of a community that reviled anything with a matching set of Breeding Male brands.

A sudden rush of sound, a faint cry, like air released from a balloon, stole Lucian's thoughts and left him with nothing but a raw, feral craving. He sprang to his feet, his entire body going forest-fire hot as a growl sounded in his throat.

Damn her. With one bite, she had made him into this, this animal, this creature of destruction, and in some way she would have to pay.

His hand fisting the knife, Lucian moved in near silence like a panther down the pitched roof and over the edge, dropping to the small balcony attached to her room. The window was a large square and, in the handful of times he'd stood there watching her sleep, he'd surmised, rather easy to maneuver through.

Darkness blanketed her bedroom, the only light coming from the streetlamps below. But to Lucian's keen gaze, it was enough to make out the furniture, the artwork on her walls and the *veana* lying in her bed. As usual, she was on her back, her dark hair spilling out over her stark white pillow. In nights previous, she had slept soundly, unmoving, like the princess Lucian had insisted on labeling her.

But tonight, she moved.

Leaning closer to the glass, his insides still blazing with heat, Lucian narrowed his gaze on her lower half, specifically on her legs as they stirred beneath the white coverlet. It was as if she were running a race in her sleep, and yet as his gaze trailed upward to her thighs, to the outline of her hips, he realized that the race she was running was the one that ended in climax.

Madness splintered his mind once again, and instead of pushing away from her window and returning to his rooftop perch as he normally did, he quietly broke the lock on her window, eased up the frame and stole inside her room. Instantly, the scent of her yet unclaimed orgasm washed over him, and he flew across the room and coiled over her like a snake. Any last shreds of stability he may have had upon entering were dead, drowned, forgotten.

The white coverlet blinded him from the act she performed, but Lucian could imagine her hands working her core, just as he could scent the dance of her fingers inside her cunt.

He snarled softly at her, at the pale, perfect face that was framed with long black hair.

No veana had the right to be this beautiful.

No veana had the right to hold him captive.

Because Bronwyn was held in her own state of captivity, her eyes remained clamped shut, but her cheeks held the delectable stain of desire, and her pink lips were parted, just enough for the ragged breaths of desire to escape. Like a dog in heat, Lucian leaned in and took one long sniff.

The mistake of it hit him instantaneously.

His fangs dropped to needle sharpness against his

lips and all he could see was blood, all he could taste was sex.

All he could do was place his blade to her throat.

Bronwyn's eyes snapped open at the feel of cool metal. "You."

"Not who you were thinking about, Princess?"

Her arms shot out from beneath the covers; her fingers wrapped around his wrist. "Get off me, you bastard!"

"Don't move."

The scent of her fear did nothing to stall him, only pushed his madness further. "Don't talk. Even your breath on my face makes me want to scratch at your skin to get inside."

Her gaze narrowed on his. "What's happened to you? You look—"

"I said, Don't talk!"

"If you're here to kill me," she said, her nails digging into his skin, "don't expect me to die easily or quietly."

Her lips pressed together, fear tensing her jaw and the skin around her eyes—though the scent of arousal still lingered temptingly in the air.

The blade still held to her throat, Lucian's fangs dropped even further as he uttered, "I hate you."

She stared up at him, unblinking, her nostrils flaring as she breathed in and out. "Hate me or yourself?"

He leaned in closer. "You've turned me inside out," he whispered near her mouth. "Do you understand that? I can't feed. I can't fuck." His head began to pound, his muscles too . . . Dammit, he wanted her mouth under his, her blood rushing over his tongue— her death on whatever was left of conscience. If he pressed the knife just a hair closer, he could have it, have it all . . . "That night you came to me—"

"I didn't plan it, Lucian—goddammit! I didn't plan to feed—"

He cut off her words, pressing the blade nearer to her throat. "Another word and I will be feeding from you."

RELEASE THE VEANA, *LUCIAN. NOW.*

Before he even had the chance to respond, the knife was ripped from Lucian's fist. For one brief moment, the cold metal hovered in midair, then shot past Lucian's face, disappearing behind him.

Lucian whirled around to face his intruder, in the back of his mind hearing Brownyn slip from the bed, taking her freedom. But his gaze, his focus was pinned on the hooded figure lurking in the shadows near the window. He hissed, "What do you want?"

"To keep you from harm," replied the ancient *paven.*

Lucian sneered at his father, the Breeding Male—the Order. "Too late."

"It will be if you continue on this path." Titus raised his hooded head toward the corner of the room. "I am sorry for this, Mistress Kettler."

Lucian turned and narrowed his eyes on the *veana* who, even in her fear, stood tall and imperious.

"I thank the Order for its help in this matter," she said, nodding at Titus. "Now, pray get him out of here before my parents awake."

Instantly, Lucian felt the pull of his father, magnet to iron. "Come with me, Lucian."

It was a solid yank, and yet Lucian was immobile, his eyes locked on Bronwyn. He uttered a pained, "I cannot."

Bronwyn turned to him then.

"She is to be mated in the morning," Titus said tightly. *SHE WILL FEED FROM ANOTHER AND HE WILL FEED FROM HER.*

"Shut up!" Lucian roared.

YOUR TORMENT WILL PASS.

"My torment has only begun!"

Lucian's gaze caught on the mark near the base of Bronwyn's thumb. The *paven*'s mark—her *paven*. Feral rage slammed through him and he shot across the room, forcing her back into the corner. She belonged to him. Her mouth, her gaze, her neck, her vein, her voice, her cunt. He grabbed her hand and pulled it to his lips. But just as his fangs entered her marked skin, he was yanked back, slammed into the one who had given him not only life, but the curse of the Breeding Male.

No blood met Lucian's dry tongue, but Bronwyn's cry of pain ripped through his black soul as Titus flashed him away.

FROM

#1 *NEW YORK TIMES*
BESTSELLING AUTHOR

J. R. WARD

THE BLACK DAGGER BROTHERHOOD SERIES

Dark Lover

Lover Eternal

Lover Awakened

Lover Revealed

Lover Unbound

Lover Enshrined

Lover Avenged

Lover Mine

Lover Unleashed